CALAMITY

Born Before Her Time

by

Pamela Mohan

CALAMITY! PRESS

Seattle

© 2020 Pamela Mohan

All Rights Reserved.

No part of this book may be reproduced, scanned, or distributed in any printed or electronic form without permission. Please do not participate in or encourage piracy of copyrighted materials in violation of the author's rights.

Edited by **Kim Mohan**

Cover, Book Design, and Silhouettes © **DARLENE**

CALAMITY! PRESS

11840 54th Ave. S   Seattle, WA 98178
http://mycalamity.me

ISBN 978-1-09835-285-1

Printed in the United States of America

This book is dedicated

to every woman brave enough to break

through the gender barrier

and follow her own dreams.

And to my husband Kim Mohan,

who is as much a sharp shooter

with a red ink pen as Hickok

was with a gun.

PREFACE

August 31, 2020
Seattle, Washington

Writing about historical characters can be tricky. Especially when historians don't have documented proof to separate the facts from the fiction. Especially when the character was a habitual liar whose own accounts of her adventures often changed in the telling. Martha Jane Canary, or Cannary as she sometimes wrote it, was prone to embellishment when it came to her skills and accomplishments. That's a fact.

Was she in love with Wild Bill Hickok? Did she marry him? Did she ride with Custer? Maybe. Maybe not.

But no one disagrees that she was a forward-thinking frontierswoman who believed gender should not get in the way of living the life you wanted, however you wanted. What she wanted was to dress like, ride like, shoot like, swear like, and drink like a man without giving up her feminine identity. A tall order for a woman to pull off in the late 1800's. By all accounts, she did achieve that goal and lived a life of unrivaled adventure that was not without its problems or tragedies.

I'm fascinated by this woman who became known as Calamity Jane. How Martha Jane Canary got that moniker is also in dispute. What's not is that she was a good-hearted person who would give her last dime to a hungry stranger, who suffered from alcoholism from a very young age, who was an expert rider and sharpshooter, and who took care of the sick during a smallpox plague in Deadwood. This is the Martha Jane Canary I've grown to love. We would have been friends had I lived in her time.

This book is a work of fiction based on her story. Much of it is based on fact, but I channeled Jane's talent for embellishment to write it the way I think she might have wanted. I allowed her to be herself.

PROLOGUE

June 6, 1903
Terry, South Dakota

If there was such a thing as heaven, Jane was certain neither that venue nor its landlord would offer her refuge when her final day on earth came and went. Didn't really matter to her. Jane's time was coming to an end, and all she cared about was being laid to rest next to her beloved Bill.

For now, she was resting on a flat rock beneath a tall Ponderosa, her loyal four-legged companion, Buddy, grazing nearby. The old stallion had taken her over snow-covered mountains, across open prairies, and through treacherous canyons—some so narrow she could stretch out both arms and touch the walls on either side as they rode through. Many of these tight spots were topped with Indian warriors holding bows and arrows, ready to release, but with Jane astride, the horse remained steady footed.

Yeah, that Buddy had been tough as nails in his prime, but lately, he seemed to spook easy. Jane figured the creature was getting jittery in his old age, and she could relate. Although she didn't spook easy, if at all, her hands shook something fierce sometimes, and the longer she went without liquor, the worse it got. Nausea, sweating, and a head that felt like a dozen wild horses were trampling over it, one after another, and then back again for a second pass, hooves that pounded against the edges of her brain, that was the wretched price she paid for sobriety. A day without alcohol was a day in hell and she was hellbent on not allowing that to happen. She took a breath and let it out in a long, heavy sigh. Sometimes she just plain ran out of her liquid medicine and those times were some of her darkest moments.

Jane raised the flask she always carried with her to her lips and took a long, luxurious swallow. She shuddered a bit, then relaxed and

1

looked around, taking mental snapshots of nature's minutia. This was one of her favorite spots. On days like today—sun shining through the branches of the pines, painting the ground with shadowy fans of all shapes and sizes, birds chirping almost in sweet harmony, just enough wind to lift the edges of her hair—moments like this she treasured above anything else her life had to offer her now. It was always a treat to sit back and take in the beauty.

Jane took another swig of the cheap whiskey—the only kind she could afford anymore—and stared down at the water in the creek bed. Unlike her, it was always rushing to get somewhere. She sat and watched as it tumbled over rocks, pushed loose logs forward, surged in its haste to move on. She was in no such hurry. There was nowhere she was aching to go anymore. Not in this life anyway.

The horse seemed content, having satisfied his need to drink. His tail swished gently back and forth, warning off pesky insects. He was her constant and only friend now, but not for long. Nothing good lasts forever. He had just about reached his limit in horse years. And Jane had just plain reached her limit. She wasn't going to leave him to die alone in this world. Jane knew Buddy would have to be put down if she wanted to spare him dying alone. She planned to take care of that sad chore soon. It was only right for her to see to it herself, before it was too late. She took another drink, trying to drown out the noise of that unpleasant thought.

Jane hadn't fared well in the last few years. She'd long since given up on keeping herself presentable. Her stringy graying hair and tattered clothes were good enough for her and, considering she was the one wearing both those things, her opinion was the only one that fucking mattered. She often forgot to eat and when she did remember to do that, the process gave her little pleasure or satisfaction. The alcohol was winning its battle to bring her down, and she wasn't doing anything to stop it. Why bother? Except for Bill and the girl, there wasn't anything on earth or beyond she could imagine loving more than the smooth, soothing liquid she'd met and befriended when she was barely more than a child. She took another draw on the flask and then corked it. The shaking had all but stopped—for now.

Jane tried to imagine a day when she would no longer have access to the alcohol she needed to calm her nerves. Even the cheap stuff was getting harder to come by. She didn't have the energy to tell the stories of her daring adventures that for years won her free booze in most saloons. Due to her age and health she couldn't work as a bullwhacker or wagon driver anymore. Whoring was out of the question, considering her poor hygiene, slovenly appearance, and ugly disposition. At fifty-one her body was aged well beyond its years, and a man would have to be beyond desperate to seek her out for sexual favors. Soon thievery would be her only option for obtaining the drink she needed to survive, even though it was killing her.

"Damned if I do, damned if I don't," she spewed out loud. The horse was the only one around to hear her, and he had stopped paying attention to Jane's outbursts a long time ago.

Jane sighed. She wondered what dying would be like. Would it hurt? Would Bill ride out to meet her? Would she be able to see him and if she was, would he look the same? Would ashes be all that was left of him, or would he still be lying beneath that damned waterfall ringed with fire? She laughed remembering that illusion. Exhaustion can do crazy things to a person's psyche.

No matter how her final act played out, she'd made it clear to anyone who would listen that her remains damn well better be laid to rest as close to Bill's as the law would allow. If her death wish was honored, she and James Butler Hickok would spend eternity together. *But as what*? She took another swig of liquor as she pondered their possible fate. Two gloriously decorated heroic angels? That idea made her laugh so hard she almost choked. It would be easier to imagine their two souls damned to hell. Or would they just end up being lifeless piles of bones? *Doesn't matter*, she thought. Jane would take any one of those options, if it meant being with Bill.

Chapter 1

March 2, 1875
Goose Creek, Wyoming

W hoa, Buddy!" Twenty-four-year-old Martha Jane Canary
pulled hard on the reins and dismounted her horse. She
had been traveling over a narrow and rugged trail winding
through a series of sandstone cliffs near Goose Creek, Wyoming. Even
though it was March, there was still enough snow on the ground for
her to make out pony tracks, lots of them. They were headed upward,
and she decided to follow and check them out.

As a scout for the US Army 9th Battalion led by Brigadier General
George Crook, it was up to Jane, as she preferred to be called, to see
what lay ahead for the soldiers seeking out any remaining Lakota
Sioux encampments that her government had ordered dispersed. Her
troops were about thirty minutes behind her.

She got back in the saddle and steered her horse in the direction
the tracks were headed. She guided Buddy around a winding path,
following the hoof prints. They rode a while before Jane noticed that
the tracks were veering off to the right into dense undergrowth. She
followed the narrow trail a short distance before realizing that the
ponies had traveled through the thicket, up to a ridge, then turned and
headed back down again.

"Damn it!" Jane muttered, "They're doubling back!" She knew
this was a tactic Sioux warriors sometimes used to surprise the troops
that were hunting them down, head on.

Jane steered her horse up the rocky ridge and back down again. A
few times Buddy's hooves slipped on loose rocks, but he managed to
hold his ground. Once they were on flatter terrain, Jane dug in her
heels. The animal thundered back through the canyon in the direction
it had come, carrying its rider toward a raging battle in progress.

4

When Jane heard shouting, whooping, screaming, and gunfire over the sound of Buddy's galloping hooves, she pulled back hard on the reins. Once the horse slowed to a trot, Jane swung her right leg over the saddle and jumped to the ground, keeping hold of the reins.

"Easy, there," she said, rubbing the stallion's head to calm him down. She tied Buddy's reins to a nearby tree branch and began a slow crawl on her knees and elbows to get within sight of the battle. As soon as she was close enough, Jane took cover behind some brush to assess the situation. It was easy to go undetected, since the two groups were so intense in their efforts to defeat each other that the noise of the battle had drowned out the sounds of her approach. And what a battle it was! Jane had seen some gruesome sights in her twenty-plus years, but nothing quite so horrible as this.

The shattered bodies of dead soldiers and Indian braves were scattered around in motionless, bloody messes. Some soldiers were so entangled with their attackers that their lifeless bodies appeared to be hugging, although there had been no such affection afforded each other in life. A soldier Jane recognized as Dan, a kind, fun-loving young man who enjoyed his liquor as much as Jane enjoyed hers, was still atop his horse, his left eye hanging from its socket and an arrow stuck halfway through his left leg. He wore both as though they were intentional accessories to his uniform. He was still firing on the renegades. Jane ran back to her horse, untied him, and hopped on his back. She rode into the melee, intending to escort Dan to safety and then take his place in battle. That's when she saw the unit's leader, Captain James Egan, take an arrow in his back. The captain slumped over in the saddle and then fell to the ground. Jane turned her horse toward the commander to rescue him from further harm or death.

An Indian brave who appeared to be younger than Jane picked a large rock up off the ground and rushed at her. "This is our land, and we won't be pushed off it!" He shouted. For what seemed like an eternity, the two just stared at each other. Jane would rather have sat down and talked about this, than be the cause of his death.

He seemed torn, the rock still held tightly in his right hand high above his head. A shot rang out, hitting the young brave in his left shoulder. He hurled the rock with expert aim before falling to the ground in anguish. Even though Jane was sitting high in the saddle, the rock connected with her head and she tumbled to the ground. Buddy panicked and reared up on his back legs. He started to run around in a circle, not sure what to do next.

"Mother-fucking son of a bitch!" Jane screamed.

She stumbled to her feet, using the sleeve of her jacket to wipe off some of the blood running down her face. Her upright advantage lasted only seconds before she felt the sting of an arrow. The sharp head stabbed her left upper arm at an angle, about two inches below the shoulder. It stuck there. Even with an arrow in her arm and blood running down her face, Jane's aim was dead on. The Indian hit the ground with a thud and would never move again.

Between the pain in her head and the pain in her shoulder, Jane was feeling a bit diminished, but she knew she had to bolster through and get the captain to safety. She reached up with her right hand and pulled the arrow out, biting her lip so hard it bled. The shoulder wound was minor, fortunately, but it hurt like hell.

I'd give anything for a shot of whiskey to help deaden this pain, Jane thought. But she knew she couldn't spare the time to do that. The captain's life was on the line and she needed to act fast.

Jane stuck her thumb and two fingers of her right hand into her mouth and gave a shrill whistle. This was a command Buddy knew well, and he reacted as he was trained to do. Within seconds the horse was at her side and Jane was back in the saddle, although not without considerable pain.

"Don't worry, Captain. I'm coming for you. Just been a slight delay," Jane bellowed as she steered Buddy toward the fallen commander. She reached Egan, quickly slid off the horse, and pulled the man up and over her shoulders.

"Holy mother of God!" Egan screamed. Jane ignored his outburst and flung the man facedown over her saddle. "Son of a bitch!" Egan yelled. Jane's only response was to pull herself up onto the horse behind him. She could see that the shaft of the arrow was too deep in Egan's back for her to remove it without causing more damage. Jane knew her captain would most likely die if he did not get medical attention as soon as possible.

"Very sorry for the discomfort, sir, but I'm just trying to get you out of here alive," Jane said, and then added, "It's going to be all right. I promise. You're in good hands."

Egan moaned with each step the horse took.

Jane ducked as arrows flew by, barely missing them. She decided that taking it easy for Egan's sake would most likely end up getting them both killed.

"Okay. No choice here, sir. We have to go fast now," she said. With that, she let out a whoop, dug her heels into the horse's sides, and rode like the wind—away from the battle. She did not stop until they were far enough from the battlefield that she could no longer hear the fighting. Then she halted the horse, got down, and pulled her captain to the ground, placing him on his right side to check his condition. She tried to be gentle, but judging from Egan's groans, she knew any amount of careful handling would most likely bring the same results. It was obvious by his now-subdued but continuous moaning that Egan was failing.

"At least I can make you a bit more comfortable, sir," Jane said. She reached into her saddle bag and removed the flask she kept with her always. She opened it, sat down beside the man, raised his head just off the ground, and poured a bit into his mouth. Some of the pain-killing liquid made it to its intended target; some spilled on the ground. Jane closed the flask and checked Egan's wound. The arrow was embedded far enough that she couldn't see its head. He wasn't bleeding out. That was a good sign, but internal bleeding was a given, and she was concerned.

Jane pulled a handkerchief from her saddlebag and wrapped her head tight with it to stop her own bleeding. She took her left arm out of her shirt sleeve and wound the fabric tightly around the arrow wound. When that was done, she took a gulp of the whiskey, let out an appreciative sigh, and then attempted to get another drink into the captain's mouth and down his gullet. Then she took her second drink. By the time that was done, the liquor seemed to have influenced the captain, and he was able to stop moaning and whisper, "Get us home. I'm afraid I'm not going to make it."

"Yes, sir!" Jane said. She picked the man up in her arms, laid him once again facedown over the saddle, and pulled herself up behind him. The average rider would have found it difficult, if not impossible, to move at any kind of speed in this position. But Jane was no average rider. She was often recognized for her horsemanship. She dug in her heels and set the horse at what might have been his fastest gallop ever. Less than an hour later, Fort Sanders was in sight.

"We're almost there, Captain. I can see the gates," she said. She also saw several riders who were setting off in her direction and called out to them for help.

"It's the captain. He's been hurt bad. He needs a doctor. Fast!" Jane bellowed.

Several soldiers raced toward her. A couple rode back to retrieve a medical sled.

It wasn't until then that Jane felt the full force of the pain and exhaustion of this latest battle in a three-month-long campaign marked by loss of troops, freezing temperatures, and hunger.

As soon as her captain was placed on the sled and pulled toward safety, Jane got down off her horse, saluted her fallen comrade, and fell straight to the ground.

Chapter 2

"Well Done, Martha," General Crook said as he approached Jane. She was sitting upright on a cot in the medical tent, sipping some hot coffee. Jane couldn't remember any of the last forty-eight hours. The bandages on her head and shoulder, however, were a sign that she had been treated. She also felt the pull of some stitches in both places that had suffered damage. She did, however, remember with full clarity the events that led up to her arrival at the fort.

"Thank you, sir," Jane said as she stood to salute the general. She felt weak and shaky, but managed to show the proper respect. And that was important to her. "Please feel free to call me Jane. As for what I did out there, it wasn't anything I haven't done before and nothing I would hesitate to do again if called upon."

Crook smiled. "Be seated, Jane, please," he said.

"Thank you, sir. They just told me I was free to go, but truth be told I am still feeling a bit woozy."

General Crook sat down on a cot facing hers. "What you did, Jane, was save a U.S. Army captain's life. You were courageous in retrieving his injured body from the middle of a deadly battlefield and getting him to safety so our camp doctor could do the rest," he said. "Because of you, Captain Egan lives to enjoy another day, and he would like to see you and thank you in person for that, assuming you feel well enough to pay him a visit in his quarters. He would come to you, but he is not quite up to getting on his feet right now."

"Hell, I can do that straight away," Jane said, making what this time was a futile effort to stand. She knew she was okay, just a bit weak from being unconscious for two days. Jane decided to stay seated for the moment, hoping the general hadn't noticed her falter.

"This must mean the captain is recovering well enough to entertain visitors?" she asked.

"I don't know about the entertaining part," Crook said with a grin, "but his recovery is going well, and he is mighty grateful to you for that."

General Crook told Jane that the captain's wound was troublesome, but Doc Jeb Crane managed to make an incision, remove the weapon, and from what he was able to observe, did not believe Egan had suffered any long-term internal damage, although there very well might be remnants of the arrow's jagged head left behind in his body.

"Won't that cause him ongoing pain?" Jane asked.

"Quite possibly, but the decision was to do nothing more now because in his weakened condition, further surgery would put him in more danger. He may be able to live with just the minimum of discomfort. And if not, when he is stronger they can address that issue. It's just a good thing you didn't attempt to pull the arrow out of his body yourself," Crook said.

"Sir, I once saw someone try to remove an arrow stuck that deep. The damned thing was barbed, and it ripped the poor man to shreds coming out. That was horrible to see," Jane said.

"Yeah, I can imagine. This one was barbed, too. Doc made a cut to enlarge the entry wound and slid a finger down the shaft to feel how deep it went and if it was lodged in the bone. He managed to remove the arrowhead. It was tricky; a very long and difficult process, but the results were successful. The captain is quite sore from the surgery and it will take him a few weeks to mend, but he's still alive and will recover well enough to be able to continue to enjoy life and to function as a military officer."

"I'm so happy to know that," Jane said. She felt proud of the part she played in saving the captain's life. Of course, without Buddy to get them to where the captain could get medical attention, and the doctor who provided that, her efforts would have been in vain.

From what I was told about your injuries, they were much less severe," Crook said. "The arrow barely broke the skin and hit some muscle, but the damage was minor and all you needed were a few stitches. As for your head, all I can say is that you must have a thick shell there. Doc said most people who take a hit that hard in the head suffer all kinds of lasting side effects. The reason you passed out was determined to be from the effects of exhaustion, rather than that of any injury. Your wounds will heal and be of no future trouble to you. As for the exhaustion, that can be taken care of with rest," he said.

"I have been accused of having a hard head once or twice that I can recall," Jane laughed. "Still, I guess I was pretty lucky."

"Indeed," Crook said, getting to his feet. "So, if you think you're up to it, what do you say we go pay the captain a visit? Not too long, though. He needs all the rest he can get," Crook said, standing and offering Jane a hand as she got slowly off the cot. She accepted and made a concerted effort not to wince. She followed the general out of the tent. He walked slower than his usual pace, aware of how much pain she was still in.

"Could you please tell me, sir, if a soldier named Dan made it back alive? You would know him to look at him, seeing as how one of his eyeballs was hanging clean out of his head and he was wearing an arrow in his left leg," she said.

The general winced and shook his head. "I'm sorry, Jane. No, Dan did not make it. His body was recovered at the battle site. We were told he fought hard until the very end," Crook said.

Jane lowered her head. "I should have tried harder to save him," she said.

"You're only one person, Jane. You can only do so much, and what you did was more than most could have managed."

11

Jane was not concerned with her own courage at this moment. It was unlike her to pass up an opportunity to expound upon her own fearless deeds, but she wanted to make sure the general knew about her friend, Dan. "Sir, you would have been so proud. Even with only one usable eye and blood gushing down his face, he still kept fighting." She stopped and shook her head. "Sorry, sir. I know it's unbecoming of a soldier to swear in front of her superiors. That's just kind of the way I'm used to talking."

Jane had used the word "soldier" loosely. She was not allowed to enlist in the army because she was a woman. The one time she had tried to buck the system ended in disaster. She told them up front that she was a woman, but an unusual one at that.

"I can do the work of three of your best male soldiers here, at least," she had boasted.

She hadn't minded being laughed at so much, she could take that. But when they told her to go home and put on a dress and act like a woman, she was furious.

"I'm a person who happened to be born a woman, not that I mind that part. What I do mind is being told that because my bits are different than yours, I am limited in what I can achieve. That's a load of stinky horseshit!" she said.

"Whoa, filly! Won't do to have you throwing a temper tantrum. You just need to go now and know your place," the commander in charge had told her.

Still, she continued to argue that she was well received and even revered when it came to her unusual skills.

"Many know me as a woman who can outride and outshoot most men with very few exceptions. And I have yet to meet any of them," she said. "If you would just let me demonstrate my riding and shooting abilities..."

"Sorry, Sis, but the rules are the rules. If you're so all-fired eager to ride into battle, maybe you should check to see if any of the government camps around here are allowing women to act as scouts. I warn you, though, your skills better be as good as you say they are, or you will be run off and sent home to do what you were born to do in the first place," he said.

She didn't ask what he thought she was *born to do*. Instead, she did as he suggested and rode out to find a government installation that would welcome her exceptional talents. And one did: Fort Sanders, where she was tested and invited to work as an Indian scout in return for food, shelter, and much less pay than the men who rode with her. She accepted that as a reality she must endure, if she wanted to do what *she* believed she was born to do.

General Crook knew that this was only one of many times Jane had more than earned her keep, and he was not going to argue with her use of the term "soldier." In fact, he recognized her as one.

"Well, soldier, after all you have been through I think we can overlook a swear word or two." He smiled at her.

"That's mighty fucking kind of you," Jane said.

Crook grinned, shook his head, and kept on walking. Jane clenched her teeth and made a mental note to hit herself upside the head later.

Egan was housed a short stroll from the medical tent where enlisted men were taken to recover. Officers had a wood structure that was by far more luxurious. After Jane's display of what she judged to be stupidity worthy of a solid fist to the head, the rest of the walk seemed to take forever.

Captain Egan's quarters were small, but clean and well furnished. He was propped up in bed by several down-filled pillows. A white sheet draped over his body covered the flannel gown he wore. Two soldiers flanked the bed and were ready to run errands at a second's notice. A small table beside the bed held a pitcher of water, a plate with some half-eaten bacon and biscuits, a bottle of bourbon, and a shot glass.

"Martha Jane Canary!" Captain Egan exclaimed when Jane and Crook walked in the room.

"With all due respect, it's just Jane, Captain," she said. "I let go of my first name years ago. I like to keep it plain and simple."

"Oh, no. You're no plain Jane, *Jane!*" Egan said. "Not even close! You're a woman unlike any I have ever seen. I'm told you rode right up to where I lay dying, all the while dodging rocks, arrows, and knives, without giving a thought to your own safety. You turned what might have been a calamitous end for me, into an ending of a much happier sort. In fact, if you don't mind, from now on you will be known to me as *Calamity* Jane. The woman who rode onto the scene of a fierce battle, endured a rock to the head and an arrow to the shoulder, yet kept on going and saved the life of a U.S. Army captain." He saluted her, then reached out his hand to her. Jane, feeling both proud and embarrassed, walked over to the bed and shook it.

"My dear Calamity! Thank you for saving my life," he said. She thought she saw a trace of excess moisture in the man's eyes.

"I am happy to learn the damage caused by that arrow is working itself toward a full mend," Jane said.

"They tell me I'll be almost as good as new in a few weeks, and that's good enough for me," he said. "The head of the arrow buried itself pretty deep in my back, but it missed my major organs. I'm damned lucky to be alive and will always be grateful to you for that."

Jane smiled. Her new name pleased her, but not in the way the captain meant for it to please her. She liked the idea of having a special name with a story of adventure behind it. She would enjoy retelling this one—how and why an army captain had bestowed it upon her—repeatedly.

"Thank you for your kindness, sir. I should let you rest now. My injuries were not so severe as were yours, as I trust you can tell by my upright position. I have been told to take a couple of days' rest and I will be good to go on the next campaign," she said.

"Jane, please accept my gift of a bottle of fine whiskey and a fresh cigar—two of the things, I am told, that bring you great pleasure."

"Oh, you don't have to do that, sir. I don't need a reward for doing my job," Jane said. She felt her face beginning to warm a bit.

"Not just for doing your job, but for doing it damn well! Accept my small tokens of gratitude. That's an order, soldier!" Egan said.

Jane's cheeks turned a bright red, but she didn't mind the heat that flushed through her face. What mattered to her was that today a brigadier general *and* a U.S. Army captain had *each* addressed her as a soldier.

"Thank you, sir. You will never know what your kind and generous words mean to me," she said.

"I'm happy to repay my debt in even the smallest way. Now I'm afraid to have to say that I am feeling a bit sleepy suddenly, Jane," Egan said.

"Rest well, sir," Jane said.

Crook motioned for Jane to follow him. Egan was already asleep when the two of them left the cabin. Once outside, Crook again praised her for her fortitude.

"Just so you know, Jane, that was not an invitation to enlist, which you of all persons know can't happen because..."

"Me being a woman and all. Yes, I get that, for now. But I don't support that notion and I don't believe it will always be this way," she said.

They walked the rest of the way back in silence, stopping just outside the tent Jane had been assigned to use.

"I would like to shake your hand once more before I take my leave," Crook said. "And seeing as how there are no rules about gender when it comes to saluting courage..."

The general took a step back and raised his hand in a salute to the woman who could fight as well as any male soldier, but wasn't allowed to be one.

"Well done, soldier. Damn well done!" Crook said. He lowered his hand, smiled, and gave Jane a friendly wink. "Yes, for your information, soldiers do swear in front of their superiors on occasion—many, many occasions," he said.

With that Crook turned and walked away, leaving Jane feeling happier than she had felt in years—ever since Bill Hickok had ridden out of her life without so much as a kind word, let alone a salute.

Chapter 3

June 1876
Fort Sanders, Wyoming

Jane had spent the next week resting and enjoying more positive attention than she had ever known before. Almost everyone at Camp Sanders went out of their way to congratulate her on her act of heroism. True to his word, Captain Egan had a bottle of Taos Lightning, a fine whiskey Jane rarely had the opportunity to sip, and not one cigar, but an entire box of cigars, delivered to her tent. She decided not to open the bourbon, but enjoyed the cigars and shared them with several of the other scouts, for which they were greatly appreciative.

Since she was the only female among the troops, Jane had the luxury of single quarters. Her tent was small, but it was all hers, and she could do whatever she wanted without being scrutinized. She could drink herself silly inside her little canvas house and no one would be the wiser. But her drinking had gotten her in trouble in the past and, at least for the moment, she was enjoying her newfound respect too much to risk losing it. A few shots here and there with her comrades was all she allowed herself at this point. An entire bottle to herself—well, that was a call for trouble.

Ten days after her arrival back at Fort Sanders, Jane received a dispatch ordering her to report for duty at Fort Custer. After serving there, Jane was ordered to the Black Hills to help protect miners. That deployment ended for Jane in the fall of 1875, when she was sent back to Fort Sanders to await further orders. She spent the fall and winter taking care of chores around camp. Tending to the horses. Taking her turn guarding the perimeter of the fort. It seemed like she spent forever waiting for her next orders to come along. She longed to be back out working as a scout.

But that's not what the army had in mind for her. When Jane's orders finally did arrive, there was nothing about being in the line of fire, or working as a scout. Or working at all.

Early in June of 1876, Jane was directed to go to Fort Laramie to spend the summer relaxing, courtesy of the United States Army. She was informed the order was a delayed reward for her many months of loyal duty and for saving Egan's life.

"We would have sent you sooner, but needed you here to carry out a few other tasks and help hold down the fort," Crook told her when she reported to him to learn what and where her next job would be.

"During your time of rest, you will be free to come and go as you wish. You can do all the riding you want, or sit quietly in your assigned quarters. Food and other necessities will be provided for you," he said.

Jane wasn't sure how she felt about this. Exhilarated, on one hand. A bit let down, on the other. She loved putting herself in harm's way. She loved the challenge. The adventure. Then again, she could go on some of her own adventures and know that there was a place to rest and be fed at the end of each journey.

Two days later, her saddlebags filled with provisions for the trip— including the prized unopened bottle of whiskey—Jane said good-bye to her comrades and took off to collect her reward.

"Hell," she told Crook when he came to see her off, "a ride of leisure knowing I have enough food and water is reward. But a whole summer to do what I want without worrying is some pretty sweet butter on my biscuit."

"You've more than earned it," Crook said. He handed her an envelope that he said contained a monetary gift. "Captain Egan, myself, and your fellow scouts and soldiers passed a hat amongst ourselves and gathered this money as a display of our respect and gratitude," he said. "Almost everyone put some money in the pot." On the outside of the envelope, someone had penned: *Calamity Jane.*

Jane swiped the back of a hand across her eyes to stop the tears that were threatening to run loose. "No one in my entire life has ever shown me such kindness," she told him. "Please tell everyone how much I appreciate this. But what would make me happy, if it's all the same to you, sir, is for you to give this to a family of a soldier recently killed in the line of duty. A family that may really need it to survive. I'll leave it up to you to decide. Besides, with the provisions you have so generously provided for my trip, I won't need any money along the way."

"If that's what you'd like, Jane, I'd be happy to see it done," Crook said. He reached inside the envelope, which contained almost one hundred dollars in paper and coins, and pulled out five dollars. "Please take this, at least, just in case you need it for anything whatsoever. You are a kind and generous person," he said.

Jane accepted the money. "If you don't mind, sir, please remove the rest of the money from the envelope. I would like to keep this vessel with my name on it."

Crook smiled and did as he was asked.

Jane thanked him and said, "Well, I'd best be off. It's been a pleasure to work with you, sir." She saluted him, then hopped up in the saddle and rode out.

It was a glorious day on the plains, the landscape speckled with all colors of wildflowers, the sun warmly caressed her back, but was not so hot as to burn or cause discomfort. She kept a slow and steady pace, in no hurry to be anywhere. She was just enjoying the ride.

Jane couldn't recall a time when she felt happier, except for—there it was again. Memories of the time she spent with Bill. She pushed Bill out her mind, which was easier to do today than it was most. An hour later, alone in the wilderness as far as she could tell, she brought Buddy to a halt, leaned forward, and placed her arms around the creature's neck. Then she sobbed like a baby into the stiff hair of Buddy's mane. Jane was not sure what led up to such an unusual release of emotions. Unusual for her, anyway. But she decided it was a combination of some leftover exhaustion, relief, and happiness at having done a good job and getting recognized for it. Bill? Yeah, he was floating around in there somewhere. Always. But she hadn't wasted a significant number of tears on the man in the past. She wasn't going to start doing that now.

When the floodgates closed, Jane dismounted, poured some water into a tin cup, and gave it to the stallion. After the horse was done drinking, Jane withdrew a carrot from her pack and put it in his mouth. "I wouldn't be where I am today without you, Buddy," she said. She rarely verbalized her affections to the animal—after all, he wouldn't know what she was saying—but she was overcome with gratitude and emotion right now, and she recognized that he was the one true and constant friend she had in this world.

After Buddy had finished his treat and rested a while, Jane got back in the saddle and continued her journey. Her plan was to ride during the day and stop and camp out at night.

Jane and Buddy rode for several hours. At times like this, when she was not on a mission, sitting high in the saddle astride her horse was the perfect time for Jane to reflect on all sorts of things. Sometimes she got so caught up in her reverie, she just about fell asleep in the saddle. She was beginning to feel relaxed to the point of nodding off six hours after leaving Fort Sanders, so she decided to start looking for a place to camp for the night. She soon found a perfect spot beside a spring and decided to call it a day.

After feeding and watering Buddy, Jane removed his saddle and gave him a good brushing. The horse snorted in satisfaction, making Jane laugh.

"Aw, Buddy. We all love a little bit of pampering, huh?" she said.

Jane built a fire, ate a piece of the dried beef included in her provisions, then lay down on the ground beneath a blue spruce tree and prepared to sleep. But as so often happened, she found it impossible to nod off with the flood of memories that liked to come out and parade through her head as soon as she dared to relax. Sleep seemed to be on the verge of overtaking her when she was in the saddle, but once she had stretched out on the ground ...

"Go away, Bill. You left my person, now I would thank you to leave my fucking mind," Jane said out loud.

The shadowy memory of James Butler Hickok, her Wild Bill, was not about to oblige, and she wondered if there would ever come a time when it would.

Jane was a tender seventeen years of age and working as a prostitute when she met the man she would always consider the love of her life. She'd heard about the idea of star-crossed lovers, but save for some brief moments when the universe let up on Bill and Jane and allowed them to love in peace, their relationship was fraught with problems from start to finish.

Jane reached over and pulled the bottle of bourbon from the saddlebag beside her. She opened it and then sat back down by the fire. She raised the bottle high above her head and said, "Here's to you, Bill Hickok, you miserable cocksucker!"

Jane took a sip and then made another toast. "And here's to the very thought of you making sleep impossible to come by." She took another, much longer sip, belched, and added one more "Cocksucker!"

Chapter 4
1869
Cheyenne, Wyoming

Wild Bill Hickok was sitting at a poker table at Jack McDaniel's Theatre and Gambling Saloon in Cheyenne, Wyoming, when Jane first laid eyes on him. She often drank there when she was not working at Miss Crystal's brothel, a whorehouse located at the edge of town, far enough from the prying eyes of both the righteous and wistful, and close enough to walk to her favorite watering hole.

Martha Jane Canary was good at many things, especially the art of dispensing sexual pleasure. She made more money at whoring than any other job she'd ever held. And there had been many of those since the age of twelve, when her alcoholic father and adulterous mother had the audacity to die within a year of each other. Their deaths left Martha, the eldest of six children, in charge of feeding and clothing her siblings. She had managed to place a few of the young ones with respectable families who yearned for a child to love. But she had to pay a monthly stipend for two others to live with foster families, and that required her to do whatever made her the most cash.

Martha much preferred bull whacking, hunting, working on the railroad, or stagecoach driving to lying on her back while a fat, smelly prospector grunted and rutted, his foul sweat dripping on her body. But she needed to do what filled her money pouch the fastest. And if that meant allowing some creep to stick his dick down her throat, or anywhere else he thought he was entitled to put it, then that's what she'd do for as long as it took.

Many of the men who frequented Miss Crystal's whorehouse asked for Jane specifically. They'd say something like: "I don't remember her name but she's very young and has some special skills like no one I've ever laid with." Or: "I want that tall redhead. Swears a blue streak and she's a bit plain but she knows how to please a man."

Jane wanted to gag when she heard the off-handed compliments her tricks paid her. "I'd just as soon bite the next fucking one off rather than suck the soured milk out of it," she'd say. And since Jane had a temper, Miss Crystal often worried that one day she just might carry out that threat. Until then, Martha Jane Canary was the brothel's biggest draw and top moneymaker.

That is why Jane could keep the hours she wanted, take breaks as desired, and drink till she rendered herself useless—sometimes beginning as early as noon—without the threat of losing her job. This was one of those days when Jane, after turning three tricks, decided to end the day early and get stinking drunk.

She walked into the saloon, over to the bar, slapped down a bag of small gold nuggets, and said, "Pour, and keep 'em coming until this morning's earnings are all used up."

The saloon's owner and namesake, Jack McDaniels, weighed the bag and whistled. "You made this much so far today?" he asked.

"I'm that fucking good, what can I say? And I'm willing to do some crazy-assed things for higher rates," Jane said. "My obligations are taken care of for the next week, so I'm spending this on my own fucking pleasure which, by the way, has nothing to do with fucking," she said.

"Okay, you got it! But no getting out of line, or I promise you I will kick your sorry ass out that door and you will forfeit the rest of the money you have not yet drank up," he said. Jane didn't always behave rationally when she was drinking, and Jack had had the misfortune of witnessing more than a few of her drunken tirades.

She might have been of a tender age, but there was nothing tender about Jane's build or demeanor. She stood five feet, nine inches tall, had muscles that many men envied, and tipped the scale at a hefty one hundred and forty-five pounds. She leaned over the bar, grabbed the man by his collar, and snarled, "You listen to me, you miserable thieving motherfucker! Seeing as how this is *your* fine establishment, I understand that you have the right to accept or reject whatever patron you deem worthy or unworthy of drinking in it. So, if my *sorry ass* gets fucked up such that you feel it necessary to toss it out the door, I'll hold no ill will against you. But I more than earned the gold in that bag and whither my ass goes, my remaining funds at the time of its departure had better fucking go right along with it, or I will hunt you down and kill you dead."

She let the man go, adjusted the crumpled dress she was wearing, and said sweetly, "Now that we have that settled, I'd be much obliged if you would commence to pour."

The shaken bartender poured a shot of bourbon and pushed it toward her.

"Thank ye kindly," Jane said. "I know my money will cover a few bottles, so I'll just take this one to a table and not bother you any further until it's empty."

Jane downed the shot, grabbed the bottle, and turned around to find a table. That's when she saw him. The most beautiful human being she had ever laid eyes on. He was staring at her, as was most everyone else in the saloon, due to her outburst. Most of the patrons recognized her and were used to her temper, but this was one of her most explosive verbal displays to date.

Bill Hickok was sitting facing the door of the saloon, as he always did, to prevent anyone from sneaking up on him. He was a wanted man, by both the law and the friends and families of men he had gunned down. He had a price on his head and was taking no chances.

Jane nodded and smiled at him. He returned her smile and nod, and then turned back to his game. He'd already won four times the money he started with, so a short time later he folded his cards, set them face down on the table, and said, "I'm calling it."

"Two pair," Matt Smith said. He laid two queens and two sevens face up in front of him.

The others had folded, except for Bill. He said, "That's a pretty good hand, Matt, but I do believe this will beat it." One by one Bill turned over his cards. Ace. Ace. Ace. Deuce. Ace.

"I'm done," Smith said, pushing his chair away from the table. "Congratulations, Bill." The others around the table followed suit and took their leave, all of them sporting considerably lighter pockets than they had when they started. But there was not one among them who dared complain in Bill's presence. The man's temper was legendary.

Bill collected his winnings, picked his glass and hat up off the table, and walked toward where Jane sat, staring at him.

"Mind if I get my own bottle and join you?" he asked.

Jane smiled. "Wouldn't care to stop you," she said.

Bill set his glass and hat on the table and retrieved a full bottle from the bartender, paying for it with a small portion of his winnings. Then he returned and sat down across from Jane, still facing the door as he had at the previous table.

"My name is Bill," he said. "And who might you be?"

"Martha Jane Canary, but I go by Jane. That name suits my personality better than Martha."

"Jane it is, then, and I think you may be right about that, judging from some of the Marthas I've known in my time," Bill said.

Jane smiled and raised the bottle to her lips.

"So, Jane, how old are you?" Bill asked.

"I'm twenty, Bill." Jane didn't hesitate to lie. She never did when a lie was more to her advantage than the truth. "But I do believe I've packed twice as many years of hard living into my time on earth," she said. "How the hell old are *you*?" she asked.

Bill threw his head back and laughed. I'm thirty-one, too old for you, by the looks of you and not your falsely stated age," he said.

Jane's face got hot. She was not used to getting called out on her lies. She decided not to pursue the matter.

"So what do you do, Bill?" she asked.

Bill savored some more of the whiskey, put his glass down, leaned forward, and said, "Right now I'm kind of between jobs, but my occupation is shooting the crap out of those who deserve to have it shot out of them," he said.

"Oh," Jane said. "If they deserve it, I have no problem—wait! I just figured it out. I've seen newspaper photos and read stories about you. You're *Wild* Bill *Hickok*."

"The one and the only," Bill admitted.

"You are my fucking *hero*, Bill," Jane told him, unable to keep the excitement and awe out of her voice. "You are the only man alive who might just be my equal when it comes to fast shooting, hard riding, and"—she raised her bottle— "hard drinking." She took a long swig and let out an appreciative belch. "Sorry about that, but it happens from time to time."

Bill threw back his head again and roared. "You are one interesting woman, Jane."

Jane loved the way he laughed. She smiled and took another swig.

The two were quiet for a few minutes, and that was fine with her. She could sit in silence and stare at this man for hours. At six feet, two inches, he was much taller than she, taller than most of the men she knew. He had long, wavy blond hair and a mustache that curled down both sides of his mouth. And those eyes—soft blue, kind of faded and tired, but so intense.

Bill broke the silence. "Anyone can drink, if they so choose. As do I. But what makes you, a very young woman, and an attractive one at that, think you can shoot and ride as fast as myself?"

"I don't just *think* that, I *know* it!" she said. "And if you want, on any given day when I'm not hung over and haven't yet begun to imbibe, of which there are many, I would be happy to show you," she said.

His calling her attractive made it difficult for her to speak without a slight tremble in her voice. "And what makes you think a person can't be both attractive *and* talented?"

26

"Well, you make a good point there, Jane. Just look at me ..."

"Trust me, I am. Can barely take my eyes off you," Jane said.

Bill roared at that one. "You've got good taste in men and whiskey, girl. And as for you proving your shooting and riding prowess to me, I look forward to that," he said. He drank the rest of the whiskey straight down and then said, "Now, if you'll excuse me, I need to get some sleep. I spent the entire night playing cards and won enough to pay for another week at Paddy McPherson's Hotel, as well as for two meals a day, and plenty of drink—which is all I require. I'll be heading off to rest there now, if you don't mind."

"Whatever you want, Bill. I don't mind it at all," Jane said, her words dripping with sweetness.

Bill smiled, nodded, and stood up. He picked his hat up off the table, put it on his head, and turned to leave. He stopped just inside the door of the saloon, then turned around and walked back to the table where Jane still sat, removed his hat, and said, "I'm thinking you look a little tired yourself. Would you maybe fancy taking a rest along with me?" he asked.

Jane's heart nearly exploded. She set the bottle down, stood up and said, "Hell, yes! Who wouldn't?"

"Bring the bottle?" he asked.

"I'll do you one better," she said.

Jane walked over to the bar and said, "I figure there are about four more bottles worth of gold left in my pouch there. Give me one of those, please, then pour the gold out of the pouch, give the bag to me, and keep the rest as credit for me to use when I come in again. That okay with you?"

The bartender nodded his agreement, did as he was told, then wrote Jane a letter of credit toward future drinking. Jane smiled and said, "Take a little off the top of that for yourself. And, uh, would you be so kind as to make me a loan of two of your shot glasses? I will return them the next time I come back for a drink. And you know I'll be back," she said.

"Sure, Jane." He gave her two glasses, and she grabbed them and the unopened bottle off the bar. Bill stepped up, took the bottle out of her hand, and slipped it into a deep inside pocket of his buckskin coat. Then he did the same with the glasses.

"See," Jane said, "this is yet another one of the many reasons I believe men's clothing is so much more useful than women's. And more comfortable, too. In fact, before we nap, if you don't mind, I'd be very much obliged if you would allow me to remove mine."

Bill smiled, plopped his hat back on his head, held out his arm for her to take, and said, "I'd be mighty disappointed if you didn't, but I don't pay."

"I just might pay you," Jane said.

Bill's laughed, winked, and said: "It wouldn't be the first time, honey."

Chapter 5
1869
The Next Day

Jane awoke the next morning happier than she'd ever thought possible. Bill was still sleeping beside her, naked and glorious. The sun fell in patterns across his body and where it lit on his long blond hair, painting individual strands with various shades of gold. She'd never seen anything so beautiful. The sugar maple trees that displayed various shades of red, orange, and gold in the fall could not hold a candle to this man's splendor. The lips, teeth, and tongue he used to probe around her mouth and her female bits the night before were even sweeter than the maple syrup those trees produced in the spring. One night, and she was ready to march into the fiery pits of hell with this man, were he to ask.

When she and Bill got back to his room at Paddy McPherson's Hotel and Diner the afternoon before, there had been little time for drinking. Right after he shut the door, Bill removed his hat and jacket and pulled Jane close. His lips and hands seared her skin. Once that door had closed behind them, there was no going back.

He slowly removed her dress, taking care to make sure his large hands lightly brushed against various parts of her body. Slow, deliberate, shudder-inducing movements that weakened her knees and left her as vulnerable as she had ever allowed herself to be. He used just the right amounts of gentle, firm, strong, and tender caresses. And he talked to her while he performed his magic on her body.

"You have such soft skin, Jane. I love touching it so lightly and watching you shiver." And, "Raise your arms up over your head, and lie very still while I explore every bit of your gorgeous body. I intend to make you moan for hours."

As he worked his hands, fingers, and tongue over and around every part of her, he said, "There are so many things I want to do to you, Jane," he said. "Close your eyes so I can surprise you with where my hands will touch you next."

Jane loved the way he took command. They made love for hours, rendering her speechless and him exhausted.

She wanted to tell him she'd never known fucking could feel so good, but he'd taken so much of her breath away, she could barely speak an intelligible word, let alone a full-on sentence.

The first time he entered her, she nearly passed out. He filled her up, then slowly moved in and out, bringing forth sensations she'd never felt before. She came first, long and violent waves of rhythmic, muscular contractions that seemed to go on forever. She felt her pelvis rise weightlessly toward the ceiling, even though his body had her pinned. He took his time and, only when he was sure she was winding down, wasted no time polishing off his own pleasure and then sank into her arms.

"Damn, Jane!" Bill said when he could speak.

"This is the first time in my whole fucking life I feel like I should be the one paying for sex," Jane said.

Bill laughed. "You did put a lot in the kitty, girl!"

She laughed at his poker analogy. "Always the gambler, huh, Bill?"

"Hey, these days it keeps me in food, booze, and housing. It's all I've got to fall back on."

Jane was still feeling the aftershocks of his lovemaking and said in between rumbles, "Hey, with your talents you could do anything," she said.

Bill sighed. "'Fraid not, honey. For one thing, I'm a wanted man and, as such, must keep a very low profile. For another, I came to Cheyenne to consult with a doctor about my failing eyesight. The prognosis is, well, shall we say, dark."

Jane rolled over on her side and put her arm across his chest. "You're going blind?" she asked.

"As the proverbial bat," Bill said.

"Mother of all fucking hell!" she said.

"That's one way to put it," Bill said. Then he pulled her on top of him and cupped a hand on each breast. "How about we forget about that other stuff for a while and enjoy the pleasure of becoming even better acquainted?"

"Whatever you say, Bill. Whatever you want," she said looking down at him, her dark red hair falling in his face. She was happy she had shampooed it yesterday.

Bill took his hands off her breasts and brushed the hair back from her face. "I don't think I've ever known a woman to say that to me. In fact, I know I haven't," he said. "Will you say that again, please?" he asked.

Jane cocked her head and laughed. Then she leaned down and whispered directly into his left ear. "I said, 'Whatever you want, darling.'"

Bill rolled Jane over onto her back, eased himself on top of her, and grinned. "Okay, then," he said.

Jane gasped as he pressed his lips to hers, his tongue probing her mouth, while his hands took another long hike across her body.

Chapter 6

Bill woke up to see Jane beside him, head propped up by one elbow, staring down at him. "Good morning, gorgeous," he said, rolling over, wrapping his right arm around her waist, and drawing her close. She laid her head on his chest and sighed.

"Hey, before I get all caught up in your sexy body again, I need to ask: just how old are you, *really*?" he asked.

"As near as I can figure, I'm about seventeen," she said.

"Why'd you lie last night?" he asked, curious but not angry.

"I just wanted you to think of me more as a woman than a girl," she said.

Bill kissed the top of her head. "You are a perfect combination of both. Your passion belies your young age and your childlike sweetness speaks to it," he said.

"And what of my uncontrollable temper?" Jane asked.

"I have a feeling you can and do control it when it serves your purpose, which is a sign of intelligence. And if that temper is not directed toward me, it's fine. Kinda fun to watch, too, judging from yesterday's performance with the barkeep."

Jane laughed. "I can't imagine ever being angry at you, let alone losing my temper," she said.

"Just remember that down the road apiece," Bill laughed.

"Speaking of down the road, I never saw you around here until yesterday. Did you just arrive in town?"

"I got here a couple of days ago. I saw an eye doctor and then played in a few poker games to secure this room. I'm paid up for a few more days, then I'm not sure what I'm doing or where I'm going."

Jane's voice was subdued when she said, "I'll be hoping you decide to stick around here, in these parts. I make good money at Miss Crystal's and only work when I want. I can help pay for this room, should you decide to stay here for a bit."

32

"Well, for today the only plan I have is to get some good food in my belly, polish off that bottle sitting yonder, and maybe find a game. That's pretty much my job these days," he said.

"What did you do before your eyes started giving you trouble?" she asked.

"I was the marshal in Abilene, Kansas, for a little while, but that ended badly," he said.

"Why? What happened?" she asked, the index finger of her left hand drawing a line down the center of his hairy chest. When she reached his navel, he put his hand over hers.

"There are two things I find I am incapable of doing at once," he said. "And they are telling a story and being seduced."

Jane pulled her hand back, smiled, and said, "Okay. Commence to telling your story, and when you are finished, I will commence to walking my fingers down below your belly." Bill sighed. "Yeah, like I'm going to be able to think straight now!"

Jane laughed. "Okay, get your mind off my fingers and tell me why your stint as marshal in Abilene ended poorly," she said.

"Yeah, that," he sighed. "Well, I think the people who lived there might've thought I was a little too quick to draw and shoot. You know this, right? You know it's imperative for you to be fast when it's you or them?"

Jane nodded. "Yes! Questions can always be asked later, if you're still alive to ask 'em."

He removed her hand from his chest and raised it to his lips. "Well, I have always employed that belief, which is why, I think, I am still alive today. And which is why I thought I could do a service for the people of Abilene, and keep them safe and all."

"Of course, you did! I'm sure you were a great sheriff, Bill." She lifted her head off his chest and looked up at him. "If I owned a town, I would want you there to keep the peace," she said.

"Are you always this sweet?" he asked.

Jane laughed. "Hell, no! Almost never. Remember yesterday? Jack McDaniel's Saloon?"

"Truth be told, I think that's what drew me to you," he said. "But you wear sweet well, too."

Jane smiled. It was easy to be sweet to Bill. "You can feel free to tell me what made your time as sheriff end badly," she said then added, "Or not, if you would rather not talk about it."

"I suppose it would be kind of good to talk about it to someone who cares to hear it," he said. And then Bill Hickok told Jane Canary about the night he killed the wrong man.

"I served in the war and then moved to Kansas when it was over. I was appointed sheriff in Hays City and later marshal of Abilene. That town had become outposts for lawless men before I arrived, and the townspeople were looking for someone to protect them. That was near the beginning of 1871 and I didn't last out the year. Three goddamn months ago, I was in a shootout with a man named Phil Coe. He owned the saloon I drank in, and he was bad to the core. As I fired on Coe, I saw someone moving toward me from the side and thought I was under attack from one of his henchmen. I turned slightly and fired off two shots. The man moving toward me was my friend and my deputy, Mike Williams, who'd come to back me up." Bill turned his head away from Jane and blinked rapidly. Killing Williams was something Bill doubted he would ever get over.

"I'm so sorry, Bill, but you didn't know. And you have a right to protect yourself," Jane said.

"Yeah, but that man had two little babies, less than three years of age, and a wife who loved him. And he was a good man, to boot. He didn't deserve to die. His death will haunt me for the rest of my life," Hickok said.

"I am so sorry, Bill. But it sounds like an honest mistake."

"It wouldn't have happened if my eyesight was still good. I knew it was changing and I should have quit. Anyway, the town held an inquest and it was revealed that my brand of frontier justice, that of shooting first and asking questions later, was not for them. I was relieved of my duties and got the hell out of Abilene before they could also learn that I'm a wanted man for killing a poker player who took my watch."

"Well, if he stole from you, how can killing him be considered a crime?" Jane asked.

"Well, he didn't exactly steal it. I gave it to him in a game, as collateral, and then, when my two pairs lost it to his full house, he wore it and taunted me with it every chance he got, until I couldn't stand it no more," Bill said.

"Well, Bill," she said, "that is a sad turn of events, but it's not as if you shot the Williams guy on purpose and as for the watch winner, sounds like he made his own bed. I've never minded using a bullet to stop a bully."

"It was the innocent people in Abilene who counted on me to look out for their well-being that I failed miserably because my eyesight is going. Mike didn't deserve to die. And I deserved to be ousted. So, from now on, I'm out of the gunfighting business. I'll earn my money as a gambler, as long as I continue to be good at that."

"We can do anything we set our minds to, Bill. An old guy I worked with on the railroad once told me that, and I believe him," Jane said.

Bill sat up, leaned over, and grabbed his pants off the floor. He pulled them on and then did the same with the rest of his clothing.

"Well, what I have my mind set on now, pretty lady, is grabbing some grub. I invite you to join me in that endeavor," he said.

"You paying?" she asked, cocking her head and winking.

"Yes, ma'am. I am paying today. But don't get used to that. I don't always win at this game of cards I now call my career."

Jane got up and pulled on her dress, minus any undergarments. Bill gave her an appreciative smirk and walked over to open the door. "After you, my dear. We will eat, drink, and enjoy the day. Tomorrow you can, maybe, show me some of your riding and shooting skills.

Then it's back to the card tables for me while you go off and earn more pouches of gold the likes of which I have never seen a woman carrying around."

"The money's great, and I need to make it to care for a couple of my little brothers, but after last night, I'm pretty sure my heart is even less into my fucking current profession than it was before I met you. And I really thought I could not detest that job any more than I already did." Jane said.

Bill laughed. "Well, don't worry about that today. Today is all about things that make us happy," he said.

Chapter 7

The next few weeks were a happy blur. Bill was Jane's whole world now, a better world than she ever imagined living in. They did a lot together. They rode. Practiced shooting targets. Watched every sunrise and sunset, side by side. They made love almost every day. Jane wanted more of Bill with every passing moment.

About a month after they met, Bill proposed to Jane. They had ridden about three miles outside of Cheyenne to have a picnic. Picnics were one of their favorite things, and Jane had spared no expense putting together a basket of fresh-baked bread bought from Elmer Cobb's bakery, some cheese Crystal allowed her to take from stock, a freshly slaughtered chicken purchased from the Laramie Butcher Shop, some cookies Jane baked herself in Miss Crystal's kitchen, and a bottle of bourbon.

They rode to a clearing in the middle of some dense brush they had discovered one day when out hunting, spread a blanket, built a fire, stuck a large wet branch through the middle of the chicken, piled some rocks to hold it over the fire, and then sat back and waited for it to cook.

Bill opened the bottle and pulled two shot glasses from the inside pocket of his jacket.

"Remember these?" he asked.

"Holy hell! I gave those to you to return to Andy," Jane said. "He's been insisting you didn't do that, but I didn't believe him. He keeps putting the cost of those glasses on my tab and I keep ignoring it," she said.

"And don't you dare even think about paying for them. I firmly believe we are the rightful owners of these glasses, considering all of the money we have spent at that saloon," Bill said.

Jane laughed. "I can buy into that belief."

They toasted each other and threw back the contents of their glasses.

They enjoyed sitting in silence for a bit, taking in their surroundings, just happy to be in each other's company. Then Bill reached out and took Jane's hand.

"I have to tell you something, Jane," he said.

"Okay, shoot," Jane said with a smile.

"Be careful. Not a good choice of words to use around the likes of me," he said.

Jane laughed again. "How about, Go ahead, Bill. Tell me something."

"In all seriousness, Jane, I've been with a lot of women, some longer than I've yet been with you. I've been blessed with the love and passion, friendship and loyalty of many, many beautiful, charming, intelligent women ..."

"What's your fucking point, Bill?" Jane was more than a little annoyed that the man she loved like crazy was waxing poetic about his past affairs.

Bill looked at Jane with an intensity that shooed the anger right out of her heart.

"The *fucking* point is, my dear Jane, that I have never in my wildest dreams thought I would meet someone like you. Someone who is so perfect for me, who I can't imagine living without. You make me happier than I ever thought possible, Jane. Happier than I probably deserve to be."

"Oh," was all she could manage to say.

"Bill stood and pulled her up with him. He kissed her long and tenderly, then said, "Jane, I want to ask you something."

"What would that be?" Jane said, her head resting just below his shoulder.

He took her face in both hands, raised it up so she looked into his eyes and said, "Skipping the intrusion of a preacher and minus the silly formalities, I would like to know, Martha Jane Canary, if you would consent to be my wife. Right here. Right now."

"What?" Jane asked.

"I said ..."

"I know what you said, Bill, but you've told me several times you aren't a man to stay in any one place or with any woman long. I had just resigned myself to knowing I would have to say good-bye to you someday and hoping that day would be a long way off. I'm confused." Jane could barely manage to get the words out of her mouth. Her heart was racing faster than a jackrabbit chased by a coyote.

"I know, but the thing is, Jane, you aren't just any woman," he said. "And I'd like to try to settle down with you."

"Are you sure?" Jane asked.

"As sure as I am that meeting you was the best thing that ever happened to me," he said.

"Then yes. Yes! *Yes*," she said, crying and laughing at the same time.

Bill kissed her, then said, "Let's kneel upon the ground, and as Mother Nature is our witness, commit to love, honor, and ride with each other as long as we both shall live," he said.

"Bill, wait!" Jane said. "I need to tell you something first."

"What would that be?" he asked.

"I've never had any desire to be a mother and I doubt I ever will," she said.

"Okay. I'm not fond of children myself, and I certainly don't want any of my own at this point in my life," he said, to her relief.

"I also don't want to be a fucking proper wife, if you know what I mean," she said.

"Not looking for a proper wife, if I even know what that is." He smiled.

"I mean, I want to be your equal. To stand beside you and ride beside you. I don't want to tend to the home while you go on the hunt," she said.

"I would never want to leave you behind when I head off for adventure. Part of the fun is having you to share that with me," he said.

Jane squealed. "Then hell, let this wedding begin!"

Together they knelt. Bill took both of Jane's hands in his, bowed his head, and said, "My dear Mother Earth, we kneel upon your sacred soil to ask you to approve of and bless this union of two souls who surely belong together for as long as you allow."

Then he raised his head, looked directly into Jane's eyes, and said, "Jane Canary, I take you for my wife as long as Mother Earth allows. Will you take me for your husband?"

Jane had tears in her eyes when she said, "James Butler Hickok, I will, as long as Mother Earth allows and beyond that. I will follow you into eternity."

They kissed; then Bill pulled Jane to her feet and kissed her once more.

"That's it? We're married? Wow! That was quick," Jane said.

"Short and sweet. Like I always imagined my wedding to be someday. What do you say we commence to eating our wedding chicken and then consummate this marriage?" Bill said.

Jane laughed. "That sounds like the perfect wedding to me."

They spent the rest of the afternoon drinking, laughing, eating their feast, and making love. One short month ago Jane had set eyes on Wild Bill Hickok for the first time. Now she was his wife. Her world could not be more perfect. For now, at least. One short month later, that perfect world would crash to the ground and break into a million little pieces. And she never saw it coming.

Chapter 8

Jane was so in love with Bill she had a hard time seeing him as anything but perfect. He had his faults, but so did she. They both drank too much. They both had hair-trigger tempers. Jane cussed too much. Bill lost money at the poker table about twice as often as he won. Jane bragged too much, which even she knew could get on a person's nerves occasionally. Bill slept too much when he wasn't drinking or gambling and flirted with other women too much. Sometimes right in front of her, as if Jane didn't exist.

Bill gambled every dime they had and then hit friends up for loans. It was hard to say no to Wild Bill Hickok. Not only did he have considerable charm, but many people were afraid of him, and handing over a few coins when he asked was a small price to pay to keep on his good side.

Bill was a gracious winner when he played cards, but not so polite when he lost. Sometimes he would turn over the table, sending bottles, glasses, and chips, and his fellow players flying everywhere. Sometimes he would just sit and brood. It was no secret that he expected those who had held the better hands to put some coins back in his, both for the honor of having played with him and for him to buy some consolation drinks.

He owed so many people there were few left to ask. And certainly not for the escalating amounts he needed to maintain his gambling addiction.

After their wedding ceremony in the woods, Jane had said she would never let another man touch her, even for money. Her financial obligations to her two brothers ended suddenly when their foster parents decided to adopt the boys and raise them as their own. That news came a day after the couple exchanged their unofficial wedding vows. So, the couple could now live off Bill's winnings and Jane's ability to hunt. Life was good as far as Jane's cloudy vision of it could see.

But one morning, claiming to be in dire straits, Bill asked her to turn a few tricks to keep him playing. He promised she could quit as soon as he hit a big jackpot again, which, he said, he was due any minute now. Then, he said, they would ride off to find a place to set down roots. He never mentioned how they would maintain those roots without any additional funds coming in, and Jane didn't ask.

Jane went back to work as a whore at Miss Crystal's because she loved him, but before long, she was turning several tricks a day, with nothing left to show for it. Bill's luck was getting worse, not better. That winning jackpot he kept talking about never materialized.

Still, Jane's way of seeing it was that they needed very little to live, and if she needed to perform unpleasant sexual acts to keep Bill in coins to support his habit, so be it. But when Jane had earlier told Miss Crystal she was hanging up her panties, the brothel owner had no choice but to bring in a replacement. There was a new girl in town, and she was the one who was now getting most of the clients

Jane was not too upset about that. Water was free, and sleeping under the stars was as good as any room with a roof. It was the days when they didn't have enough money to use for drink that were problematic.

On those days Jane would saunter into the tavern alone, approach the bar, turn to face its patrons and ask, "Who wants to hear my story about how even as a small child I was already being recognized as a girl who could outride and outshoot any male?"

Often the men would humor her, more for a good laugh than anything. The drinks would flow, and so would the words out of Jane's mouth.

"I was only fourteen years old when I was hired as a pony express rider. I had to carry the mail fifty miles, sometimes, over the roughest trails in the Black Hills country. It was a dangerous route, but my reputation as a rider and quick shot were widely known," she said.

And after that introduction, she followed with various tales of ambushes, attempted highway robberies, and Indian attacks—all of which she managed to come out unscathed from, to heroically deliver the mail where it needed to go.

While Jane held everyone's attention, Bill would saunter into the saloon, stand near, and as the shots were bought for her, he would grab one here and there. When they'd had their fill, Jane would say something like, "That's it for today, boys. But I'll be back later tonight, maybe, to share with you my story of the day I took down three road robbers who had surrounded a family's wagon. Those fellows didn't know what hit them!"

It was eight o'clock at night after a day of meager earnings at the whorehouse when Jane stumbled into Jack McDaniels' saloon. She had gone through a bottle of whiskey while sitting in their tent for two hours waiting for Bill to come home. She had left for Miss Crystal's to pick up some tricks around noon, about the same time he went to take part in an afternoon poker game. When the bottle was empty, and Bill was not yet back, she decided he must be winning, and she would go sit at the saloon and drink some more until he was done.

When she walked into the saloon, the first thing she saw was Bill sitting at a table with one of the whores. He was drunk and had one of the woman's blonde curls twirled around his fingers.

"You filthy whore!" Jane screamed as she charged the table. Both Bill and the woman dove for cover as Jane knocked over the table, causing the drinks on top of it to go crashing to the ground.

Jane went after the woman next, grabbing her by her hair and dragging her out the door. Bill tried to pull Jane off the poor girl, and Jane hit him in the mouth with her fist.

They were both thrown in jail for causing a public disturbance while drunk. They spent the night in separate jail cells, but forgave each other the next day, when they were sober.

They were approaching one-month of marital "bliss", which Jane had every intention of turning into a huge celebration, when Bill delivered the worst news Jane thought she would ever hear.

43

They had just raced five miles out and then back again to Cheyenne, calling it a tie as they crossed the finish line together. Bill and Jane rubbed down and watered their horses, put them in their stalls at the livery stable, and then went off to the saloon for some drinks.

This day they had some coins to spare. and Jane was tired from riding. She was happy she would not have to think up yet another tall tale to be able to drink her fill.

She and Bill entered the tavern. Bill bought a bottle and asked for two glasses.

"I've been asking repeatedly for you to return the two you borrowed months ago, or at least pay for them," McDaniels told them. This made Bill angry, but Jane said, "We don't need no fucking glasses. The bottle's fine to drink out of."

They sat down at what had become their favorite table—the one Jane was at the day they met. Bill was looking more tired than usual this day, and Jack's reminder about the glasses put him in a foul mood.

"Don't you dare ever give him back those glasses," Bill said, shooting an ugly look in Jack's direction.

"Oh, don't worry about that. He's probably just in a bad mood today," Jane said. "I'm more worried about you. Are you feeling okay, Bill?" she asked.

"Yeah, just wondering what to do next. Where to go from here," he said. He was staring down at the bottle angry about being denied a glass. "I love the way a glass looks when the light hits it," he said. "Especially when it's filled with this sweet amber liquid."

"I know what you mean," Jane said. They drank in silence for a bit, enjoying the quiet, until a man Bill often played cards with approached their table.

"Hey, Bill, want to join us in a game later this afternoon?" the man asked.

"Maybe," Bill said without looking up.

The man stayed put and pushed a little harder. He obviously wanted Bill in the game. "Well, we only have one seat open, and if you take too long to decide, someone else might grab it," he said.

Bill looked up and glared at him. "Okay," he said.

"Okay you'll play, or okay if someone else takes your seat?"

"Okay, buddy, you can do whatever you want as long as it does not include standing here, breathing down my back, and asking me any more questions now," Bill said.

"I don't think Bill's feeling well today, so you might just want to consider putting someone else's ass in that spare seat," Jane said.

A man named Donald Spores, who had overheard the exchange, more because Jane had a loud voice than because he was eavesdropping, called from his table a few feet away: "Son of a bitch, Bill! Your girl not only wears the pants in your relationship, but she uses them to control you, too."

Several patrons laughed at that, which enraged Bill. He shoved his chair back from the table, took a few quick steps toward the man, grabbed him by the neck, pulled him up out of his chair, and growled, "If you want to see the sun set tonight, you motherfucking ass, I suggest you shut your damn mouth now and never open it again in my presence." The guy nodded in agreement and Bill dropped him. Then Bill turned and walked out of the saloon.

Jane got up, glared hard enough at those around her to keep them from making any further comment, and ran after Bill. He was walking toward the stables when she caught up with him. "Don't listen to the asshole, Bill. You and I know I don't control or speak for you. I was just trying to avoid an ugly scene," she said.

"It's not your fault," Bill said, slowing his pace a bit. He reached the stables and sat down on a bench outside the door. "Jane, would you sit with me a spell?" he asked.

"Of course, Bill," Jane said. She was happy to know he did not blame her for the previous confrontation.

Jane was sitting to the left of him, and he reached out and took her right hand in his. But he didn't look at her. His head was hung such that the only thing he could see now was the ground.

"What's wrong, Bill?" Jane asked.

When he didn't answer, she asked again, in a different way. "William Hickok, I swear you are scaring the piss out of me. Talk to me!"

Bill raised his head, but looked off into the distance. There was no eye contact.

"I'm restless, Jane," he said. "I told you I never like to stay in one place long."

"Yeah, I fucking know that. So, what's keeping us here?" Jane asked. "I'll go anywhere you want, Bill."

He turned and looked at her, and without saying a word, she knew. But he did speak, and she later wished he hadn't.

"I also told you I don't stay with anyone long. I'm a loner. I'm sorry," he said.

Jane's emotions had never been as conflicted as they were at that moment. She wanted to scream. Cry. Swear. Beat the living crap out of him. Shoot him dead off that bench. Bury herself in his arms. But she was not going to beg.

"What the fuck did you mean when you said I was perfect for you, Bill? You made a vow akin to the 'until death do us part' in a normal wedding ceremony. Do we look goddamn dead to you?" she cried.

"I recall saying I'd try my best. At the time, I thought I could do it," he said.

"Do it? What exactly the fuck is *it*?" Jane asked.

Bill sighed. "Stay with someone long-term, Jane," he said.

"Someone? Am I just *someone* to you, because I could swear I remember you telling me I was not just any woman the day you asked me to marry you," she said.

"You know that was just a romantic moment. It's not as if it was legally binding or anything," he said.

"Or anything. To you, apparently, it was nothing. To me, mother-fucker, it was everything. How dare you play with my feelings like this?" Jane was furious.

Bill didn't answer.

"I see," she said. "Well, what's stopping you, then? Go. Take off," she said.

"It's just the way I'm made, Jane. I don't really have a choice in the matter," he said.

"Bullshit!" she said.

"Jane ..."

"No, I don't want to hear it. You don't want a life with me, then fine. I don't need any explanations as to why."

"I was planning on staying a couple of days, to give you a chance to get used to the idea. Maybe soften the blow," Bill began to explain.

"What the hell kind of fucking blow are you talking about?" she said. She was as close to popping her cork as a shaken-up bottle of bubbly. "I was fine before you slithered your way into my life, you miserable, motherfucking asshole. I'll be no less fine when you go." Tears weren't often a part of Jane's makeup, and that was one thing she was grateful for now.

Bill stood removed his hat and said, "I do love you, Jane. I'm just not the staying sort."

"What a crock of horseshit," she said. "Just go. Go! You don't see any fucking ropes holding you down, do you?" She stood, crossed her arms, and glared at him.

Bill went into the stables and returned a few minutes later, holding the reins of his saddled horse.

"Pleased to have made your acquaintance, Martha Jane Canary," he said, taking off his hat and bowing.

For one of the few times in her life, Jane felt like she was going to cry. She mustered a half-smile and said: "Good-bye, cocksucker. Wish I could say the same," she said.

47

Bill put his hat back on his head and mounted his horse. He looked down at Jane and said, "Until we meet again."

Jane didn't miss a beat. "Better hope we don't because if we do, I will shoot you on sight."

Bill threw his head back and laughed, infuriating Jane. When he saw her reaching for her pistol, he dug in his spurs and raced away, out of Cheyenne and out of Jane's life.

She stood a few minutes, watching his dust, thinking *What just happened here?* Then she turned and walked back to the saloon. She entered the tavern and announced for all to hear, "Buy this girl a drink and keep 'em coming," she said, pointing both of her thumbs at her chest.

"Ask your prissy boyfriend," yelled one man who was not in the saloon during the previous confrontation. "He seems to like women who support him. Where is he, anyway?"

Jane's eyes flared, like a bull about to charge. "Wild Bill fucking Hickok and I just got divorced. He rode off into the sunset, the lying son of a bitch!"

The poor man didn't see coming what happened next. Jane was on him like maggots on a dead bison. It took two large men to pull her off the man, and by then his face was a bloody mess.

McDaniels was walking toward Jane, with every intention of tossing her out of the saloon.

"Aw, Jack. Leave her be," one of Jack's regular customers said. "The girl's having a bad time. I'll buy her a few drinks if you let her stay, and I'm sure a few others will, too. Right, boys?"

Several men nodded and verbally confirmed they would contribute.

"See? You just might turn a good profit tonight," Jane's benefactor said.

Jack considered the financial gain in allowing Jane to stay, but warned her, "If you lay a hand on one more person inside this bar, I will kick your butt out of here without hesitation."

True to their word, several patrons at Jack McDaniels' saloon laid their money on the bar, so Jane could get her fill of whiskey. By the time she stumbled out of the saloon late that night, she could barely remember her own name, let alone anyone who went by the moniker Wild Bill.

Chapter 9

Jane woke up late the next morning, lying in an alley in a pool of urine and vomit. "What the fuck?" were the first words out of her mouth. She looked up to see the Cheyenne Hotel and diner owner, Paddy McPherson, shaking his head, and probing her with his foot.

"Jane! What the hell are you doing? It's a wonder you haven't been trampled to death!" Paddy said.

"Go away and leave me alone," Jane growled. "I just want to sleep forever."

"And you may very well get your wish if you don't do something about your current state of affairs and the drinking that got you here," he told her.

"Get up!" he said gruffly, grabbing her left arm. Dealing with Jane in the shape she was in was no picnic, but he did not want to leave her lying there. Paddy pulled a flask from his jacket pocket and offered it to her.

"Here, take a sip of this. It's the only thing I fear will rouse you from your stupor," he said. Then he added: "But just one sip!"

Jane took the flask and raised it to her mouth. When Paddy decided she was taking too much, he pulled it out of her hands.

"Now go clean yourself up. And put on some clothes. You seem to be missing the bottom part of your dress. Afterwards, come see me at the diner and I will give you something to help get rid of some of the side effects of your overindulgence."

"You got something that will make forget about the only man I've ever loved?" Jane asked.

" 'Fraid not," he said, his tone softening. "He'll never settle down with one woman. Why should he, when for some inexplicable reason he can have any number of women he wants?"

News had spread quickly that Bill Hickok had ridden out of Cheyenne the previous afternoon. There was also talk of him leaving behind some serious debts. The sheriff had been approached by several of Bill's note holders, who asked him to make Bill pay or throw him in jail.

"Listen, I'm sure he didn't leave you because he wanted to. Your man was in a heap of trouble. He ran up a lot of credit and failed to pay. His debts here are huge," McPherson said.

Jane sat up and looked at the man standing over her. She knew that Bill had owed some people money. He had, in fact, asked for money from her many times and, of course she gave it to him. She would have given him anything he wanted. The thing was, he had never come back with anything to show for it.

They had been asked to leave the hotel for lack of payment. She was telling a whole lot more bar stories to keep them liquored up. Most of their food was provided by her, and it had become a daily chore for her to ride out and hunt down a meal.

Still, although it crossed her mind from time to time, she did not grasp the seriousness of the situation until now.

"How much do we owe you, Paddy?" she asked.

"It's not your debt, Jane. Don't worry about it. Bill's the one who rented the room, and for a bit he was paying on time. All I have to show for your last two weeks there is a cigar box holding your IOUs," he said.

"It's my debt, too," Jane said. "I always pay my bills. You hold onto that cigar box and its contents and I will pay them one by one until they are all gone."

"I'm so sorry, Jane. I just want you to take care of yourself," Paddy said. "Do you want some help up?"

"I can do it, but thanks for caring," Jane said.

He walked away, and Jane managed to get to her feet. She headed for the creek to bathe the stench away. She washed off her soiled clothes and took a nap while she waited for them to dry, lying naked under a tree. When she woke up, she felt a bit better physically, but her heart was aching to hold Bill. She also realized she would have to turn a lot of tricks to pay off Bill's debts. The only obligation she knew about for sure was the hotel and diner, but Jack said Bill had left owing many people. Jane had no idea how many IOUs were floating around Laramie.

Why didn't he trust her enough to let her know how bad things were? She would have gone back to whoring full time until their debts were paid. Or, maybe he was afraid of being thrown in jail until the money was forthcoming—which to her was a ridiculous way to deal with such a situation. How was a person supposed to make money to pay their bills if they are behind bars? But if that was the case, she would have ridden out of town with him and they could have started over somewhere else. She could always make money doing something. And, once they had enough to pay off his debts in Cheyenne, he no longer would be threatened with being thrown behind bars.

Jane put on her clothes again and decided not to take Paddy up on his offer for what she figured was coffee and food. She chose instead to head to the saloon to retrieve her buckskin pants she hoped no one had taken.

As Jane approached the saloon, she groaned at the sight of three prim and proper women standing in front of the entrance, each holding a Bible.

"Good morning, Miss Jane," one of them said. Jane recognized her as Silas Jonas's wife.

"Good mornin', ladies," Jane said, removing her hat and holding it to her chest. "Is it fucking possible that you're all here to buy me a much-needed libation?"

All six eyes staring at Jane narrowed in disapproval.

"Wow!" Jane said. "It's almost like your peepers all think alike." She winked to give the appearance of having a sweet disposition, which she sometimes did have. But not today.

Dolly Jonas cleared her throat and forced the slightest of smiles. "Jane, we are proper ladies and, as such, do not desire to be subjected to your vulgar language."

"Well, Mrs. Jonas..."

"Oh, please, call me Dolly," she said.

"Dolly. Ah, I've only ever known you as the wife of a man named Silas. Delighted to make the acquaintance of your own, separate person," Jane said. "But here's the thing, Dolly, I'm mighty thirsty right now, and the only thing I know that will quench that thirst is right inside that door you're blocking. So, I ask you kindly, please get the *fuck* out of my way."

Dolly and the other two women held their ground. "Or, how about you joining us for a cup of tea in the hotel dining room?" Dolly asked, each word laced with sugar.

Jane put her hat back on her head, never taking her eyes off Dolly. Then she looked at the other two women and asked, "Are you two able to speak? Cause I have not seen your lips do anything but pucker, like you just ate something sour," she said.

"Of course, we can talk!" the woman standing to Dolly's right said with no small amount of venom.

Jane held her hand out in greeting. "Good! And your name is?"

"Mary," the woman answered. She did not reach out to take Jane's hand.

Jane put both hands on her hips. "Well here's the thing, Mary, Dolly, and—you other one. I don't care for tea and I don't care for preaching, so I think I will just decline your kind invitation, of which the tea is offered but the preaching is certain to be on a plate alongside the biscuit."

Mary turned to the other two women. "She's a lost cause, sisters. We might as well move along."

"Mary! No one on this earth is a lost cause," Dolly said. Then she addressed Jane. "Please give us a chance to share God's love with you,

Jane. He can help you defeat the devil you carry around on your shoulders."

Jane slowly turned her head to the left and then to the right, checking out her shoulders. "I see no one hitching a ride. What I do see are three busybodies who need to move aside or be moved in the most unpleasant of manners. In other words, ladies, *get those fat asses out of my way!*"

Jane lunged toward them and the women stepped aside. Then all three dropped to their knees and began to pray.

"Oh, Most Heavenly Father, please lay your hands on our sister, Jane. Remove the foul language from her tongue and the need for liquor and violence from her system. In your name..."

"Jesus," Jane spewed, then walked into the saloon, leaving the women behind.

Mary stood up first and called after her. "Yes, Jane! Yes. Jesus is His name! Please let us speak to you about him."

Jane ignored her and approached the bar. "Give me a goddamn shot," she snarled. Andy, the bartender on duty, did as he was told. Jane picked up the glass, carried it back to the swinging saloon door, lifted it up to the women as if to toast, and said, "This, ladies. This is what speaks to me."

She put the glass to her lips, tilted her head, and let out a sigh. She nodded toward the trio of proselytizers, and then turned and walked back to the bar. "Keep 'em coming, Andy," she said, then added in response to the bartender's raised eyebrows, "Put it on my tab. You know I'm good for it, one way or the other."

"My boss told me not to serve you until you clear up yours and Mr. Hickok's tab," Andy said. "The shot I just poured you was on the house because you seemed poorly, Jane. But no more until we wipe the slate clean here."

"That goddamn son of a bitch!" Jane swore, pounding her right fist on the bar. Andy took a step back, uncertain where this was going.

"So, what the fuck is the bottom line, Andy? What the hell does the cocksucker think I owe him? Never mind the fact that I must have boosted your sales last night," she spat.

Andy ignored her argument. He knew she was right because he had done the accounting that morning, but that didn't change the fact that he had orders from the boss to collect a past debt before issuing any more credit. He pulled a sheet of paper from a shelf behind the bar, looked at it, and said, "Well, including that incident with you shooting the mirror that used to hang behind this bar, thus depriving it of its ability to reflect, you are in arrears a total of nineteen dollars and twenty-five cents," he said. He decided not to mention the shot glasses, but they were included in the bill.

Jane sighed. She had forgotten about her brilliant display of some mighty fine shooting the previous evening.

"I don't suppose we could call that useless piece of reflective glass a prop, used by myself to entertain your clientele, thereby causing them to linger and, thus, spend more money on booze?" Jane knew she didn't have a prayer, but had to try anyway.

"Gotta pay up, one way or another, before I can pour," Andy said, holding his ground.

"All right. Add another quarter to my tab and pour one more shot to fortify me, while I go back to my place of employment to change into a dress and turn some tricks. I will have your goddamn bill paid in no time at all, plus enough for several more sips," she said.

Andy ignored her request for the second shot.

Several hours later Jane returned with enough money to pay off hers and Bill's debt and set herself up in drink for the night. It had been a busy day at Miss Crystals. Men had been in and out of the Brothel all day long, and there had been enough work to keep all of the whorehouse employees busy. Jane had not only serviced seven male clients, she had also slipped her hands in some pockets while her clients were distracted by her pleasuring techniques.

It was well after dark when Jane called it quits for the night. There was nothing stable in her demeanor when she left the saloon. She figured she would just lie down in an alley again and sleep it off. That was where she was headed when she saw the familiar face of a man walking briskly toward her. He looked worried, but that was Doc Johnson's usual expression.

Jane asked, "Hey, Doc, where you going to in such a hurry?"

"Silas Jonas's wife fell and hit her head a bit ago. She has a pulse but won't wake up," the old man said.

"Dolly? I was just speaking with her this morning," Jane slurred.

"You know Mrs. Jonas?" Johnson asked. "Jane, come with me. You may be able to help comfort her," he said.

Jane had a soft spot for any innocent man, woman, child, or animal who was sick or injured. It was one of what she considered to be her many weaknesses.

"Okay, Doc. I'm drunk as a skunk, but I'll see what I can do."

"No surprise there, Jane," Johnson said as he kept walking. "Just try to keep up. We're in a hurry here."

Jane turned in his direction and did her best to keep up with him. Twice she stumbled and fell, but Johnson didn't stop to help, and she got back on her feet and caught up with him as fast as her compromised condition would allow. It seemed to take forever for them to get to the Jonas house, which was on the edge of town.

Silas Jonas was waiting outside the modest wood cabin, wringing his hands in despair. He did not seem any less drunk than Jane.

Silas had sent his ten-year-old son, Seth, to get Doc Johnson and bring him back to the cabin. The doctor had told the boy to wait in his office until he examined his mother. He didn't want the child to be at home if Dolly died before he could help her.

"What happened, Silas?" Doc asked. The boy had not shared with him the details of his mother's injury. But the doctor was pretty sure he knew what had happened, since it was no secret around town that the man could be a mean drunk.

"I don't know, Doc," Silas answered. "One minute she was yelling at me for coming home sloppy, and the next thing I knew she was on the floor." He tried to suppress a sob, but failed. "I think she hit her head bad, Doc," he cried.

"You son of a bitch," Jane shouted, raising her fists in front of her and stumbling toward the distraught husband.

"Jane!" the doctor bellowed. "Not now! We have to see to Mrs. Jonas."

Jane lowered her fists and followed Johnson inside the cabin. Dolly Jonas was lying on the floor in front of the house's wood stove. Silas had covered her with a blanket and put a pillow under her head. In a moment, Doc ascertained that her breathing was shallow, and her pulse was slow.

Johnson told Jane to bring a kerosene lamp closer to him. When that was done, he pried open one of the woman's eyes, and then the other. Then he checked Dolly's head, asking Jane to allow it to rest in her hands while he examined the skull. There was a gash in the back of the head that Johnson said would need to be sewn up. But she had not lost much blood. Her face was beginning to swell, as was her wound. And there was bruising around the eyes that indicated internal bleeding.

Doc opened his bag and extracted the tools of his trade. It took ten stitches to close the wound. Then the doctor stood up and told Jane to help him move the woman to a bed. Silas showed the two into a room with a large bed that was topped with pelts of various animals sewn together to make a blanket. Silas pulled the cover away, and Johnson and Jane laid her body on a straw mattress covered with white poplin. They covered her, and then the doctor nodded for Jonas to join him near the door of the bedroom.

"Silas, I don't know for sure how this happened, but it's pretty obvious to me that a good assumption would be that your wife was shoved with a great deal of force and hit her head on the steel edge of your wood stove. She's alive, but in a coma. Whether or not she comes out of it or even lives through the night is something only God would know. If she does live, she may never again be able to speak or function like a normal person. If she dies, then I reckon that will make you a murderer, and if the townspeople don't get to you and string you up first, I will be here to whip the living shit out of you and then hang you myself."

"Oh, I'm right there with you, Doc," Jane said. The passage of time and the trauma had sobered both Jane and Silas a bit. Silas sat down on the only chair at a table, put his head in his hands, and sobbed.

The doctor ignored him and turned to Jane. "Would you mind sitting here with her tonight? I have a woman I need to check who is close to giving birth, if she hasn't done that already," he said.

"Yeah, I'll stay. I owe Dolly one. I was kind of rude to her this morning," Jane said.

Doc gave Jane a quizzical look, but decided not to ask.

"I'll tell Seth about his mother's condition and send him back to be with her. It will be good for both Seth and his mother to have you here, Jane," he said, then added, "If there is any change, for the better or worse, send Silas here to fetch me."

He looked at Silas. "We may not know the outcome of your actions for days or weeks or even years, but whatever the case, I hope God has mercy on your soul, because you won't get any from me."

The doctor nodded at Jane and then left. Jane gave Silas her worst scowl and then went into the bedroom to sit on the edge of Dolly's bed.

She stroked the woman's hair and told her she was going to be okay. "You have to pull through this, so we can tussle outside the saloon again. That was kind of fun, don't you think?" Jane took an angry swipe at the tears that had started to roll down her face. "You meant well, and I should have known that. I should have been nicer to you. You listen to me, Dolly Jonas, goddamnit! You pull through this and I promise I will fucking sit down and drink a cup of tea with you

58

and your lady friends. And you can tell me all about being saved and shit. Fuck! I'll have two cups with y'all. So, come on, Dolly! Pull through this. We sinners need you."

Jane was exhausted and had sobered up enough to feel hung over. Her head was aching, and she needed sleep. She laid her head down on the comatose woman's legs and sobbed hard, loud, and long.

Chapter 10

J ane tended to Dolly Jonas daily. The woman regained consciousness after a few days, but needed a lot of help. She suffered from debilitating headaches, and Doc put her on laudanum, an opium-based drug containing morphine, to help ease the pain. The laudanum, however, made her disoriented, and she needed to be watched during her waking hours.

Her son stayed close by, but seemed lost and scared. Silas ordered him out to tend to the animals and farm chores. Once one task was finished and the boy reported that to his father, Silas had another all lined up for him.

Jane tried to engage the child in conversation from time to time, but he seemed afraid to say much of anything, instead just shaking his head when asked yes or no questions or shrugging his shoulders when asked what he would like to eat, how he was feeling, or any question that needed any personal disclosure. Jane assumed Seth Jonas had also suffered at the hands of his abusive father over the years.

For his part, Silas was, at first, contrite and begged his wife's forgiveness.

The day Dolly began to stir, Jane sent Silas to fetch the doctor. Doc Johnson examined the woman for nearly an hour before determining that, with the proper care and patience, Dolly should recover to the point of being able to live a normal life.

Silas broke down in tears, laid his head on his wife's chest, and said, "Thank you, Jesus! I promise, from this day forward, I will never lay hands on my wife in anger again! Dolly, I am so sorry!"

The woman heard her husband invoke the name of her lord in a genuine expression of gratitude and put her hand on his head. *Jesus* was a word he had previously used only as a profanity. "Oh, Silas, I have waited for the day to come when we would walk together in praise of Jesus, our heavenly father," she said.

"Please forgive me, Dolly," her husband cried.

"Of course, I forgive you, Silas. And I praise God that you have seen the light," she said.

Jane wanted to vomit. She did not trust this man's sincerity for one second. Doc told Silas that Dolly needed to rest as much as possible and said they should all leave her to do that. Doc gave the woman a teaspoon of laudanum, Silas gave her a gentle kiss on her head, and Jane told her to call out if she needed something.

The rest of that day, when Silas was around, Seth trod carefully, as though the ground was covered with a mixture of egg shells and broken glass. As for Silas, he brooded, moped around, and asked a few times if there was anything he could do.

Jane told Silas that yes, there was plenty he could do. The cows needed milking, chickens needed feeding, farm needed tending by someone other than his son, who did all the work while he, Seth, sat feeling sorry for himself.

"You're shoving all of your work off on this boy, Silas. It's not right. It's one thing for a boy to help with chores, but it is not his responsibility to run this farm," Jane said.

Silas had grudgingly gotten up and gone off to join Seth in tending to the farm. A couple of days after Dolly regained consciousness, Jane asked Silas if he would mind going into town and gathering some supplies.

"I ain't got no money, Jane," Silas said.

Jane still had the rest of the money she left the saloon with the night Dolly got hurt, because while tending to Dolly, she hadn't had a chance to spend it on booze. She gave him a few coins and explicit instructions to buy some canned peaches, beans, sugar, and bacon.

Silas went out to fetch the provisions and came back a few hours later carrying a bottle of bourbon. He sat down at the table, opened the bottle, and began to drink. Jane heard him come in and, thinking he had returned with the food, came out of the bedroom where she had been sitting with Dolly while the woman slept. Seth followed Jane out, and when he saw the bottle in his father's hands, he bolted back into the bedroom and closed the door. Jane didn't blame him for not wanting to stick around.

"Hey, Janie! Take a swig yourself. You've earned it," Silas said. He was slurring his words, indicating this was not his first drink of the day.

"Where's the food I sent you to get?" Jane asked, ignoring his offer to join him in drink. She hadn't had any liquor since the night Dolly got hurt. Jane accepted that it was her responsibility to oversee this woman's recovery, since her husband was a useless human being in her eyes.

"There's plenty of flour for biscuits, eggs to gather, and dried beef. She can fill up on that," Silas said. "In fact, while I appreciate your help these last few trying days, there's no need for you to stay here any longer."

In truth, Silas was tired of Jane's sour stares in his direction. It was time for her to move along so he could resume his life without threat of a lecture or a scowl from Jane.

Jane walked over and picked up the bottle off the table, corked it, and held it out to him.

"I think *you* leave," she said. Her voice was so calm that Silas found her words laughable.

"Oh, do you, now?" he said, standing up and grabbing the bottle out of Jane's hand. "Well, little lady, this is my abode and that's just not gonna happen."

Jane snatched the bottle back out of his hand, moved away from him, uncorked it, and dumped its contents on the floor before Silas could react. She grabbed the neck of the now-empty bottle and brandished it as a weapon. Silas laughed.

"You bitch! Do you think I'm afraid of a woman holding a bottle upside down? Not only am I not afraid of you, but I'm going to make you pay for wasting good liquor," he sneered and began staggering toward her.

Silas stopped when Jane pulled her revolver from her holster.

"Listen, you miserable cocksucker, you have two choices here. One, gather a few of your belongings and leave peacefully or two, I will put a bullet through your thick, ugly skull," she said.

Silas just stood there, not knowing what to do. "How 'bout you put the gun down and we talk about this?" he said.

"No talk necessary. I will not negotiate with any man or woman who puts their hands on innocent victims to cause them harm for no reason whatsoever. You're one of those people. And you're neither innocent nor a victim. Shooting you would be an act of justice as well as a kindness to the rest of the world. Now either start walking or I start shooting," she said.

Silas realized he didn't have a choice in the matter, grabbed his hat, and walked out the door without saying another word. All he really wanted to do was drink in peace, anyway. And he certainly could not do it here, with this woman watching his every move.

Jane stood at the door and watched to make sure Silas kept walking away from the cabin. When he had been out of sight for a while, Jane lowered her guard and her gun. She set the empty bottle back on the table and looked at it longingly.

Jane sat down, feeling all the exhaustion the events of the last few days had produced. She rested her head on the table and fell fast asleep. She didn't wake until early the next morning, when she found Dolly standing over her with Seth at her side.

"You dear, sweet woman, you have no idea what an angel you are, do you?" Dolly asked.

"Fucking mother of god, woman, you near scared the piss out of me!" Jane said. "What the hell are you doing out of bed, Dolly?" Jane said.

"I woke up feeling a little better and decided it would be a good time to get back on my feet for a little bit, at least," she said. "I even managed to make us some coffee."

Jane got to her feet and offered the woman her chair. "At least sit down while I pour it," she said.

Dolly accepted the offer and sat.

Jane poured two cups of coffee and placed one in front of Dolly.

"Sorry we only have one chair. Silas was always going to make us another," Dolly said. "But Seth and I use those crates in the corner and they work pretty well. Why not pull one over and join me?" Dolly said.

"Don't mind if I do," Jane said. She pulled the crate up to the table, got two plates, placed a day-old biscuit on each, put them atop the table, and sat down.

The two women ate and drank in silence for a bit. Dolly spoke first.

"I overheard what went on out here last night," she said.

"Most sorry I had to do that, ma'am, but your husband ..."

"No need to apologize," Dolly said. "That man is pure evil when he is drinking. It's good you made him leave."

"Guess I should be more tolerant, seeing as how I'm a drunk myself, but I swear on the name of your Jesus, even in my most inebriated hours, I have never laid a hand on or shot a bullet through anyone who did not fucking deserve it. Sorry about the swearing."

"You have nothing to be sorry about, Jane. Whether you believe it or not, I know you're one of God's favorite children, and your goodness comes through even with all of that swearing and drinking," Dolly said.

Jane was touched more by this woman's kind words than any she'd heard before. "That's mighty nice of you," she said, her voice a bit faint.

For a few more weeks Jane stayed with Dolly and Seth, until she was certain the woman could fend for herself and take care of the boy. Silas did not return. Jane learned that he had been caught stealing a horse and was sent to Fort Sanders to face trial. If found guilty, which evidence suggested he would be, he would be executed by hanging. She did not share this information with Dolly and Seth. They may have found out on their own, but never spoke about it.

The day before Jane planned to set out on her own, Dolly surprised her with a gift. Jane's horse, which she had kept in Dolly's barn while staying there, was getting on in age, and Jane had known for a while she would need to find a replacement if she was going to travel overland at the speed she liked to go. The last long, fast ride she had taken on old Jim, while racing with Bill, had been a great exertion for the animal, Jane had noticed. And she had taken it easy on the horse ever since.

Seth, whose chore it was to see to the horses, had grown to love the old stallion. One day he explained to his mother that Jane's horse would be good for them to use around town, but not for hard travel. He suggested a trade involving a young, barely broken stallion that Silas had brought home intending to train but never got around to doing that.

Jane was inside the cabin gathering her belongings when Dolly called to her from outside.

"Jane, could you please come out here for a minute?" Dolly called.

When Jane stepped outside she saw Seth holding the reins of the young stallion.

"Jane, Seth and I have a favor to ask you. Seth has grown fond of your horse, Jim, and would like to know if you would consider trading him for this one we have no use for," she said.

"We figure, being as good a rider as you are and all, you will be able to train this one to work better for you," Seth said.

Jane reached out and touched the animal's snout. She rubbed her hand gently along his neck and walked around him, admiring every inch.

"Do you mean it?" she asked, looking at Seth and Dolly. "You would trade my horse for this beauty?"

Dolly smiled and said, "Yes, we mean it."

"But this horse is so much more valuable than mine. You could get a good price for it, and I don't have the means to give that to you," Jane said.

"You have paid for this horse ten times over," Dolly said. "Seth and I want you to have it, and Jim will serve our needs much better than a horse neither one of us can ride or control."

"Deal, Miss Jane? Please say yes," Seth begged.

"Deal!" Jane said. "Yes!"

"Thank you," Seth told her. He handed Jane the horse's reins and then said, "Excuse me, please. I need to go tell Jim the good news!"

Jane looked at Dolly and smiled. "I think my old, loyal Jim is going to live quite well in his old age."

"You've made my son very happy. Thank you," Dolly said.

The next day, with just the buckskin clothes on her back, her shotgun, her pistol, a flask filled with water, and some biscuits and bacon, Jane was ready to leave Cheyenne behind for good.

"I am mighty beholden to you, Jane. I hope your travels are safe, and your life is blessed from now through eternity, and if you don't mind, I will pray about both of those things," Dolly said.

"I'd be grateful if you did. Shoot. It couldn't hurt, right?" Jane said.

Jane gave Seth and Dolly each a heartfelt embrace, said a fond farewell to them, and then turned the horse around to head out.

"Miss Jane, wait!" Seth called.

Jane turned the horse back around and said, "What is it Seth?"

"I was just wondering, Miss Jane, if you have chosen a name for your new buddy yet?"

Jane threw her head back and laughed. "I had not, but I think you just helped with that."

"What do you mean?" Seth asked.

"From this moment on, I will call my new friend here, *Buddy*!"

Jane turned around, mounted Buddy, and rode off to the sound of Seth clapping and Dolly laughing.

Chapter 11
June 1876

I t was near dawn when Jane finally fell asleep. She had spent the night allowing her memories to have their way with her. Strands of various-colored ribbons danced around her brain like carefree children cavorting around a May pole, weaving in and out, over and under, until they were all braided around that one central figure.

Sometimes when this happened, she would fight to turn off all thoughts and feelings having to do with Bill. Sometimes she succeeded. But that was rare. Often, the force with which they catapulted into her mind was so strong she had no choice but to let them run their course.

Those Bill ribbons were every color of the rainbow, except for the black ones. Black did not belong in a rainbow. Or on a May pole. The bright reds, soft blues, greens, yellows, pinks—they all had a place there. But black was for funerals and grieving. And still, the black ones insisted on joining the others.

It had been a glorious time, that short period she spent with Bill. They had fit so much life and love into a few short weeks, and though it ended badly, most of the time she didn't regret having started it with him. Sometimes, however, she wished they'd never met. She knew her heart would never be the same again, and sometimes she didn't know if that was a good thing or a bad thing.

Last night's hike along the trails of her past meant there would be no miles traveled today in her trip to Laramie. By the time she awoke, evening had arrived: A full moon had replaced its sunny counterpart, and Buddy was chewing on some grass.

"Well, that was one hell of a trip we took back in time last night, huh, Buddy?" she said to the horse, who neither understood her words nor answered her question.

Jane made a fire, brewed some coffee, and baked some beans. She gave Buddy a carrot and spent the next several hours trying to make sense out of the first twenty-five years of her life. Jane knew it was pointless to play the "what if" game, but sometimes she couldn't help it. What if she had been born in a world where girls got to do the same things boys did? What if her parents had been fine, upstanding citizens who had properly provided for their children? What if she'd had a childhood that was filled with happy times playing with her siblings, fishing with her dad, going to school, being taught she could do anything she set her mind to? What if, indeed?

That was the problem with the "what if" game. *What if* didn't fucking matter. All she'd ever had to work with is *what was*.

Jane sighed, got up and gave Buddy a hug, and then lay back down on the ground. She fell asleep around midnight. Tonight, thankfully, the thought of Wild Bill Hickok was no more than a pleasant note in the musical repertoire of her past.

Jane rose early the next morning, refreshed and eager to resume her journey.

Chapter 12
June 1876
Fort Laramie, Wyoming

A day later, the log wall surrounding Fort Laramie came into Jane's view. The U.S. Army had purchased the former privately-owned trading facility in 1849 and turned it into a government military camp. The camp was a sprawling complex; the Army had wasted no time constructing new buildings for stables, officers' and soldiers' quarters, a bakery, and a guardhouse, among other things. Fort Laramie was considered the principal military outpost on the Northern Plains.

Jane felt a sense of pride mingled with excitement as she approached the camp. She rode through the open gate and up to the visitor center. She dismounted, tied Buddy's reins to a post, and went inside.

"Can I help you?" a soldier standing behind a counter asked.

Jane removed her hat and said, "Name's Jane. I'm here for a promised session of two months' rest and relaxation."

"I was told to expect you. Army hero, or something like that?"

"Something like that," Jane told him, her tone a bit icy. "I saved the life of one of your organization's captains. So, yeah, something like that."

"So that's what all the fuss is about. Well, welcome, Jane. I have been told to direct you to your very own small cabin on the opposite end of the soldiers' barracks. We have several of them reserved for visitors and esteemed guests. I'm sure you will find it quite comfortable."

He pulled a key off a hook on the wall behind him, where several others like it were hanging, and put it on the counter in front of her.

"You are in number seven," he said. He checked a ledger and told her, "You will find a basin for personal hygiene, a toothbrush and powder, a bowl of fruit, a loaf of bread, some dried beef, a bed with down comforter and pillow, a sleeping gown, a box of cigars, and two bottles of bourbon."

He looked up at her. "Um, I'm sure those last two items are a mistake. Please forgive me if I offended you."

"No offense and no mistake. My tastes are widely known—by most, but not all," Jane said with a grin.

The soldier cleared his throat. "Well, then. Your mount can be boarded at livery two, stable number seven. Anything else you may want or need, you can ask for and all efforts will be made to see to it that you have them," the young man said, then added, "And there are a large variety of items that can be purchased at our expansive trading center."

"Thank you kindly," Jane said.

"Oh, and I am supposed to tell you that you are welcome to dine three times a day at the appointed times posted at Commissary Two."

"Well, it would seem I am to rest and relax in style," Jane said. She was delighted by her good fortune.

She thanked the soldier, picked up the key off the counter, and went back outside to retrieve Buddy. She decided to walk him to the stable, groom him, and make sure he was comfortable and had all he needed before going to her quarters. Buddy was going to get a well-deserved rest here, too. He had earned it as much as she had.

As she was leaving the stable, Jane saw General Alfred Terry walking toward her. She removed her hat and saluted. He shot a salute back at her.

"Welcome to Fort Laramie, Calamity Jane. And thank you for your heroic deed and brave action. Captain Egan is a close friend of mine. My world would have been a very sad place without him in it."

"You're most welcome, General Terry, but as I told the fine captain, I was just doing my job," Jane told him.

"A job very well done. If the army ever decides to let women enlist, you would be the first female soldier I would want in my unit."

Jane blushed. She could get used to all this adulation.

Over the next several days, Jane was the perfect guest, asking to help when she saw a way to contribute to the everyday chores around camp, comforting the wounded who were brought there from battle, enjoying long rides with Buddy, and drinking just a little alcohol to ensure she didn't do anything disgraceful.

During her second week at the fort, Jane started playing cards with some of the soldiers who had taken a shine to her. They liked the fact that she wanted to be "one of them," as she often stated, and admired her many talents. They also enjoyed sitting around listening to her stories—some would say far-fetched—of incredible acts of courage. Still, she was one of the most entertaining people most of them had ever seen away from the theater stage.

Jane loved these sessions with these soldiers she looked up to. But with all that camaraderie came an escalation in her drinking. And when she was under the influence of a significant amount of alcohol, Jane's priorities were often skewed.

Nearing the end of her third week at Fort Laramie, Jane was now more often drunk than sober, had been chastised for two events involving unauthorized shooting in the middle of the night, and had lost all sense of propriety. On the night that brought her down, she committed a criminal act involving the theft of government property. Namely, stealing some of the alcohol kept in a supply shed at the camp. An act punishable by hanging.

Chapter 13

Jane walked into the commissary around four o'clock and was greeted by several choruses of "Calamity!" from soldiers already gathered there for the evening meal. She smiled and walked over to a long table where many of the calls originated. A half-dozen men were sitting there, enjoying bowls of pepper pot soup, plates loaded with meat and vegetable pie, corn bread, and custard, and cups of steaming hot coffee.

"Dare I assume you are all in extra good spirits today, and could that be because this is your day to be paid for your fine service to the U.S. government?" Jane asked.

"Our pants are indeed weighed down with some substantial coinage," Ezra Cooper said, sticking his hand in his pocket, withdrawing a fistful of coins, and dropping them on the table. "I think I'll be heading for the trading post after dinner to buy me something to drink in celebration."

"I like the way you think, soldier," Jane said. "I will like it even more if you decide you want to share with someone special."

Ezra scratched his head, then turned to the soldier sitting next to him, put his arm around the man's shoulder, pulled him close, and said, "Well, I guess Thaddeus here is about as special to me as anyone."

Thaddeus Young, who was small in stature but known for his ability to take on almost any man twice his size, shoved Ezra away so hard the man toppled over and fell off the bench.

"I think Jane was talking about herself, you rummy old cove!" Thaddeus said.

Ezra took the rejection well, laughing as he got up off the dirt floor and took his place back at the table.

"Pardon me for my error in judgment," he said, looking at Jane and bowing his head.

"I'm pretty certain all will be forgiven once you share a few glasses of your trading post purchases with her later," Lucius Evans, another of the soldiers in the group, said.

Jane nodded, excused herself, and went to retrieve some food and drink. After she had what she wanted, she went back and sat down with the soldiers.

"Well, I for one am happy y'all got your monthly stipends today, and would be pleased to partake of whatever liquid reward you use those coins to purchase," she said.

"I'll share my tea with you anytime, Jane," Garrett Young volunteered.

Jane cleared her throat. "My choice of the word 'whatever' was made in unfortunate error. To clarify, I would remove that word and change 'liquid' to liquor—a much better and more accurate telling of the liquid to which I refer."

"Well, I will be happy to share my hard-earned drink with you, Jane, but for a price I believe you can afford to pay," Ezra said.

Jane swallowed some coffee, belched, and said, "Of course I will share some stories with you fine gentlemen. Just keep in mind that I am a much better storyteller when the liquid of which I previously spoke is at my immediate and continuous disposal."

All the soldiers roared.

"I do believe we're all in for a fun evening!" Lucius said.

"I think it might be advisable for us to meet up after dark outside of this encampment," Jane said. "Say, about a quarter mile south?"

They all agreed that sounded like a good idea.

"Great!" Jane said. "You bring the bottled fruits of your labor and I shall bring my scintillating stories of one woman's—"

"Yeah, yeah. We know. Just bring something we have not yet heard," Ezra told her.

Four hours later the party was in full swing with nearly a dozen soldiers and Jane sitting around a blazing campfire, all well on their way to various stages of intoxication. Jane was free with her affections while freeing several of the men of some of the coinage left in their pockets.

"You look like you need some company," Jane would tell first one soldier, then another. Only one in the group turned her down. Nathaniel Smith was leery of Jane, having seen how nasty the woman could get when she was drunk.

Jane didn't seem to care when he pushed her away. She just went on to the next, spending time with each of the men. They fondled her female bits; she fondled their pockets. By the time the whiskey ran out and most of the men had left to head back to camp, Jane's britches were heavy with coins.

Ezra, Lucius, and Jane were the only three left. They were enjoying the final drops from some of the bottles.

"Too bad the trading post is closed at this hour," Ezra said.

"Yeah, too damn bad," Lucius agreed.

"I certainly haven't even begun to quench my thirst," Jane chimed in. She belched loudly and then said, "You know, the officers keep some of their private stock in the supply shed. I saw several bottles there when I was helping one of the kitchen hands put some food away a few days ago."

"I've heard that, but how do we get into the supply shed?" Ezra asked.

"A key would be nice," Lucius said.

"Don't s'pose either of you have one," Jane said.

Both men shook their heads.

"You?" Ezra asked Jane.

"Nope," she said.

The three of them sat in dejected silence for a few minutes. Ezra almost nodded off.

"I'm thinking there should be a way to get into that shed without the use of a key," Jane said suddenly.

"The only way I can see that as being possible is if we break in," Lucius said.

"So, what are we waiting for?" Jane asked. She got up and started walking toward the camp, with Lucius and Ezra following, like sheep being led to slaughter.

Chapter 14

Martha Jane Canary's brain pushed its way through several layers of fog, trying to find some clarity. Her head felt like it was cracked in a million pieces. She was sure her eyelids were being held down with lead weights, making it next to impossible for her to lift them open.

Jane vaguely remembered drinking with some soldiers at the government outpost where she was staying. The camp was located fifteen miles north of Laramie, South Dakota. Jane had been there for three weeks, enjoying her reward for saving the life of Captain James Egan. Yesterday was payday and Jane had used her storytelling abilities to dupe the soldiers into parting with their hard-earned cash and keeping her shot glass filled with liquor. She remembered they had run out far too soon to suit her. But everything after that was a blur.

She had no idea how she ended up in the guardhouse.

The air inside the small structure smelled like freshly brewed urine seasoned with stale vomit. Her stomach churned loudly, and bile rose in her throat. She winced as she swallowed it back down again.

The only light inside the guardhouse came from cracks in the walls where the lumber used to build the structure did not quite flush together, but there was enough sunlight leaking through those cracks to assure Jane that morning had come.

She lifted her head off the ground and tried to raise her torso into a sitting position. As she bent at the waist, her head lolled to the right a bit and she forced it left, overcorrecting and falling onto her side.

"Son of a bitch!" Jane cursed and pushed with her right hand to get upright. She sat for a few minutes, thinking about how to manage the art of standing. She was about to roll forward on all fours to begin the upward push when she heard the chain across the outside of the door rattle.

"Fucking bastards locked me in?" she said out loud. "Well, we'll just see about this. Show your cowardly dog face," she growled as the door slowly creaked open.

Sunlight rolled in the door and grew brighter the wider it opened, forcing her to shut fast her sensitive eyes. "God damn that's some powerful light," she swore.

It took a few minutes for her eyes to adjust, but she slowly forced them open as a large shadow standing inside the door frame blocked some of the blinding light. A tall man with shoulder-length hair and a mustache that swept across his upper lip and down each side of his mouth stared down at her.

Oh, holy hell! I must've drank so much I'm seeing things that can't be there, she thought.

Then the apparition spoke. "Hello, Jane," it said. "You're looking mighty hungover, pale, shaky, your beautiful hair matted with vomit, a far cry from the vision of loveliness I remember."

The sunlight streaked through his long blond hair and highlighted the delicate stitches of his embroidered buckskin jacket. She knew this was not a drunken vision.

"Motherfucking Bill Hickok, as I live and breathe...."

"Barely live and breathe, from the looks of you," he corrected her.

"I wasn't aiming to ever see you again. Where's my pistol when I need it most?" she said.

Bill looked stern. "From what I hear it has been removed from your person, as well as other effects, save for your clothes, due to your behavior," he said.

Jane wondered what she had done, but didn't want to ask. Instead she said, "I don't need a gun to scratch your lying eyes out, cock-sucker!"

Bill laughed. "Yeah, kind of the way I remember your final loving words to me before I rode out of Cheyenne."

"Rode out of Cheyenne owing hundreds of dollars which I had to work myself near to death to pay off," she said.

"I'm not proud of that, Jane. And you tell me what I owe you and I will pay you back in full," he said.

"What? You? Or with money from the wife I heard you went and got yourself married to—a fancy woman back east with tons of money, if my information is correct," Jane said.

"Your information is spot on. I did marry a wonderful woman with a high standing in society. Her name is Agnes," he said.

"Never mind the fact that we were never formally divorced," Jane said, with the slightest tinge of animosity.

"Well, never having been formally married, you know, I didn't think that would be an issue," Bill Hickok told her. Then he added, "Guess I don't need to ask how you've been?"

"I've been just fine, except for this momentary lapse in judgment," she said, not adding that she had no idea what her lapse of judgment had involved.

"Good to hear," he said, then asked, "Do you know why you were locked up?"

"Nope. Not a fucking clue. And I prefer to keep it that way," she said.

"Well, what you prefer is not gonna happen in this case. Necessity dictates you listen to me for a minute, because the information I have to impart affects your immediate future," he said.

God, he did look magnificent standing there. Jane felt a sudden urge to make herself presentable, as well as that old familiar stomach-flipping sensation she used to get when she gazed upon his countenance.

"Okay, but hold that for a bit. I need to go tidy up my person in that creek yonder," she said, pointing toward her intended open-air bathhouse.

"I suppose you're gonna need some clean clothes, too," he said.

Jane smiled. "You're fucking right about that. And if you don't mind, please round up something of the female variety," she said.

"Information recently imparted by the captain of this camp indicates that you have grown accustomed to exclusively wearing clothing of my gender's variety," Bill said, raising his left eyebrow in a teasing gesture.

"Your information would be as correct about me as mine was about you," she said, "but since you opened that door I have me a sudden and inexplicable urge to want to dress like a woman again, even if only for a little while," she said.

"I trust that your sudden and inexplicable urge to dress in feminine attire has nothing to do with me because, as we've already established, I'm married, Jane. Legally and all," Bill said.

Jane stuck her head outside the door and looked around. "Is she here with you?" she asked.

"No. She is waiting for me at our home in New York State. I'm here to help my friend, Charlie Utter, set up his postal delivery business and try my hand at some gold prospecting. I hope to return to her in a couple of months' time," he said.

"A couple of months, huh? A lot can happen to change one's plans and the state of one's heart in that amount of time," Jane said.

Hickok stared at his former lover. He had thought about her often since he had left her behind in Wyoming. But he had a wife now. A good woman who did not thrill him the same way Jane had, but who was a whole hell of a lot more stable.

"Be careful out there. There are some high-ranking officials who are none too pleased that you accepted their generous gift and used it to take advantage," Bill told her.

"You should be careful out there, too. Hear tell there is a woman you once married who has every reason to follow through on her previous threat to shoot you," Jane said. As if she could. As if she would. Bill didn't react.

Jane wondered what the hell she had done. "I remember nothing of the previous evening," she said, "having been besotted by some mighty fine liquid refreshment," she said.

"Well, the soldiers you got thrown in the stockade for being your accomplices remember, as do some of their buddies who say you deftly removed them from beneath the burden of their coins. So, at the captain's insistence, you will be joining my wagon train heading for Deadwood." He grinned.

"I accept your fine invitation to join your wagon train," Jane said, thrilled that her sudden travel plans to wherever it is Bill was heading had been arranged for her.

"It's not an invitation," Bill said. "It was put to me as non-negotiable, in return for keeping a noose from finding its way around your neck."

Jane's eyes grew three times wider. "You making that up, Bill Hickok?" she asked.

"Oh, hell. Go clean yourself and make it fast. We're leaving here in a half hour," he said.

Jane let out a loud happy "Whoop!" that did her pounding head no good at all. But she was happy, even if painfully hung over. She turned and left to attempt to make herself presentable for the only man she would ever want.

Bill was back, and this time she didn't intend to ever let him leave without her. She wasn't sure how she was going to achieve that seemingly impossible task, because he was married and all, but she would find a way, or die trying.

Chapter 15

Jane was floating on her back in the middle of the creek, enjoying the sun bathing her face and the front of her body, when she heard Bill calling her.

"Jane, I got something for you to wash up with," he said. "Catch!"

Jane stood up and caught the bar of lye as he tossed it to her. Her breasts glistened with the sun-kissed water dripping off them. Bill turned his head.

"I got a dress from one of the girls traveling with a Deadwood saloon owner," he said. "Sorry, but I wasn't able to procure any undergarments to go with it."

"Oh, that's okay. I prefer to go without, as you may recall," she said.

Bill was glad he had turned away earlier. The tiniest hint of a smile crept across his lips. Best she didn't see that.

"I told you, Jane, I'm married now," he said.

"Which kind of amazes me, the fucking married part, because I remember you telling me that day you walked out of my life that you just weren't the type of person to be tied down," she said, her tone a bit angrier than she felt. "But here you are, all married up and tied down to one woman who, interesting enough, is thousands of miles away."

"I'm older now, Jane, more settled than I was a few years ago. Anyway, you and I would not have made a good union. We both drink too much, and you fucking swear too much. Agnes keeps me grounded." He said.

"Grounded, huh?" Jane said, making a special effort not to swear or to point out that he had just done so himself. "You don't look very grounded to me, out here on the prairie heading to one of the wildest prospecting towns in the west."

Bill sighed. "I'm going to Deadwood to stake a claim I'm hoping will pay off and then head back home to my wife," he lied. His real

81

reason for joining Charlie Utter's wagon train was to escape the rigorous boredom of domestic life.

"You'd best stop lying to yourself Mr. *Wild* Bill Hickok," Jane said.

Bill turned to face her. His tone was tinged with anger when he said, "And you'd best enjoy your bath, because we're pulling out of here at noon and I've promised a certain officer I will make sure you leave with us, much as I already regret that agreement. Now if you'll excuse me, I need to go help my friend, Charlie, load some provisions."

He turned and was walking away when Jane said, "Better be some fucking bourbon amongst those provisions, Mister Married Man."

Bill kept walking, but the slight smile had returned.

When Jane was as clean as she was going to get, she stepped out of the creek and onto the river bank. She sat in the full sun drying herself for a bit, then slid the dress over her head. It was a lightweight cotton and felt fine against her skin, which was good because it was more than a bit snug. The green in the blue-and-green pattern was the color of her eyes. She wished she had a mirror, so she could see how she looked. She sat on the bank waiting for her other clothes to dry. Using her fingers as a comb, she sorted out her long auburn hair, picking through tangles until her hair was smooth and lay nicely against her shoulders. She was lost in thoughts of the past and her too-brief romance with Bill when a female voice startled her out of her reverie.

"My dress looks nice on you," the woman said. Jane turned and looked up at her.

"Well, as I live and breathe, if angels exist, you must be what they look like," she said.

The woman blushed. She was younger than Jane, with a sturdy yet delicate frame and the most gorgeous blonde hair Jane had ever seen. Her skin was light, and her cheeks had a slight pink glow to them, like the painted face of a porcelain doll.

"Your dress, huh? No wonder my jugs are popping out of it," Jane said, looking at the girl's smaller bosom.

The stranger ignored Jane's comment. "My name's Trixie, and I'm part of the wagon train I'm told you're joining, Miss Canary," the girl said. She was carrying a warm biscuit. She tore it in two pieces and offered one to Jane.

"Name's Jane, full name Calamity Jane. I've dropped the Canary part because of being renamed by a general whose life I saved a few months ago. And I wasn't really given a choice about joining your wagon train," Jane said, accepting the biscuit and tearing off a large chunk with her teeth.

"I'll just call you Jane, if you don't mind. And I heard about your forced exit from this camp and the reason why. That's why I brought you this here biscuit. I figured your innards must need something right about now to sop up all that alcohol you stole and consumed."

Jane swallowed what she'd been chewing and scolded the girl. "Don't you worry about the state of my digestive system," she growled. "I stole it?"

"Yeah. And hey, not worried at all. You're the one who fucked yourself up. I was just trying to show some kindness and consideration," Trixie spat back. "Would it fucking trouble you too much if I sat down?" she asked.

"No, I don't suppose it would *fucking* trouble me at all," Jane answered.

"Wanna know about the wagon train you didn't choose to be part of?" Trixie asked.

"You're mighty sassy for such a delicate-looking flower. And you cuss as bad as I do," Jane said, then added, "Actually, as a matter of fact I'd like to know what apparent criminal behavior I am accused of participating in. What happened last night?" she asked.

"Can't tell you what I don't know, so I'll just tell you what I do," Trixie said. "I heard you and a couple of the soldiers broke into the supply shed, helped yourself to a whole lot of drink that did not belong to you, and then got drunk right then and there. The men with you had enough sense to go back to their quarters. No one seems to be saying exactly who accompanied you on your little crime spree but somehow they figured it out. You passed out and were found there very early this morning by one of the kitchen hands looking to retrieve some flour for morning biscuits. Not surprised you don't remember anything."

Some of it was coming back to her now that Trixie had jogged her memory. "So, tell me about this wagon train I've been forced to join, as well as its occupants, if you don't mind," she said.

During the next several minutes Trixie told Jane that, as she understood it, the wagon train was led by a man named Charles Utter. "Charlie, they call him." She said he was heading to Deadwood to start his own shipping company, and most of the travelers on board were prospectors hoping to hit it rich. A few wives were along for the ride, as were she and four other women her new boss, Al Swearengen, had hired to work as whores in his saloon called The Gem Theater. Trixie figured she would earn some money, get fed and clothed, and have a roof over her head until, eventually, she met the man of her dreams and left whoring behind to devote her life to him and their five children. She seemed excited about the prospect of all of that.

Jane stared at the woman as if she was viewing some carnival sideshow freak.

"Okay, first of all, rare is the decent man who comes along wanting nothing more than to marry someone in your profession, Trixie. Trust me. I know. Second, how the hell do you know how many children you're going to have, and who would fucking want that many snotty poopers anyway? And third ... shit, I forgot what three was."

"Well, aren't you the high and mighty one," Trixie said.

"I'm mighty, and I'm proud of that because I've learned to take care of myself. Falling in love with the right man is okay, but wanting to do nothing but wipe the butts of his brats and serve as his slave is crazy. I know love, but my idea of sharing a life is to ride alongside him, do the same things he does, work toward the same goals," Jane said.

"Hell, I don't want to do any of that," Trixie said, "but I would dearly love to have a job where I could work with numbers. I just love playing around with arithmetic, adding and subtracting things."

"Well then, you should do that," Jane said.

Trixie looked sad. "Not likely gonna happen, being fucking female and all," she said.

"Nope. It won't. Not unless you make it happen," Jane said. She had tired of this conversation. She got up and checked her shirt, pants, britches, and underwear. "I'll probably need to put these on before we ride out, if I'm going to be any help along the way," she said.

"Oh, you should keep the dress on," Trixie said. "It looks attractive and you might make some money along the way. Besides, it's fine for what women are expected to do."

"Okay, I'm sure I'll regret asking, but what are women expected to do on this trip?" Jane asked.

"We mostly walk alongside the wagons and gather buffalo chips to use for starting a fire, and make the vittles for breakfast, lunch, and supper," she said.

"I imagine a dress suits those tasks just fine, but not for what I do. Yes, I'll be fucking happy to build the fires and make some meals. But I'm primarily a hunter and expect to provide fresh meat along the way. I'm also a mighty good bullwhacker, and I can't swing that whip the way I need to in feminine attire, if you know what I mean. Plus, what happens when we need to cross a river that's being particularly difficult? No, I'll keep the dress on long enough to take a stroll by Bill's wagon and let him see what he's been missing, then change into more suitable attire."

"Bill? As in Mr. Hickok?" Trixie asked.

"Formerly better known as *my* Mr. Wild Bill Hickok," Jane said.

"But he's married and faithful to his wife," Trixie said. "He has turned down services offered him by me and some of the other girls because he said he values his marriage and wants to stay true to his vows. I think her name is Alice. Or Agnes. Or something like that."

"Well, Trixie, here's some information for you. Before he married egg face, or whatever her name is, Bill and I were man and wife. Lovers. Friends. Partners. I let him walk away, but now that I've got him back in my sights, I don't intend to make the same mistake twice."

Trixie laughed. "Well, this trip just got a whole lot more interesting," she said.

Chapter 16

Bill Hickok and Charlie Utter were putting the last of the supplies in Bill's wagon when Jane arrived, wearing her dress and carrying a wrapped bundle of her creek-washed men's wear.

"Calamity Jane, reporting in for our pending journey to that thriving metropolis of Deadwood," Jane said, giving her head a slight tilt and flashing a silly grin Bill's way. Neither Charlie nor Bill paid any attention to her, so she continued, "I've got my own horse. His name's Buddy. Got him from a woman I cared for after her husband knocked her unconscious the night after you walked out on me, as a matter of fact, Bill. Anyway, I won't need any special accommodations, save for at night when I assume a tent will be provided for my overall comfort and safety," she said, the smile still plastered on her face.

"We don't have any extra tents, Jane," Bill answered without looking her way.

"That's fine. I'm okay with sharing. And since it's been brought to my attention by your very own self that you are my escort outta here, I reckon I'll be sharing with you, Bill."

Both Bill and Charlie looked at her now, and Jane took advantage of the moment by lifting the skirt of her dress and trilling around, thus providing a glimpse of her uncovered female bits.

"By the way, I'm mighty grateful and much obliged to you for providing this dress that, I'm told, showcases some of my best assets," she said.

Charlie Utter turned and looked away, but not before seeing more than he would have felt comfortable seeing. Bill stood his ground, as did his eyes.

"You're welcome, Jane," he said, "and you do look fetching in that dress, but as I told you, I'm a married man and, as such, not likely to be tempted by your charms. And no, we're not sharing a tent. You can have the tent. I'll sleep on the ground."

"Suit yourself, old married man. But I swear, if you had been this boring when I was married to you, I would have been the one to ride off into that sunset, leaving *you* in *my* dust," she said.

Bill winced. If there was one thing he hated being called, it was boring.

Jane interrupted his thoughts. "Now, I am going to change into my working attire, so I can help hitch up the wagons, which would be a difficult job dressed like this." And with that, she pulled the dress up over her head and began untying the bundle of buckskin clothing. She dressed slowly, delighted to see that Bill was watching her every move. Once clothed, Jane picked the dress up off the ground and folded it neatly. She walked over to Bill and handed it to him. "I'll let you hold onto this, and anytime you want to see me in it again, you just give me a holler," she said.

She turned away and walked off to retrieve her horse.

"Bill..." Charlie started to try to talk to his friend, but Bill waved him off.

"Don't worry, Charlie. Jane's quite a woman, but she wasn't right for me years ago and she's not now," he said.

"She is one hell of an unusual woman," Charlie said. "I'm not so sure I could handle her."

Bill laughed. "I'm pretty certain no man alive could handle that woman," he said. "As I recall, however, it was a hell of a lot of fun trying!"

Charlie grinned. He sometimes envied his friend's wild and hard-living ways, as well as his way with the ladies. But he knew those times had to come to an end, for Bill's sake. Bill was slowly losing his eyesight, had sworn to Agnes that he was done gun slinging and gambling, and if all that held true, maybe he at least could live a happy life with a woman who was recognized as a fine, upstanding business woman.

Bill, on the other hand, had used a desire to make his fortune prospecting for gold for a couple of months as an excuse to hit the trails and get out from under the domestic cloak that now sometimes smothered him. He was sincere in his intentions to remain faithful to this woman who had been his friend and at his side long before they married. He owed a lot to her. And he was certain he could also keep his promise to stay clear of the card tables. But it did feel so good and so natural to him to be riding into the wilds again.

Charlie made the rounds and checked to see if all members of the wagon train were ready to go. Then, as the captain of the entourage, he gave a nod to the group's scout to set off ahead and find a suitable campsite for the night. Once that was done, Charlie Utter rode to the front of the line of wagons, circled his right hand beside his head, and bellowed, "Forward ho!"

Jane and Bill rode side by side for the first hour, mostly because he knew he couldn't ditch her, not that he really wanted to do that, and partly because he enjoyed riding with someone who could handle a horse as well as Jane.

Jane felt content in a way she had not known since she and Bill parted ways. This felt right again. She was certain it was right. It was one of those things you just knew in your soul. This man was her destiny, and she would do anything in her power to remain in his company.

Jane saw Trixie walking beside one of the wagons with some other women she knew must be part of the whore contingent being transported by the saloon owner. "Gonna walk with my friend for a bit, Bill," she said. He nodded and pulled on ahead as she dismounted.

"How's the budding romance going?" Trixie asked Jane when Jane walked toward her, leading Buddy by his reins.

"I reckon it's going okay," Jane said.

"Was he swept away by the vision of you in my dress?" Trixie asked.

"So much so he nearly fucking drowned in the vision of me in your dress," Jane said.

Trixie nearly lost her balance laughing. The terrain was rough, and walking alongside the wagons took concentration. Taking a tumble was a common occurrence, but many preferred strolling alongside the wagons to riding inside them. The canvas-covered wagons were suffocating inside on a hot day like this. Plus, passengers were constantly jostled up and down and side to side as the wagons clambered over the uneven trail.

Dan Dority, Al Swearengen's procurer, chose to ride his horse most of the time, with sporadic trips to his wagon, where he would pleasure himself off and on throughout the day with one of his protégés. He called it testing them out for any special skills that might help them make more money once on the job in Deadwood. Jane called it bullshit. She and Trixie had not been walking together long before Dan stuck his head out of the back of his wagon and summoned her to him.

"Ugh!" Trixie said quietly to Jane before yelling that she was on her way. "It's so hot and he smells so bad, but there are always a few shots of liquor involved, so off I go," she said. "See you later, Jane."

"Later," Jane said. As much as Jane would have loved a shot or two of liquor right now, there is no way she would climb into a wagon and service a slimy devil like Dan.

She got back on her horse and rode to where Bill was. "Hey, if someone was parched and wanted to get unparched, where on this goldarn wagon train would one go to do that?" she asked.

"There's a rainwater barrel in the wagon Charlie and I share," Bill said.

"Yeah, that's fucking great and all, but this is a different kind of parched," Jane said.

"Well, whatever the hell kind of parched it is, that is all we drink when we're riding," Bill said.

"Okay then, maybe I will get me some of that water," Jane said. "Is there a drinking device for this wet nectar of the gods, or do I have to dip my fucking face in the barrel to partake?"

Bill pulled on the reins of his horse and stopped dead in his tracks. He had tried to stay stone-faced whenever Jane spoke, but the thought of her sticking her face in a barrel full of water was too funny. "If you climb into said wagon, you will find a ladle next to the water barrel," he said, grinning.

"Wait! Is that ... why, I do believe it is! Don't look now, Bill Hickok, but your mouth is fucking turning upward," she said. Jane didn't wait for him to respond. She turned her horse around and trotted back to what she liked to think of as their wagon. She dismounted and tied Buddy's reins to the back of the wagon, then crawled up inside.

The wagon was filled with prospecting tools, food, water, and other goods. She saw her dress resting atop what looked like a canvas tent. Jane smiled. At least he hadn't thrown it away. She looked beside the water barrel and found the ladle. She lifted the lid off the barrel and dipped the ladle inside. The water was warm, but still refreshing. Jane refilled the ladle and then put the cover back on the barrel as Bill was climbing into the wagon.

"I see you found it," he said.

"I did, thank you," Jane said, her words as sweet as syrup dripping from a maple tree.

"I'm a bit parched myself, so I thought I'd join you in a drink," he said.

"Certainly," Jane said as she began to remove the lid from the water barrel.

"No, not that," Bill said. "The fine folks at your former camp gave me something even better for agreeing to take you off their hands."

He pulled a bottle out from under the folded-up tent and popped off the cork. "We're not supposed to be doing this during traveling time, so don't tell, okay?" he said.

Jane gave her head a solemn shake back and forth and pinched her lips together to indicate she wouldn't.

Bill grinned and handed her the bottle. Ladies first?" he asked.

"Don't mind if I do," Jane said, grinning from ear to ear. She took a generous gulp, wiped her mouth with the back of her hand, and handed the bottle to Bill. He smiled and raised the bottle to his lips. Then he replaced the cork and took a deep breath.

"Reinforcement," he said. "Now we'd better get back to our rides." He stepped aside to let Jane leave first. She brushed against him as she passed, lingering a few seconds longer than necessary.

"I've missed you, Bill Hickok," she said quietly, then climbed out the back of the wagon, got on her horse, and rode ahead.

When she was gone, Bill said, "I've missed you, too, Jane."

The two rode apart from each other the rest of the day, but when it came time to camp for the night, Jane sought Bill out.

"I'm going to get a fire going for us. What kind of provisions do we have for a meal?" she asked.

"We have plenty of beans, bacon, and the makings for biscuits," he said.

"Dried beef will work with the beans, and I'll make biscuits to go with them. Tomorrow I'll ride out and get us some fresh meat," she said.

"Really? I don't shoot as well as I used to, but I wouldn't mind riding along," Bill said.

"Wouldn't mind having you along," Jane said with a smile. Then she set to work building a fire, using buffalo chips she'd gathered along the way as fuel.

"I'll get your tent set up while you make dinner," Bill said.

He had just finished with the tent and Jane was putting the finishing touches on their food when Charlie came by. Jane was not happy to see him.

"Charlie and I eat together," Bill said. "I meant to tell you to make enough for three."

"I think we can make it work," Jane said. She forced a smile for Bill's sake, but would just as soon have bitten Utter as look at him.

The three ate in silence until Charlie spoke. "Bill, you can share my tent with me tonight. It's big enough for the two of us. Just bring your own blanket."

Jane glared at him.

"That's mighty fine of you, Charlie, but I don't mind sleeping under the stars. I'll be fine."

"Suit yourself, but we have a fortnight of travel ahead, so if you change your mind, the invitation is open."

"Thanks, Charlie. Right now, I'm going to go walk a bit, and when I come back I'm going to drink a bit. Jane, feel free to get the bottle I told you about earlier and start without me. I'll be back soon," Bill said.

Jane got up and retrieved the bottle from the wagon. She pulled out the stopper and handed the bottle to Charlie, who took it and lifted it to his lips. Charlie continued to hold the bottle, instead of offering Jane a swig. He cleared his throat and took another sip. Then, apparently fortified enough to address her, he said, "Miss Canary, I think it would be a good idea if you just left my friend, Bill, alone."

"Did you hear me ask for your fucking advice, Mr. Utter? Cause as near as I can tell, I didn't," Jane spat back.

"Look, I know all about your previous romance with Bill, but he's settled down now with a woman who keeps him out of harm's way. Away from things that could be a hazard to his health and overall well-being. I just want what's best for him," Charlie said. He offered the bottle back to Jane. She pulled it from his hands, plugged it, set it down beside her, and glared at Utter.

"If she's so good at keepin' him safe, what the hell is the motherfucker doing out here, in godforsaken hostile territory? Huh? How come she couldn't keep him safe at home? Maybe a safe life is not the kind of life Bill wants. Maybe this is the kind of life that suits

93

him best. What do you say to that, Mr. fucking know-it-all Bill's best friend?"

Jane pulled the cork out of the bottle and took a long swig. She saw Bill approaching, smiled, and passed the bottle back to Charlie.

Charlie refused the offer and stood. "Bill, I'm going to get some rest. I'm feeling pretty tired tonight," he said.

"Okay, Charlie. Sleep well," Bill said.

After Charlie left, Jane handed the bottle to Bill.

"I think I'll turn in, too," Jane said.

"How 'bout sitting a spell and helping me finish this bottle?" Bill said.

Jane smiled. "Don't mind if I do," she said.

They sat in awkward silence by the fire for a while, sharing nothing but a bottle of whiskey. Then Bill cleared his throat and asked, "So, other than stealing government bourbon and drinking yourself silly, what have you been up to during the last eight years?"

Jane laughed. "Well, for one thing, I have acquired a new name," she said.

"You're married?" Bill asked.

"No," Jane laughed. "I performed an amazing act of bravery during a battle with some renegade Sioux and saved the life of a commander. He gave me the name Calamity and I kind of like it. So henceforth, I will be called Calamity Jane," she said.

"Calamity, huh?" Bill said. "That's a name your parents should have given you at birth."

"I'd have been much obliged if they had," she said.

Another few minutes of silence followed, but this time it did not seem so awkward. It felt comfortable sitting here by the fire with him. Comfortable enough for Jane to ask, "Are you happy ... with her, Bill?"

"She's a good woman. She takes care of me. I no longer fear dying alone," he said. "After I left you, I got myself into some pretty bad situations. In truth, I should be dead now ten times over."

"That's a whole lot of hypothetical dying," Jane said. She wondered what he might have done to put himself in danger, other than probably leaving a trail of debt behind him wherever he went.

"It's just that I have such a hard time staying in one place for too long, Jane," he said.

"You're not telling me anything I didn't already know, Bill."

He smiled. "Yeah, I guess you do. But I figured if I could be married to someone as stable and grounded as Agnes, I'd change my ways and maybe live a little longer."

"And here you are," Jane said. "Far away from all that safety and stability."

Bill polished off the bottle. "It didn't take more than a couple of weeks to start feeling that longing to be traveling on again. Charlie saw it and, being the friend he is, invited me to accompany him on this journey, promising my wife he would send me back safe and sound when it was over. The theory is, if I can get free and do this sort of thing occasionally, maybe I'll be able to be content with being settled most of the time."

"Interesting theory. So, you have no intention of prospecting for anything other than a good gambling saloon, am I fucking right?"

"I promised Agnes I would stay away from the cards," Bill said.

"I'm sure you did, and if she believed it, she doesn't know you as well as I do," Jane said.

Bill grinned. "And on that note, I'm gonna follow Charlie's lead and lay this tired old body down for the night."

"Good idea. Want me to tuck you in?" Jane asked.

"I want you to crawl inside that tent and try, for just one night, not to do anything to live up to your new name," Bill said.

Bill lay down on a blanket he had spread out on the ground beside the tent. He was asleep within minutes. Jane lay awake in the tent, listening to him breathe. No music she had ever heard sounded as beautiful as that.

Chapter 17

The travelers in Charlie Utter's wagon train began their day at the first hint of dawn. When Jane crawled out of Bill's tent, several fires within the circle of covered wagons had been started and whatever was available for breakfast was being prepped for cooking.

Bread, biscuits, and muffins were being fashioned out of the dough made and left to rise the night before. Neither Bill nor Jane had done anything to prepare for breakfast. Fortunately, Charlie had. He had a fire going, coffee brewing, and was cooking a pan of bacon and eggs. Charlie was stirring the pot and sipping coffee from a metal cup.

"Mornin', Charlie," Jane said as she approached the man.

"Mornin', Jane," he said without looking up.

"Don't s'pose you want to share some coffee and grub for me to take Bill," she said.

"I always make breakfast for Bill, which is why you see all this food cooking. Coffee, too. I just assumed you might be hungry, too, so I made enough for all three of us," he said.

"Mighty kind of you, 'specially considering you don't fucking like me and all," Jane said.

"I don't dislike you, Jane. I'm just looking out for my friend."

"A friend who's miserable living the life of a city dude, which he's not and never will be," Jane said.

Charlie sighed. "I know, Jane. But he was bound to die if he had gone on drinking, gambling, and shooting his way out of situations he got himself into."

He poured some coffee into another cup and handed it to her.

"Mighty grateful, Charlie, for both the coffee and for looking out for *my* friend and, I might add, *my* husband before he married Agnes.

But the thing is, what fucking good is living if to do that you have to be kept in a cage?"

Jane took a sip of her coffee. She wasn't surprised when Charlie didn't answer.

Chapter 18

A short time later Bill awoke and joined his traveling companions. "Mornin', Bill," Jane beamed, barely able to contain her excitement at the mere sight of him.

"Mornin'," Bill growled. "Charlie making me breakfast is a daily occurrence without which I would be hard-pressed to carry out my day. Coffee, Charlie! Please. And thank you."

"Here you go, Bill. Looks like pleasant traveling weather today," Charlie said.

"Pleasant hunting weather, too, right, Bill?" Jane said.

Bill nodded and sipped his coffee.

"I didn't know you were planning on hunting today, Bill," said Charlie. "Do you think that's a good idea, considering your eyesight? We have plenty of supplies to see us through to Deadwood."

"Bill's asked to join me in a little hunting expedition for some fresh meat today. No one's asking him to do any of the actual hunting," Jane said, giving Charlie a warning look.

Bill sat quietly, eating and waiting to see how Charlie would respond.

"Well," he said with a mixture of resignation and irritation, "the horses have been fed and watered, but we still need to clean up the campsite, take down the tents, load the wagons, and yoke the oxen. I s'pose I can do that all myself while you two—"

"Great!" Jane said. "C'mon, Bill, let's go shoot us some antelope. Or rabbits, at least."

"Can I finish eating first, Jane? What's the goldarn hurry?"

"Take all the time you want, Bill. I think I'm just excited about getting fresh meat for the fine travelers on this wagon train," Jane said. She sat back down and smiled at him.

"Also, after I'm done eating, I think we should both help Charlie here with morning chores," Bill said.

"That would be nice," Charlie muttered, looking down into his coffee mug as if there was something worth watching there.

"Whatever you say, Bill," Jane said.

Bill set his cup down and looked at Jane. "You didn't just say that," he said.

Jane giggled. "I wondered how much you remembered, Bill," she said.

Charlie looked confused.

"I remember it all, Jane. I remember it all. But remembering the past won't change the present," he said.

Charlie stood up and began clearing the breakfast debris.

"Let me help you, Charlie," Jane said, and took the plate right out of Bill's hand. "Done with this, I assume?" she asked.

"I am now, Jane," Bill growled.

Charlie just shook his head and went about the business of cleaning up and putting out the fire.

"More coffee before Jane tosses that too, Charlie?" Bill's request sounded so pathetic Charlie almost laughed.

"Sure thing, Bill. Something tells me you're going to need all of the caffeine you can get today," Charlie said.

"O-Kay!" Jane stood up at that and announced, "I am going to pack some supplies for our day of hunting, and get my horse. When you're ready to ride, Bill, I'll be waiting for you at what will be the back of the wagon train once the oxen are hitched and the wagons are lined up."

She set off to retrieve Buddy from the spot where he was tethered. "Thanks again for the grub, Charlie Utter. And for watering and feeding Buddy."

Bill stood up and nodded his appreciation to Charlie. Then he followed Jane to get his own steed. Charlie shook his head at how quickly Bill had forgotten his admonition to Jane about helping with the chores before riding off. Well, he should have been used to it by now, Charlie thought. Bill Hickok wasn't the most ambitious man Charlie had ever met. In fact, quite the opposite.

Once Bill and Jane had loaded their saddlebags for their day-long journey, they rode out side by side, enjoying the crisp early morning air, the songs of the thrushes and meadowlarks, and the sun climbing upward.

"Whoa," Bill said after they'd been riding for about a half hour.

Jane, who was riding a bit ahead of Bill, pulled Buddy to a halt and turned in her saddle to see why Bill had stopped.

"Something wrong?" she asked.

Bill swung his right leg over the saddle and stepped to the ground. He looked up at her, smiling. "Hell, no. For the first time in a long time, Miss Calamity, something's right. I just wanted to stop and enjoy the moment. I could live out my days and then die happy doing nothing but this from dawn to dawn."

Jane looked confused. "Hunting?" she asked. "We haven't even started yet."

"No, riding free," he said.

Jane smiled. "I was joshing with you on that one, Bill Hickok," she said.

Bill smiled. He got back up on his horse. "Okay. Moment enjoyed. I reckon we'd best be continuing on to the hunting grounds to treat some weary travelers to decent food tonight," he said.

"We'll make it a party. One huge campfire cooking meat for all," she said.

Within a half hour after reaching the hunting grounds, Jane quickly dispensed with the lives of two jackrabbits who made the mistake of sitting up on their haunches to find out what was approaching. Bill shot a mallard in a reedy swamp and then followed up by killing a prairie fowl. The two gathered their prizes, tied them and flung them over their saddles, and then moved on, keeping an eye open for deer and antelope.

They dismounted when they found a spot they where could remain hidden and where plenty of fresh grass would attract their prey. Jane sat on her haunches, hopeful to have some target practice appear soon. Bill sat on the ground beside her, stretched out his long legs, and leaned back on his elbows.

"There's one," Jane said quietly.

Bill sat up and squinted. "Hell, he must be a good hundred and fifty yards away," he said.

"Closer to two," Jane corrected.

"I don't care how good you are, Jane, that's an awful long way..."

Jane took three quick shots.

"Did you get him?" Bill asked, straining to see.

"Yep, and would have gotten both of his brothers, too, if the first shot hadn't scared them off," Jane said, grinning from ear to ear.

"I reckon I'll go gather while you maybe can retrieve some of that venison and water from your saddlebags and then maybe take the flask out of mine. I hope you don't mind, but I took the liberty of opening another one of the bottles in our wagon and pouring some in my flask," she said.

When she got back with her newest prize Jane found Bill had spread a blanket on the ground and laid out a few pieces of venison, some crackers, a canteen filled with fresh water, Jane's flask, and an unopened bottle of whiskey.

"I was thinking ahead, too," he said.

Jane smiled. "Your style never fails to impress me, William Hickok," she said.

"I'm even more impressed by your shooting," he said.

Jane laughed. "Finally, you acknowledge that I'm a better marksman than you?"

"I wouldn't go that far," he said. "In my younger days I could have shot two anything to your one," he said.

"Well, Bill, these aren't your younger days," Jane said.

"Don't remind me," he growled.

They ate and drank in the kind of silence that is caused by a peaceful, overall happy feeling. If Jane could have bottled this moment, she would gladly have poured her whiskey from her flask to store it.

Bill was the first to speak. "I don't know about you, but this not-so-young man could use a little closed-eye time," he said.

"Sounds good, but not too long. I want to shoot some more food to make sure everyone at camp gets to partake tonight," she said.

"I heard there were a few more hunting parties going out today, so between the lot of us, I think there will be plenty," Bill said.

They both lay back on the blanket, what was left of their meal and the drink between them.

"I still love you, Bill," Jane said quietly.

Bill didn't speak, but the hand he reached out to take hers said all she needed to hear.

They drifted off to sleep, waking about an hour later to find the area filled with deer and antelope. This time Bill shot at the ones within the range of his limited vision and Jane fired away on those more distant. When they were done, they had collected a deer and an antelope.

"I think this is all we can carry," Bill said, as he set his gun down and prepared to gather the dead animals.

Jane agreed and together they collected the food, tied it to their saddles, and set out to reconnect with the wagon train, which was within an hour or so of stopping to camp for the night.

As it turned out, the travelers had just pulled into a campsite and were forming the circle of wagons when Bill and Jane caught up to them. The sight of all the fresh meat thrown across their saddles caused an uproar.

"Our heroes!" Trixie yelled.

Several of the men ran out to greet them and help remove the carcasses and carry them into the circle.

They learned that the other hunting parties had returned before them and were also successful in their endeavors.

"One fire in the middle," Jane bellowed. "We all eat together tonight."

Once the meat was cleaned and roasting on the huge fire that had been built for the occasion, travelers began gathering to enjoy the festive atmosphere. Several bottles were passed around and, when the meat was ready to be consumed, they all dug in with little restraint.

"We're all acting like we're starving," Jane said, her mouth full of rabbit and well on her way to feeling no pain.

Charlie shot Bill a look as if to say, "How charming is that?" Bill, however, was not receiving the message. He laughed at Jane's lack of etiquette and continued to feed his face and wash the meat down with some of the other travelers' fine liquor.

After dinner a few fiddles were brought out and Al's girls, as they'd come to be known, invited several of the single men to dance.

When the music and the fire began to fade, Bill asked Jane to relate the story of how she had come to be called "Calamity Jane." She was all too eager to oblige.

Her words were slurred, her voice was a little too loud, and the story changed some from its original telling, but no one minded how she spoke and no one knew the original story anyway. Jane spent the next hour with all eyes on her and all ears eager to hear.

"Well, those of you who don't yet fucking know me and have not yet heard of my many brave and daring deeds might be surprised to know that you are looking at the person who, not so long ago, faced hundreds of renegade Indians who had surrounded the horse of Captain James Egan, rushed in with no regard for my own life, grabbed the dying captain, threw him across my horse, and rode him to the safety of Fort Sanders, all the while suffering arrows in both legs, both arms, and my back."

Several in the group seated around the fire stared at Jane in awe.

"See, I was working as a scout for the U.S. Army Ninth Battalion led by Brigadier General George Crook, only it wasn't an official position because I'm a woman and, as such, not entitled to be fucking paid or recognized as a government employee. Even though I was welcome to do what none of the male soldiers could do that day and fucking save the life of a captain, which is a huge case of steaming horse poop if you ask me," she said.

She took a sip from the near-empty bottle closest to her and then continued.

"I'm telling you, I have fought the U.S. government tooth and fucking nail to recognize that gender matters only when it comes to whether you stand up or squat to pee and that's all. Otherwise, I can do what any man alive can do, and in most cases, even better."

"But what about the name you were given?" Bill asked.

"I'm getting to that part, Bill. Rein in your fucking horses," Jane said.

Bill and several others laughed. They were all enjoying Jane and her storytelling.

"So here I am, half alive, riding into Fort Sanders with a nearly dead captain, and I was given a hero's welcome—not that I knew that at the time. As soon as I knew the captain was safe, I passed out and didn't wake up until several weeks later. Although in terrible pain, I tried to tear myself from my bed and find out how the captain was doing, hoping to God I would find him alive and well. I was unable to stand and collapsed on the floor, or so I am told. Another week passed before I once again regained consciousness.

"I awoke to find General Crook himself standing by my bed. He shared the good news with me that Captain Egan was recovering well, having fared better than myself, and told me that as soon as I was strong enough to do so, he would like to see me."

Jane got up, walked to where another bottle sat unattended, took a long drink, and then went back to where she had been sitting and continued.

"I said of course I was strong enough, but doctor's orders were that I not be allowed to leave my bed."

" 'Don't worry, Jane,' the general said to me. 'The Captain will come to you as soon as I tell him you're conscious.'

"So it wasn't more than a few minutes later that Captain Egan walked in and stood by my bed. I was a little groggy, but remember him saying, 'I want to shake your hand, soldier. You deserve the highest honor given to any soldier for your bravery, quick thinking, and daring acts with no regard for your own welfare.'

"'It was just part of my job, Captain,' I said. 'I'm happy to see you're alive and well.'

"'Well, Martha Jane Canary,' the captain started to say.

"Then I corrected him. 'It's just Jane, Captain,' I said. 'I let go of my first name years ago. I like to keep it plain and simple.'

"Then the captain said back to me, 'Oh, no. You're no plain Jane. Nosireee! From now on, you will be known as Calamity Jane. The woman who rode into the scene of a major battle, endured a rock to the head ...'"

"Wait! You didn't tell us about the rock," Charlie said.

"Well, what do you fucking expect, Utter? I had so many injuries I can't always remember them all. Besides which, I don't want to exaggerate. I'd rather just tell the story if you mother fuckers don't mind," Jane said. She was quite annoyed.

After several choruses of "Go on, go on!" from those listening, and some unfavorable looks directed at Charlie for interrupting, Jane continued.

"Anyway, the captain saluted me, told me I could ask anything I want of him or the U.S. government, offered me a free rest and relaxation in Fort Laramie at the government's expense, and a few days later held a ceremony where I was given a large sum from the government and some assorted presents from the captain, and was applauded by every member of that camp's unit."

"Wow," Trixie said. "You must have been so proud!"

"Was then, still fucking am," Jane said.

"So why didn't you become a paid soldier, if they recognized you as such?" Charlie asked.

Jane sighed. "Because, Charlie Fucking Utter, like I already told you, I squat to pee."

"They should have made an exception in your case," Trixie said.

"Yeah, well, that didn't happen," Jane said.

"What are you planning to do now that the army no longer looks upon you so kindly, due to ...?" asked Trixie.

Jane cut her off. She looked directly at Bill and said, "I have another mission of a secret nature I am working on as I speak."

Charlie cleared his throat and Bill stood.

"I don't know about the rest of you," Bill said, "but these old bones need to rest for a few hours, which is about all we have left before we head out tomorrow." He turned to Jane, bowed slightly, and added, "Thanks for a wonderful party, Miss Calamity Jane."

Jane blushed. "Thank yourself, Bill. You shot half of the food we ate tonight."

"Yes, true. But you told the best story," he said.

With that, he walked away toward their campsite. Jane stretched and yawned loud enough to make a point. "Guess I'm worn through and through, too." She got up and addressed the people still sitting beside the fire.

"Thank you all mighty kindly for indulging me and my tale. If you liked that, I have a whole bunch of others you might want to hear. But now I am going to rest," she said. Jane tipped her hat and started to walk away.

"Trixie, get in here," she heard Dan Dority bellow.

Trixie got up and called after Jane. "Hope your mission is accomplished soon," she said.

Jane kept walking, a smile spreading across her face. *Me, too. Trixie. Me, too,* she thought.

When she got to the tent she found Bill sleeping beside it, same as the previous evening. She crawled inside, lay down, and fell asleep dreaming about Bill, their picnic, and his hand closing over hers when she told him she still loved him.

Chapter 19

Jane had gone to bed shortly before eleven and had only been asleep for a few hours when she woke to hear someone calling her name outside the tent.

"Jane? Jane, wake up!"

Jane roused herself, sat up, and stuck her head out of the tent to see a near-hysterical Charlie Utter. It was still pitch dark outside, and Charlie was holding a lantern.

"What the fuck's wrong with you, Charles?" Jane asked.

"Jane, have you seen Bill?" Charlie asked.

"No, Charlie, because of I was sleeping in this tent alone and haven't seen anyone yet this morning, which considering how dark it still is, has not begun to grace us with its fucking presence," she said.

"Well, he came over to my tent a couple hours ago, all upset about something. Said he'd had a nightmare and was going to take a walk and work some things out in his head. Next thing I knew, I heard a horse galloping away from camp. I checked, and Bill's horse was gone. I figured he would come back after a while, but it's been too long and I'm worried."

Jane crawled out of the tent, still clothed from the night before. She stood scratching her head and trying not to worry.

"He probably just wanted to ride, Charlie. He used to do that when I was with him. Day or night, something was bothering him, he would ride for hours," she said.

"I met him shortly after he left Cheyenne—"

"Me. He left *me*," Jane corrected him.

Charlie ignored her. "And in all these years that I've been his friend, he has never just taken off for this long. And I promised Agnes —"

"Well, if he did run off, it was certainly not because of me," Jane said, venom dripping from her words. Hearing the name of the woman Bill had gone and married drove Jane nearly insane. "We are getting along just fine. Better than fine, as a matter of fucking fact. And if anything, the thought of returning to *her* probably is driving him to distraction."

Charlie sat on the ground and covered his face with both hands. Jane felt kind of sorry for him.

"Look, if it will make you feel better, we can ride out and look for him," she said.

"Where? I don't even know what direction he was heading. And I have a wagon train full of people counting on me to keep this journey on its proper course," he said.

"Hell, I used to work as a scout for the army. If anyone can find him, I can. I'll ride out a few miles in a circular route," she said.

"Thank you, Jane. I'd be much obliged," Charlie said.

Jane saddled Buddy, hopped on his back, and started out to the east. If she was being honest with herself, she would have to admit she was a bit worried, too. What if he had just decided to take off again? What if he was going back to his wife? What if he was hurt somewhere out there? These are things she didn't even want to admit as possibilities, even though she knew they were.

Every quarter mile, Jane would stop, call out Bill's name in the darkness, and then continue, trying to cover the entire area around the wagons. She was about five miles into her search pattern, now traveling in a southerly direction, when her call was answered.

"Jane," Bill Hickok called back. She rode in the direction his voice had come from and found his horse tied to a tree and Bill sitting on a rock nearby.

"Bill, what the hell are you doing out here?" she asked.

"Well, if you must know, I was trying to get some time to myself to think about some things," he said.

Jane got off Buddy, tied his reins to the same tree as Bill's horse, and plopped down beside the man. "Sorry to intrude, but your friend, Charles, woke me up all panicky about you telling him you were going for a walk and then riding off on your horse," she said. "I told him I

109

know you to do that when you have something pushing at your mind and not to fucking worry, but..."

"Were you worried?" Bill asked.

Jane looked at him and then grinned. "Yeah, I won't lie, I was a bit, Bill. But mostly that you had decided to go back east and that I would never see you again."

He was quiet after that. She stood and said, "You came out here to have some time alone, and now that I can go back and report you are alive and well to Mr. Worry Wart Utter, I will take my leave and let you be," she said.

She was getting back on Buddy when Bill softly said her name. "Jane?"

"Yes?" she answered.

He looked up and at her and said, "Mind if I sleep in my tent tonight? I have been having trouble with bad dreams and I think that will help."

Her heart went out to him. "Of course, Bill. Whatever you need. Hell, I'm fine with sleeping under the stars. Done it most of my life. You take the tent," she said.

Bill stood up then, took hold of Buddy's halter, and said, "I was not meaning for you to sleep outside the tent with me in it," he said.

"I don't understand. What about Agnes?" she asked.

"She's a wonderful woman, but in truth she bores me to tears," Bill said. "As soon as I saw you, well maybe not as soon as I saw you, you did look disgusting, your hair full of vomit, and all—"

"Bill! For the love of God!"

"Even with the deplorable shape you were in, all those memories started to run right back at me, like wild horses spooked by a pack of wolves, trampling any illusions I may have had about being able to endure a life in the city with a woman I love but am not excited about," he said.

When Jane remained silent he said, "Look, I know my reputation with women is terrible. You should also know that I could do the same thing to you as I did in Cheyenne. I'm just... right now..."

"Shut up, okay? I'd be honored to share your tent with you tonight and as many nights as you are willing to stay. Even if it means getting my heart broken all over again," Jane said.

She got down off her horse and wrapped her arms around Bill. They stood there, not moving, not speaking, barely breathing. Then Bill put his right hand under her chin, lifted it, leaned down, and gently kissed her lips. After a few more minutes of enjoying the moment of their reunion, Bill spoke. "Let's ride back to the wagons together. Charlie probably has breakfast started and I'm hungrier than I've been in a long time," he said.

"Me, too," Jane agreed. "Um, but one question, first. Who's going to tell *your* friend about our new sleeping arrangements?"

Bill grinned. "Seeing as how he is *my* friend, as you were clever to point out, I will be happy to do that. There are a lot of things I need to talk to him about. He's a good friend. He'll understand some of it, and what he doesn't understand, I know he will accept," Bill said.

Bill waited until Jane was astride Buddy, then untied his horse, hopped in the saddle, and together they rode back to the wagon train. The sun was just beginning to poke up over the rocky horizon when they rode into camp.

"Why don't I feed and water our horses to give you time to talk to Charlie alone?" Jane said. "I'll be there in a bit and join the two of you for breakfast."

Bill gave Jane an appreciative look and slid off his horse. He handed Jane the reins, squeezed her hand gently, then turned and walked away to face Charlie.

When Jane finished her chores a half hour later, she found the two men sharing a meal together. Charlie stood up, gave her a hug, and said, "I'm mighty beholden to you for checking on Bill this morning."

"Morning? More like middle of the fucking night," she said.

111

They all laughed.

"And you're welcome," Jane said.

"Bill told me he has decided to stay on in Deadwood, rather than going back east," Charlie said. "I told him I have no problem with that, but that I hope he's sure about what he is doing."

Charlie fixed a plate of food, handed it to Jane along with a cup of coffee, and addressed Bill. "It ain't my business, but as your friend, I would urge you to stay away from the card tables and keep your hair-trigger anger in check. Deadwood has no laws and from what I hear, it is not the best place for someone with your reputation and habits to spend more than a short time, which is what I intended when I let you talk me into bringing you there."

Bill didn't respond. For a long time now, he'd had a feeling his days were numbered. That was the theme of his recurring nightmares. Someone was going to shoot him dead. And he knew, somehow, it wouldn't be long. It was because of this premonition that he had decided he wanted to spend his remaining days with Jane.

Two weeks after Charlie's warning, the wagon train rolled into Deadwood. To celebrate, Bill and Jane put on quite a show with some fancy riding and shooting their guns in the air. It was a glorious moment.

Chapter 20

J ane's first look at Deadwood as she rode into town would have made most women recoil in disgust. Centennial Road, running along the slope directly above the town, gave new arrivals a view of the one and only street that ran the length of Whitewood Gulch, just below the mouth of Deadwood Creek. The street twisted and turned, mimicking the gulch beside it, and in some places, was so narrow it could barely accommodate a wagon.

It had been raining for a few days before the wagon train's arrival, and the crooked street held so much water that no one could walk without mud clumping around the bottoms of their garments. Considering that horses, buffalo, pigs, mules, oxen, and other creatures used that street, guided by their human owners to get from one place to another, it was a safe bet that mud was the least objectionable substance underfoot.

As if that weren't enough, several bodies of animals lay where they had died, causing a stench that reached one's nose long before one reached Deadwood's only street.

The town was crowded, with lean-tos and tents sprinkled among the wood buildings, many of which were in the process of being built.

Jane and Bill's display of fun horsemanship was not as impressive as usual, considering the state of the street they rode in on. Still, several onlookers cheered. They'd heard about and eagerly awaited Wild Bill's arrival in Deadwood, and, although Jane was the lesser known of the two, many had also heard of this woman who preferred to dress and live, at least in most ways, like a man.

The town appeared to be filled to the brim with all sorts of people seeking to set up a home, prospect for gold, start a business. A steady stream of newcomers entered Deadwood at all hours of the day and night, some on horseback, a few in stagecoaches, and some, like Charlie Utter's group, in wagon trains. Many people walked into the gold prospecting camp with all their worldly possessions on their backs.

Charlie had written ahead and sent a deposit for the rental of a storefront just off the main street. It was a modest wood building, just on the edge of the encampment of a large contingent of Chinese immigrants. The structure had a good roof over it and a door that locked, but no windows, which made it dark inside, but Charlie with Bill's assistance, intended to take care of that within the next day or two.

Charlie pulled his wagon up in front of his new place.

"Help me unload, Bill?" he asked.

Bill turned in his saddle and looked at Jane. "Would you mind scouting out a place for us to set up camp while I help my friend here unload?"

"I can do that," Jane said, smiling from ear to ear at the words "a place for us to set up camp."

Charlie said, "We should be done in an hour or so."

"I'll be back then, hopefully with good news about our campsite," she said.

Jane rode off, and Bill got down off his horse. "I don't know about you, Charlie, but I'm parched," he said. "How 'bout we mosey over to one of what looks like a dozen or so saloons and get us a drink or two?" Bill's smile was infectious, but Charlie was immune to it.

"How 'bout we unload first, take the wagon to the man who has agreed to buy it from me, and then get that drink?" Charlie said.

Bill sighed. "We'll do it your way, but if I die of dehydration..."

"Which would be out of the question considering we still have some water left in the barrel," Charlie said. He knew his friend was not inclined toward manual labor.

Bill grudgingly agreed and, during the next hour and a half, unloaded one item to Charlie's three. But finally, they were done.

You go on and deliver the wagon and oxen to your buyer. I'm going to wait here for Jane. She should be back soon," Bill said.

114

"Why don't we meet down the street at Saloon Number Ten? I noticed when we rode in that it was a little less crowded than some of the others," Charlie said. He didn't tell Bill, but he hoped a little less crowded meant that a poker game was a little less likely to be taking place. He'd promised Agnes to keep Bill away from the gambling tables, as best he could, and even if Agnes was out of the picture for now or forever, Charlie intended to keep that promise, for Bill's sake.

Bill agreed, and Charlie set off. Ten minutes after he left, Jane came riding up to Charlie's new place with a huge grin on her face. "Wanna go see where we're resting our heads tonight?" she asked Bill.

"What I really want to do is get a drink," he said. "The ground will still be there later."

Jane agreed. "I guess it will at that."

Bill told Jane about Charlie meeting them at the Number Ten Saloon. Together they rode that way, dismounted, tied their horses to a hitching post, and went inside.

Wild Bill's distinctive appearance was known by many in these parts, and he was recognized as soon as he walked in the door. Most people stopped talking, and those in his path parted way to allow him to get to the bar. Jane followed close behind.

"Two shots, please," Bill told the bartender, placing two coins on the bar.

Bill and Jane toasted each other, threw them back, and Bill ordered two more. While the barkeep was pouring, Bill turned to face the hushed patrons and said, "No need to worry, folks. I'm not here to start any trouble. Just to live my life in as near to peace as I can, maybe do a little prospecting, play some cards, and drink a bit." He reached back, picked up the shot glass off the bar, and said, "To peaceful coexistence."

Several of those in attendance raised their own glasses in response.

Bill bought a bottle from the bartender, and he and Jane sat down at an empty table. Jane was surprised by it but didn't ask him about his expressed intention to "play some cards." He could do what he wanted, as far as she was concerned. She was just happy to be back with him. And it had happened a lot sooner than she had dared to hope.

Charlie met them after a while, had two shots of whiskey, and said he was going to go back to his place and get some rest. There was much work to be done tomorrow.

"If you were not able to find a decent campsite, Jane, the two of you are welcome to sleep at my place. Your bedrolls and blankets are there waiting," he said.

"That's mighty kind of you, Charlie, but I did find a place, so I reckon Bill and I should follow you back and recover some items for the night and then go there," she said.

"Yeah. I'm pretty tired and wouldn't mind laying my head down for the night," Bill said.

"I'll buy a fresh bottle to take with us," Jane said.

Charlie thought Jane was hiding something, but he didn't know if he was just tired or still unhappy about his friend's betrayal to his wife. He also was not happy with Jane buying another bottle to take with them. Agnes had told him that she hoped Bill would keep his drinking down to the minimum because she was worried about his health.

Jane came back with the whiskey and the three of them returned to Charlie's place. After gathering their bedrolls, crackers, beans, and jerky, Bill asked Charlie where he had put the tents. Before he could answer, Jane spoke up. "Oh, we won't be needing tents," she said.

Both men looked at her like she was crazy. The weather had turned a bit chilly, and a tent could make the difference between sleeping in comfort or shivering most of the night.

Before either of the men could comment, Jane said, "I bought us a cabin, just outside town."

"You what? How in the world...?" Bill asked.

"Well, I rode around looking for a place for us to land, saw this abandoned shack, made some inquiries, learned the owner was trying to sell it at a price no one wanted to pay, and bought it. Fifty dollars," she said.

"Where did you get that kind of money?" Bill asked.

"Oh, on the last payday I was at Fort Laramie I was given my monthly stipend and the soldiers were given their generous pay. I'd say they unwittingly contributed quite a bit to our new life in Deadwood."

Charlie stood in shocked silence. Bill seemed delighted. He picked Jane up and swung her around. "That's my girl! Let's go see our new home."

Jane and Bill said their good-nights to Charlie, retrieved their horses, and rode to the outskirts of town where they would settle down for the night and, Jane hoped, for a long time thereafter.

The cabin had a kerosene lamp with some fuel left, and they lit it and looked around. There was a wood table, two chairs, a basin, and a wood stove. There also were a lot of spider webs and evidence of other critters that had camped here before them. There was no door, but Bill promised he would put one on in the next few days.

Bill used the little bit of wood that was there and lit a fire. Then they sat down at the table, raised their glasses, and toasted their new home. Tomorrow they would set about fixing the place up. To they would celebrate.

"To us?" Jane asked.

"Indeed," Bill said.

Chapter 21

August 2, 1886
Deadwood, South Dakota

For the next few weeks, Jane and Bill lived in their cabin on the outskirts of Deadwood. He played cards some nights to feed them, but if they had all they needed at any given moment, he and Jane spent their days riding and their nights drinking and making love.

August 2, 1876, began like most other days. Jane waited for Bill to tell her if he was staying home or needed to find a card game.

"I think I need to fill the bank," he told Jane as they were lying awake that morning. She snuggled close and told him to do what he thought was best. She never argued with Bill, nor did she try to control him or his actions. He was not winning at cards any more than he did when she had first settled down with him in Cheyenne. The difference was that he was not betting such high stakes as he did back then, so the losses were much more tolerable. And the wins were enough to financially sustain them.

"I think I will find a daytime game or two today, so we can have a celebratory dinner tonight," he told her.

"What are we celebrating?" Jane asked. To her, every day with Bill was worth a celebration.

"I wrote Agnes a letter asking for a divorce because of me loving and wanting to be with you for the rest of my life. I was hoping you would take it to Charlie to be mailed while I'm playing cards today," he said.

Jane let out a whoop. "Oh, that's the best reason to celebrate ever fucking was!" she said. They made love and then got up and dressed. Bill gave Jane half of the money in his pocket, which might have lasted the average couple a week or so, and told her to go buy a pretty dress, the finest bottle of bourbon she could find, and some pork from the butcher.

"Any particular color you want this dress to be?" Jane asked.

"Surprise me," he said. "And don't forget to mail the letter."

After Bill left, Jane spent an hour or so tidying the cabin. Then she set out to tend to her errands. The first place she stopped was at Martha's Dress Shoppe.

"Good morning, Jane," Martha greeted her when she walked in the door.

"And a mighty fine morning right back at you," Jane said. "I need something special to wear on a date tonight," Jane told the woman.

"Oooh, you and Mr. Hickok going someplace special?"

"Well, Martha, anywhere I go with Bill is special, but tonight we will stay home, light the stove, spread a blanket on the floor—because we like picnics indoors and out—and eat, drink, be merry, and celebrate our love," Jane said.

"Well that sounds delightful," Martha said. "I have only this week received a shipment of dainty frocks with ruffles that are perfect for such an occasion."

"I'm afraid I'm not the dainty type. But I think what I would like is something in white, maybe a ruffle at the bottom, and, um, low cut on the top," Jane said.

"I think I have just the thing," Martha said. She disappeared into a back room and returned with two dresses. One was white organza over satin, no bottom ruffle but low cut. The second was a pale-yellow cotton with a button-up bodice, also low cut, with ruffles all the way down the skirt. These were the sort of dresses Martha ordered for her clients who worked the saloons. The dresses for proper ladies were not so fancy. Martha held them both up and said, "I have my ideas about which one of these you will love wearing most."

Jane reached out and pointed. "This one. Definitely," she said.

Martha smiled. "I was right," she said.

"It's a lot of money at ten dollars and fifty cents. I can give you a discount and call it ten even," she said.

Jane tried on the yellow dress, and she and Martha were both impressed at how perfect a fit it was.

"Yes, I would be happy to buy this one," Jane said. She knew Bill would love it.

"Excellent choice," Martha said and then asked, "Would you like me to box it up for you?"

"No, thank you," Jane said. "I think I would like you to box up the clothes I came in with and I'll wear this one."

Martha did as she was asked. Jane paid for the dress and left the shop, feeling prettier than she had ever felt in her life. She was happy it had not rained for several days and the mud had dried up. She held the skirt of her dress slightly off the ground, stepped around animal excretions, and thus managed to keep the bottom of her new dress clean.

She glided down the street, appreciating the stares she was getting from men and women alike. When she got to the Chinaman's butcher shop she purchased a premium pork loin and set off to pick up a bottle of liquor from The Gem.

As she was walking away from the butcher shop, she spotted Charlie Utter's store and realized she had forgotten to bring Bill's letter with her to be mailed. She decided there would still be time to go back home and retrieve it after buying the bourbon. So, her next stop was the Gem Theater.

As she walked up to the saloon, she saw Al Swearengen standing on the second-floor deck outside his office, where he could often be found. He liked standing up there, feeling like he was above everyone. It also gave him the opportunity to keep his eye on what was going on around him.

"Hey, Jane, why are you dressed so fancy?" Al asked.

"Don't worry about my attire," Jane said. "I've come to buy a bottle of fine whiskey, and I want to open it myself and taste it before I pay."

Jane did not trust Swearengen, for good reason. She knew he often opened bottles and watered them down. Sometimes he would take the high-priced whiskey, pour half into an empty bottle, then fill both bottles with the cheap stuff, thinking no one could tell the difference. And most didn't. But one thing Jane knew well was the difference in taste between fine whiskey and the cheaper stuff.

She looked up at Al and added, "I want to watch you take it off the fucking shelf, check the seal, and then open it myself and give it a taste because of the fact I don't trust you any farther than I can fucking throw you."

"Jane, Jane, Jane, you judge me unfairly, and your language does not match that pretty dress you're wearing," Swearengen teased. "Come inside. I'll pull a doozy of a sealed, unaltered bottle off the shelf. But it's gonna cost you."

"That's fine. I can pay. But I want to watch you pull it, I want to be the one to open it, and I want to taste it before I pay," she said.

"So you already fucking said and I already fucking heard." Al mock-saluted her and said, "I'll be right down."

Jane entered the saloon and waited for Al to come downstairs. She greeted the bartender and told him she was waiting for Al. Before long, the saloon owner came bouncing down the stairs, walked over to Jane, took her hand in his, and kissed it.

Jane pulled her hand away and swore at the man. "Don't you ever put your slimy mouth on me again, you motherfucking cocksucker," she said. "Just pull me a goddamn bottle."

"Whoa! Do you talk to your Wild Bill like this? I guess we all have our individual tastes in women," Al laughed.

Jane just glared.

"Sorry, but you look like such a proper lady, I thought you might want to be treated as such," he said.

Al walked over behind the bar and took a bottle off the top shelf. He handed it to Jane.

She inspected it and determined it was properly sealed.

"Do you want to know how much it is?" Al asked her.

"Well, if you expect me to pay you I guess I'll need to know how much it is," she said.

"That is my best bottle, the last one I have until next month's shipment, and it costs twenty-five dollars," he said.

"Holy Mother of God!" Jane said. "Do you have anything cheaper?"

"Yes," he said, grinning, "but none of the less expensive bottles are sealed, and thus do not meet your strict requirements."

Jane glared at the man and opened the sealed bottle.

"Dan, give the *lady* a glass," Al said.

"Not necessary," Jane said and raised the bottle to her lips.

"I hope you know you are now obligated to pay for that," Swearengen said.

"Wow! No problem," Jane said. She corked the bottle, set it down on the bar, and dug the last of the money Bill had given her out of the pocket of her dress. She had twenty-six dollars and some spare coins.

"How about if we negotiate the exorbitant price of this bottle, good as it is, because what you are asking for is akin to the average low-down road robber." She said.

Before he could answer, a man came running into the saloon shouting, "Wild Bill Hickok's been shot! Saloon Number Ten!"

Jane felt the blood drain from her face. She left the meat and the whiskey on the bar, bolted out the door, and took off running down the street. She flew through the doors of the saloon moments later and saw Bill lying in his own blood.

"He's dead," a man leaning over Bill's lifeless body said.

Jane could tell that from where she stood, without needing to check for a pulse. She walked over to Bill's body, sat down on the floor next to him, and reached out, pulling his bloody head to her chest

122

and cradling it. She rocked back and forth slowly, quietly sobbing and kissing his forehead, then lips. Doc Amos Cochran came up behind her. He squatted next to her, took one look at the head wound, and knew no man could live through getting his brains blown out the way Bill had.

"Does anyone know how this happened?" Doc asked.

"Yeah," the saloon owner spoke up. "He was playing cards and Jack McCall walked in and, just like that, shot Wild Bill Hickok in the back of the head. I doubt Bill ever knew what hit him."

"But Bill never sits with his back to the door," Jane cried.

"That's a fact," Doc said.

"It was the only seat left and Bill said, "'What the hell. I'm tired of worrying about it.'"

"Jane," Doc said, taking the woman's arm, "Let me get you out of here."

Jane looked up at Doc and told him, "I will never, ever, let this man go. He's part of my fucking heart and soul, and I will carry him with me till the day I die."

Some of those standing around Jane and the corpse of Wild Bill Hickok thought she meant that in literal terms. Doc knew what she was saying. "You're right, Jane. You don't ever have to let go of your love for Bill. But as for his body, someone needs to get it up off this floor and take it to be prepared for a proper burial."

Jane kissed her lover's forehead one last time, gently laid him back down on the floor, and then, with Doc's help, got to her feet.

She stood and stared at Bill for several minutes, then turned and left the saloon without saying another word. It occurred to her that he would never see the dress she bought to please him. There would be no celebration tonight, or ever. Just a succession of days and nights without him. Of wanting to hold him, touch him, talk to him. The only true happiness Jane had ever known had been ripped from her arms. Twice. How was it possible that a few short hours ago Bill had been laughing, talking, breathing, and now...?

Jane walked toward their home, passed The Gem, and then turned around and walked back. Al was standing behind the bar. He'd heard the shot was fatal.

"Jane, I am so sorry," he said. He'd never really cared for Hickok, or Jane either, as far as that went. But he thought it was the right thing to say, and Al Swearengen prided himself on saying the right thing when it seemed to be called for.

"Where's the stuff I left here?" Jane asked, showing little emotion.

"I've got it right here for you, Jane. I didn't know if you'd come back for it or not, so I put it on this shelf behind the bar," he said.

He pulled the pork loin out and tried to hand it to her.

"Keep the meat," she said. "I'm not hungry. All I want is the fucking bottle."

Al handed her the bottle. She reached into the pocket of her dress and pulled out twenty-five dollars, no longer caring to negotiate.

Al took her money without comment. He knew he had overcharged her by five dollars and was happy he hadn't tried to water the whiskey down after she had run out of the bar.

But he might as well have. It wouldn't have mattered to her at this point. She no longer cared about the taste, just the effects.

Chapter 22

Jane returned to the place she and Bill had shared for too short a time. She opened the bottle she had purchased from Swearengen and took a long sip. Jane wiped her mouth with the back of her left hand and shook her head, staring at the creek through the open doorway. She sat down on the fur coat Bill had laid on the floor for the two of them to share and once more raised the bottle to her mouth.

The envelope with Bill's letter in it was on the table where she had left it. She took another gulp of the whiskey, then corked the bottle, got up, and placed it on the table next to Bill's letter. She ran her hand across the wood and smiled. They had shared many happy meals at this table. They had laughed together at this table.

And once, when Bill told her how scared he was of going blind, they had cried together at this table. And now on this table sat words he had fashioned with his own hands. She had forgotten to take the letter with her, or it would be on its way to Bill's legally wedded wife. Now grieving widow. Scorned woman who need never know that, if Bill had not died, she would have been his ex-wife.

Jane picked up the envelope and turned it around in her hands a few times. She had many faults, but snooping was not one of them. Still...

"You're dead, Bill. Gone forever from this world," she cried out loud. "Damn you for being dead, Bill! Damn you for sitting with your back to the door of that fucking saloon!"

Jane suppressed a sob, set the letter back on the table, and took another sip from the bottle. She walked over and stood in the doorway for a while, wondering how everything could look so normal. The trees around her should have withered and died when he did. The clear blue sky might at least have the decency to turn gray and cover itself with angry, swirling clouds. Birds were still singing, and that was not right.

"Shut the fuck up!" she screamed, covering her ears with her hands. But that didn't help. She still could imagine the furious sound of thunder following deadly bolts of lightning. Her world was torn from beneath her feet, yet it looked as normal as it had hours ago, when everything really was normal and right.

Jane turned back and looked at the table.

"Bill, might your last written words bring needed comfort to my soul, such as to warrant me invading your privacy? I sure don't want to post this missive such that your wife's agony upon learning of your demise is made a heavier burden to bear when learning of your infidelities. It will be fucking hard enough for her to get news of your death, without her having to further learn that you were planning to leave her ... *for me,*" she said.

Jane walked over to the table and picked up the letter. The name Agnes Hickok and the address were facing her. Agnes Hickok. Oh, how that name burned like a hot poker piercing Jane's heart. Agnes would now forever be Mrs. James Butler Hickok. She, Jane, would never carry that surname.

Jane took a deep breath and held it for a few seconds. Then she let out a long, halting sigh. She'd been through a lot, but this? This was just too much to expect a body—anybody—to bear. She picked up the bottle and gulped in a desperate move to make the pain go away.

Jane and Bill had often talked for hours into the night about how this time they would have a legal and binding nuptial. She would take his name and they would be the most famous couple in history. They would make piles of cash traveling around and telling their stories. They'd work at entertaining folks, not at prospecting gold. That was what they were born to do.

The gold they would earn from their tales of derring-do and displays of superior shooting would be as great as if they had laid claim to a goldmine. And twice as much fun. They even thought about the fact that Bill's eyesight would soon be gone. They knew when that time came they would find other ways for him to entertain a crowd.

Maybe he could train horses to do fancy tricks. They hadn't gotten quite that far in their planning.

Now that would never be. Jane took another sip of whiskey and turned the letter over. She took her time breaking the wax seal. Then she pulled two handwritten five-by-eight-inch pages from the envelope.

"Bill, I truly am sorry for not respecting your privacy, but you're not here and these words are all I've got now, even if they were meant for another," she said.

The letter was dated August 2, 1876. It began:

My Dearest Agnes,

First, I want to thank you for marrying the sorry likes of me. I will never know what made a woman like you, so intelligent, refined, and of your own independent means even consider courting this wild cowboy. But you did, and for that I will always be grateful.

Were I to expound upon your beauty and virtue, it would take much more ink and paper than I have here at my immediate disposal. So please try to remember all the ways in which I have verbally addressed your wonders in your very company.

Jane sniffed loudly and reached for the bottle. "Were you here in my very company, my dear Bill, I would not hesitate to tell you how much this letter, so far, makes me want to fucking vomit," she said, then pulled the second page from behind the first. She sniffled, took a deep breath, and continued to read.

"The thing is, Dear Agnes, I have never been one to settle down for long. Do you remember me telling you that on more

than one occasion? So, for me, love has always been temporary—until the next time. But I've finally met a woman who is so like me that I will never feel tied to a place or a person exclusive of all others.

I am so very sorry to inform you that woman is not you. Her name is Jane and she allows me to be my own person— in every way. I knew her and had a romance with her years before I met you. I've never really gotten her off my mind. Because of that, and so many other things, I love her and believe I always will.

Agnes, you don't need me and eventually I would just make you miserable, even worse than this letter does. Please show me this final act of love and grant me a divorce so I can marry Jane. If you ever need me, I will be there as a friend, family, and former lover.

Dear Agnes, I will love you forever if you agree to do the one thing that finally will make me happy.

Bill.

Jane set the letter back down on the table. The words "I love her and believe I always will" played over and over in her mind. She knew he loved her. He'd said those very words to her, and here she had them where she could read them repeatedly, as often as she liked, forever.

But the letter was addressed to another woman and, as such, was not hers to keep.

The sound of hoofbeats coming toward the cabin made her jump. Jane went to the doorway and saw Charlie Utter hitching his mount to a tree. He reached into his saddlebag and pulled out a bottle of whiskey and a bag with some bread and dried beef.

128

"I thought you could use some company and..." Charlie held up the bottle in one hand and the bag in the other.

"Oh, Charlie. What am I going to do without him?" The floodgates holding back Jane's tears broke, and she sank to the ground sobbing.

Charlie entered the cabin, set his offerings down on the table, and sat down next to Jane. He put his arms around her and did the best he knew how to comfort her. He was an awkward man who hadn't held a grieving woman before, and he was not quite sure what to do. So, he just held on and let her cry until there seemed to be no more tears left to come—at least for now.

Charlie went outside and gathered some kindling to start a fire in the stove. It was cool for August, and the night air could be more than chilly. Without a door, or someone to snuggle with... Well, he just thought it might help to have a fire.

After he got the fire going, Charlie took a kerosene lamp off a hook on the wall, lit it, and set it on the table. He noticed the letter but didn't mention it. The way he saw it, the letter wasn't any of his business.

"It's a letter Bill wrote to his wife, asking for a divorce so he could be with me. I'm not inclined to send it and heap even more distress on her," Jane said when she noticed Charlie looking at it.

"He told me he was planning on doing that," Charlie said. "Mighty kind of you not to send it now."

"I can't imagine she came even close to loving him as much as I do, but what fucking good would it do to let her know he was planning to leave her?"

"None at all," Charlie agreed.

They sat quietly for a while. Then Jane said, "The thing is, Charlie, I want to hold on to the part of the letter where he says he loves me. But I could send the first page, which gives no indication of his betrayal, only praise for her many charms. But it is not signed by him and it would give the appearance of being incomplete. I can read most

129

words just fine, but I never learned to form the letters that make them. And even if I could, my penmanship would not match his."

Charlie was quiet for a minute, mulling over the situation. "Well, what would you think of sending the first page, along with a short note that it was found, unfinished, among his possessions?"

Jane liked that idea. "And would you be the one to kindly write that short note?" she asked.

"I'd be happy to do just that," Charlie said.

During the next half hour, Jane and Charlie came up with several points they thought a proper note of this sort should cover. Then Jane handed him a sheet of paper, a pen and some ink, and began to dictate:

My Dearest Agnes,

By now the news of Bill's death has made its way to you. I am so sorry I did not do a better job of protecting him. I know you must be very disappointed in me. And I don't blame you. I want you to know that Bill found the trip to Deadwood quite enjoyable. I hope you can take some comfort when I tell you the light in his eyes and happiness he exhibited while riding toward our destination would have done your heart good.

As his closest friend, I want to tell you what a huge loss this is for me, too. I am sending a box of his possessions I thought you might want to keep, along with what appears to be a letter he began writing shortly before he was killed. He often spoke about you, and his love for you. Please accept my heartfelt condolences, along with this package. I hope in some way it helps you as you heal.

Respectfully, Charlie Utter.

Jane finished the bit of whiskey left in her bottle and then opened the one Charlie brought. She went to a cupboard and removed the only two glasses she had. They were the shot glasses Bill had refused to return to the saloon in Cheyenne years earlier. She handed one to Charlie, tears running down her face as she poured whiskey into his glass, then filled hers. Holding the glass up in front of her, Jane said, "Here's to you, my dear, dear Bill. I tried to do the right thing for your wife. I think it is what you would want. Someday we will lie down together again. Until that time comes, please let this toast serve as my vow to never stop loving you."

"To Bill," Charlie said.

Daylight was almost upon them when Jane passed out at last. She had finished the second bottle, mostly without Charlie's help. At times during the night she sat rocking back and forth, not saying a word. Other times she alternated between soft sobbing and loud, pitiful wailing. It broke Charlie's heart to see her like this.

Charlie stood up and covered Jane with a blanket. He picked up his hat, the first page of Bill's letter, the note to be added, and the envelope addressed to Agnes. He blew out the lantern and placed it partially atop the second page of the letter to make sure it would stay in place. The wind had picked up a bit and it was almost as drafty inside the cabin as it was out.

Charlie shook his head as he looked at the open space where Bill had promised to add a door. It came as no surprise to Charlie that Bill had never gotten around to doing that.

Charlie put the hat on his head, letter in his pocket, and took his leave. There were tears running down his cheeks as he mounted his steed. "Oh, Bill," he cried. "I don't know what I'm going to do without you, my friend."

131

Chapter 23

Jane still wore the dress with Bill's blood on it when she stumbled into Doc's office late the next morning. Her right hand was wrapped around the neck of the now-empty bottle of whiskey. Her face bore splotches made of tears mingled with dried blood, created when she had tried to swipe her tears away with the bloodied sleeve of her dress.

"Oh, Doc, what am I going to do without Bill? He was my best friend," she cried.

"I sympathize with you, Jane, but drinking yourself to death will not bring Bill back from the grave," Doc said, his tone gentle.

Jane raised the bottle to her lips in hopes of getting a last drop out of it. Then she wiped her mouth with the back of her hand, held the bottle up in front of her, and said, "This here and my horse, Buddy, are the only friends I have left in this world, Doc."

This time Doc's response was anything but gentle. "Damn it, Jane! You have a lot of friends. I count myself as one among them. I know what Bill meant to you, but you must pull yourself together. You have many years ahead of you, if you don't do yourself in by drinking."

"I appreciate that, Doc, but I just don't feel like living this troublesome life any longer. For me life has been nothing but a hard time sandwiched between harder times," she cried.

"You want to talk about hard times, Jane? This morning I tended to a woman who was giving birth to twins—both dead before they got to experience one second of life. A month before that, this same woman's seven-year-old daughter died from influenza. Last week I had to tell a hard-working farmer that unless I cut off both of his infected legs, he would die. He chose to live, but I have no idea how he is going to feed himself or his family minus the only two legs he had. And two weeks ago, I had to inform a wife and mother of three children that her status had changed to widow. And you know what, Jane? Not one of those people I just mentioned chose to wallow in self-pity."

"Well, fuck you, Doc. I ain't them," Jane growled. "I'm tired of having the only thing I ever wanted in life snatched away from me—not once, but twice. And this time there is not even a glimmer of hope that I will see him again."

A hard pounding on the doctor's door interrupted their conversation.

"Christ Almighty, now what?" Doc said as he hurried to the door.

Doc did not recognize the man before him, who was holding a limp body.

"Get him in here," Doc said, stepping aside and gesturing toward the only bed in the small shack. The stranger did as he was told.

"What happened?" Doc asked.

"He's terribly sick," the man said.

Jane and Doc took a close look at the patient now lying on the bed.

"Holy shit, Doc! I know what those sores on his face mean," Jane said. "This guy's got smallpox, and if he has it ..."

Both Jane and Doc turned to look at the person who brought the sick man in, but he was no longer there. He had sprinted away as soon as he heard the word "smallpox."

"I've seen this before," Jane said. "Had it myself as a child. It spreads like dried brush set afire."

"You had smallpox?"

"Yes," she said. "Nearly died. After yesterday, I wish I had."

"But you didn't, and there was a reason, Jane. You are now immune to this disease and can help me care for what I fear are a whole lot of people in this town who are about to get sick."

Doc took Jane by the shoulders and looked her straight in the eyes. "Jane, this is not a pretty sickness, as you know, and you are newly grieving, so if you want to turn and walk out of here, I'll understand. But if you can find it in you to help me with this situation, you will do a lot of good for a lot of people. I fear it will take both of us twenty-four hours a day to treat all the people who were probably exposed and about to be God-awful ill."

Jane looked at the man whose job it was to take care of hundreds of miners, dance hall girls, cowboys, and prospectors and wondered how he did it. She told him, "I'll help you, Doc. I don't have anything or anyone to live for at this point. I might as well use my time trying to make the stricken feel a little less miserable," she said.

"Good, Jane. Thank you! The first thing I'll need you to do is to go clean up, sober up, get some rest, and then get the hell back here as soon as all of that is achieved," he said.

"Okay," she said.

Jane went back to the cabin, took off her dress, and put on her buckskin britches and jacket and then headed for the bath house. It would take more than a dunking in the creek to get the blood and dirt off her.

There was no one standing in line when Jane arrived at the bath house a short time later. She walked up to the counter where the proprietor, Amos Smith, sat working on his ledger. Jane still had traces of blood on her face. Amos seemed shocked to see her there, and stood to greet her.

"Jane, I heard about Bill's killing. I am so sorry. I hear they caught Jack McCall, the bastard who shot him in the back, and he is on his way to the Federal Court in Yankton to be tried for murder," Amos said.

"Good! I hope he swings from the noose choking for two days before death overcomes him," Jane said.

"I share that sentiment. In the meantime, what can I do for you?"

"Look, Amos, I know men are the only ones allowed to bathe here, but I'm wondering if you could make an exception? Doc has a very ill patient at his office right now and needs my help. I need to be as clean as possible to do that," she said.

"There's no one in there right now and this is my slow time of day, so you have at it and we won't tell anyone." Amos, like so many residents of Deadwood, had a soft spot in his heart for this woman.

"Much obliged, Amos." Jane reached into the inside pocket of her jacket and pulled out thirty-five cents, the posted cost of a hot, half hour bath.

"It's on the house, Jane, with my deepest sympathies for your loss," Amos said.

"Thank you kindly, sir," Jane said.

"I have all the buckets filled and heating. Use as much water as you want. I'll put the closed sign on the door and lock it until you are done and dressed," he said.

Jane tipped her hat and then disappeared behind the curtain separating the office from the bathing room. The room held four metal tubs, which were emptied, rinsed out, and half filled with tepid water each morning. Two of them had not yet been used this day, so Jane had clean water to add some heat to. She took two of the buckets off the fire, one at a time, using a mitt to cover the hot handles, and lowered each into one of the clean-water tubs. When the buckets were empty, she removed her clothes and lowered her body into the tub.

The warm water felt good, and she lay back for a bit and closed her eyes. She pictured Jack McCall with a noose around his neck while she stood high on a platform, holding the rope that would hang him. Then, using brute strength fueled by unbridled anger, she swung McCall round and round in a wide arc, till his feet were almost level with his head, his eyes bulging clean out of their sockets. This scene replayed itself in her mind a few times before she decided she'd better let go and get busy with scrubbing. Once she was satisfied that she was clean enough, she stepped out of the tub and climbed into the other clean one to rinse off. This time she didn't add any heat to the water, hoping the shock of going from warm to cool would sober her up faster.

When she walked out the back of the bathhouse, she felt refreshed and her head was clear. She thanked Amos for his generosity and then headed for Seth Bullock and Sol Star's hardware store. Of the two, Jane liked the affable Star more than the brooding Bullock. Sol was

135

the one she saw when she entered the store. He was sitting next to Trixie and the two were leaning over a ledger, heads close together.

"Hey there, you two," Jane said.

Both looked up and Sol stood immediately. "Jane, may I tell you how sorry I am about Bill?" he asked.

"You may, and you did, thank you," she said. "May I ask what you and my friend, Trixie, are up to, all huddled together?"

Sol blushed but Trixie just grinned and said, "You may, and you did."

Jane had heard that a romance was brewing between the Jewish hardware store owner and her friend, but she did not know that one was teaching the other accounting.

"I see you are as much a smart ass as the day we met," she told Trixie, allowing a slight smile to cross her face.

Trixie's return smile was warm and tinged with pity. "I, too, am sorry about your loss, Jane. And as for what we are doing, Sol is teaching me how to manage the store's books, in anticipation of hiring me in the very near future," she said.

Jane thought back to the day Trixie had told her such an event was not likely to happen.

"So, you have changed professions?" Jane asked.

Trixie looked up at Sol and said, "Not entirely, yet. But I'm hoping."

Again, Sol blushed.

"As a matter of fact, I'm due back at The Gem as of about ten minutes ago. Nice seeing you, Jane," Trixie said, and patted Jane's shoulder as she walked by.

Once Trixie was gone, Sol asked, "What can I do for you today, Jane?"

"Mr. Starr, if you have not heard already, you will soon. The smallpox plague has come calling in Deadwood. So far, only one person we are aware of. I told Doc I would help him care for our current patient and any others who will surely follow suit. I'm on my way to tell Doc that I am loaning the use of my cabin as a sick house for as long as there is a need. I've come to ask for some things to do that but have no means to pay at this moment. I'm hoping you will extend me some credit," Jane said.

Seth Bullock had walked in behind Jane and heard her request. The two partners didn't make any financial decisions unless both agreed.

"Seth?" Sol asked.

"Give her whatever she needs," the other man said. "There is a meeting set for two this afternoon at The Gem to discuss what money each of us can contribute to send some riders off to procure the vaccine from various sources. We need to keep this from sweeping through the entire town. I had to stop by Doc's cabin to tell him about the meeting, and already he has three patients down with the disease."

"Holy hell!" Jane said. "Would you please take six cots, some spittoons, three kerosene lamps, kerosene, what cooking utensils you can spare, and a few bedpans to my cabin?"

"We will," Sol said.

"And Charlie Utter stopped by this morning and purchased supplies to put a proper door on the cabin," Seth told her.

"Thank you both, kindly," Jane said. "I will go now and help Doc transport the ill."

Jane's grief and her need to drown it in alcohol were overshadowed, at least for the moment, by her need to help heal the sick. And that was a good thing for both her and the people she would help save during the next few weeks.

Chapter 24

By the end of the first week Jane's cabin and surrounding tents were converted into a hospital. Eight men and one ten-year-old boy had contracted smallpox.

Doc, Jane, Trixie, Seth, and Sol took turns tending to the needs of the afflicted, with Jane and Doc working twelve to eighteen hours every day. Jane didn't drink to excess during this time, but whenever she got a break, she would go out back, where she had set up a tent and bedroll, and indulge just enough to take the edge off. Even in the most hectic of times, when there weren't enough hands to press wet cloths to foreheads, or three or four-people decided to vomit at once, or her thoughts should have been drowned out by the screams from poor souls with pus-filled sores that covered their bodies, Bill was never far from her mind. The memory of him followed her around every waking second.

Gary, the ten-year-old boy who had come down with the pox, was the most ill, yet the least likely to complain. Jane took a liking to the boy and whenever possible gave him the most attention.

"How're you doing today, sweetie?" Jane asked one morning, about a week after the boy had been brought to the cabin.

"I'm just praying to the Lord above that I live through this, Miss Jane," Gary said.

"I happen to know, having been spoken to by the Lord above about this very thing early this morning, that you are going to get well," Jane said, stretching the truth considerably.

The child's eyes lit up briefly, and he smiled and drifted off to sleep.

Jane took a clean cloth and went outside and dipped it in the creek. She came back in to find Doc standing over the child with a concerned look on his face.

"His fever isn't breaking, Jane," Doc said.

"If anything, it seems to be on the rise," Jane agreed.

138

"I'm worried. His blisters are so large and there are so many of them. And the pus does not seem close to draining and forming scabs," he said. "Anyway, we're doing all we can for him. Just must keep him as comfortable as possible. In the meantime, you've been on duty for near twenty straight hours now. Why don't you go lie down and I will stand watch? Trixie should be here soon, too."

"Doc, would it help to bring his fever down if I keep applying cool compresses to much of his body, changing them as soon as they begin to heat up from his fever?" Jane asked.

"It might, but you need to get some rest before you collapse, and I have several patients here to attend to. I can't spend all of my time on one," he said. Just then Cam Baker, whose illness was the most serious of all, began calling out for help.

"You go see to Cam," Jane said. "If it's all the same to you, I'd like to spend my rest time tending to the boy."

Doc put his hand on Jane's shoulder, nodded, and walked away.

When Trixie walked in an hour later, Cam Baker was in his final hour on earth. He was severely dehydrated from vomiting, in excruciating pain, and his fever was so high he was delirious.

Trixie shook her head and got to work helping other patients. Jane had not stopped applying cooled cloths all over Gary's body, hoping to bring the boy's fever down. This effort involved trips to the creek every fifteen minutes. Jane was not only about to drop from exhaustion, but beginning to feel the effects of alcohol withdrawal. During one of her trips to the creek, she stopped by her tent and took a swallow of liquor. But it was not enough to ward off the shaking.

Whether it was from sheer tiredness, the effects of the beginning of withdrawal after going for more than a day practically without drink, or what Jane was beginning to see as a hopeless situation, her emotions got the best of her.

Jane was putting fresh compresses on the boy's legs when she cried out, "*God damn it all!* I never give you a second thought because I do not believe you fucking exist. But this little boy lying here dying

139

does. And in return for him giving you the honor of believing in you, the least you could do, if for some reason you *do* fucking exist, is to listen to his prayers and make him well. What the fuck kind of a god would let a sweet little boy who's never done no one a bit of harm, suffer like this?"

Doc had just finished pulling a sheet over Cam's face. He walked over and put his hand on Jane's arm, calming her down somewhat.

Trixie looked up, but went back to her attempts to get Nels Christianson to take a sip of water. "Come on, honey. You need to get some fluids back in your system," she urged Nels.

"Cam has succumbed, Jane," said Doc. "Would you please help me get him out to one of the graves? Then we need to burn his blankets, sheets, and anything else he may have touched," he added with a heavy sigh. It was clear the man was beyond weary.

"No need for either of you to do that," Seth Bullock said. He and Sol had arrived about the time Jane was cussing the almighty, but no one noticed them walk in. "Sol and I will tend to it ourselves. But first, we need to tell you that the first of the riders have returned from Cheyenne with the vaccine. If you can spare the Doc here, we need him to come immediately to administer it."

"Oh, that's good news!" Trixie said.

"You go, Doc," Jane said. "Trixie and I can handle this."

"I've got no choice," Doc said. "The sooner we get everyone in this damned town vaccinated, the sooner we can stop the dying."

As Doc left, Seth and Sol walked over to Cam, picked up the entire cot with him on it and carried it out the door. They buried the man, said a few words out of respect, and then threw the bedding on the fire.

When they came back inside the cabin, Sol said, "Seth and I thought we'd stay and help while Doc inoculates as many townspeople as possible. Then, hopefully the good Doc can get some much-needed rest before he collapses and we are left without medical aid. Jane, you, too. Go lie down a bit. We'll come and get you if there is a need," Sol said.

"I can't leave the boy," Jane said. "He needs constant tending."

"Tell me what to do and I will provide the constant tending until you return. I will come and get you if there is any change," Seth said.

"Jane, please take a rest, or you will not be any help to this boy or anyone else," Trixie pleaded.

Jane finally agreed and, after telling Seth in painstaking detail how to apply the compresses and how often to change them, stressing that the boy's lips needed to be kept moist, and making Seth promise again to come get her if Gary's condition worsened, she went out back to lie down. After taking two long swallows of whiskey, she lay down and fell fast asleep.

Chapter 25

Bill was lying on a cot beneath a rainbow-colored waterfall, the water cascading all around, but not on him. He was not moving, and Jane wondered if he was asleep. Then she remembered he was dead. She couldn't see the wound in the back of his head because he was lying on his back. He couldn't even turn his head, but somehow, he knew she was there.

"Jane, you came. Please help me. I've got the worst headache imaginable," Bill cried out, breaking the silence and startling his former lover.

"Well, of course you've got an ache in your head, you goldarn fool. You've got a hole the size of a fist in it. Why wouldn't it hurt?" she asked.

"Jane, please don't yell at me, seeing as how I'm fucking dead and all. It's hard enough to handle what's going on without you being all pissed off and everything," he said.

Jane didn't respond. She was still trying to understand the weird scene spread out before her.

"Do you know what happened to me?" Bill asked.

"Yeah, what happened was, you were shot in the back of the head by a man named Jack McCall. What did you ever do to him, anyway?" she said.

"So, it was Jack McCall. Why, that motherfucking poor loser! I never done anything to him but take his money fair and square in a game of five-card draw," Bill said. "I sure didn't see *that* coming!"

"Of course, you didn't see him coming, you ridiculous, negligent fool! Would you happen to remember why that was?" Jane asked.

"Don't know," Bill said. "Maybe I went blind before I got shot?"

"No, you did not go blind before you got shot, stupid motherfucker. You allowed yourself a lapse in judgment and common sense. You could have seen him just fine if you had not had your back to the fucking door where he walked in!" Jane was now screaming at him.

She was furious with Bill. He'd caused her so much pain for no good reason. His carelessness had ended their dreams of growing old together.

"And what's this about you not taking your usual precautions in seating arrangements because you thought your days were numbered?" she pressed on.

"In hindsight, it would appear I was right," he said, then added, "You can't see my face, but I just winked. Remember how much you used to love my wink?"

"There's some sort of weird barrier between us and I can't get to you, or I would throttle the hell out of you," Jane seethed. "Can you move at all?"

"Nope. Only my eyes, lips, and missing tongue, and, as for your threat, I would be fucking happy having the hell throttled out of me because it is quite clear that hell is where I'm residing—at least for the moment," he said.

Jane couldn't help but giggle. "You're dead, got your brain shot clean out of your head, yet you're still able to think, talk, and make jokes. That is so fucked up!"

"Yeah, well, your brain is presumably intact, as is the rest of you, and I'm still funnier than you ever were," he said.

"There is nothing funny about the depths of despair to which I have sunk," Jane said. "It's been hell without you, Bill. I have never felt this bad in my entire miserable life."

"Well, guess what? I find myself feeling a bit bad and in a bit of a pickle, too, Janie. Wanna flip a coin to see which of us is worse off?" he said, then added, "I just threw another wink your way."

"I may be breathing, Bill, unlike you, but I might as well be dead for all life matters to me now that you're gone. And don't fucking call me Janie."

"That's sad, but let me put it to you this way, *Jane*. I've been lying under this cock-sucking, albeit beautiful waterfall, bone dry because whatever powers rule the universe decided—*why the hell not throw*

143

yet another burden his way—parched as hell and unable to catch a fucking solitary drip on my tongue which, as we have already discussed is not there because it suffered some fucking collateral damage when my head was shot up," Bill said.

"This is not real," Jane said. "I need to stop talking to you before I go insane, and don't even think about telling me I already am, or by god I will hunt you down and kill you all over again in the afterlife if there even is one despite my seeing it lying right here before me, if that's what this is." Jane knew she was rambling. She tended to do that when she couldn't make sense out of something.

"Jane?" Bill asked, his tone suddenly fearful. "Am I in hell?"

"I don't know about you, my dear Bill, but I most certainly am."

Suddenly the waterfall was surrounded by fire.

"Help me, Jane! For the love of God, help me," Bill screamed.

Jane tried, but couldn't get to him.

"Bill!" Jane screamed repeatedly, until her voice was hoarse. Her screams must have eclipsed the dream, because when she awoke, Trixie was holding Jane in her arms, smoothing her hair out of her face, saying, "It's going to be okay, honey. I promise."

Jane, drenched in her own nightmare sweat, fell back to sleep in Trixie's arms. The next time she awoke, she felt rested. And that was the last time she ever dreamed about Wild Bill Hickok.

144

Chapter 26

Seth, Sol, and Trixie were all standing by Gary's bedside when Jane walked back into the cabin. Her heart sank, as she feared the boy had passed while she was sleeping.

"Oh, no! You promised you'd come get me if he got worse," Jane cried, stopping just inside the doorway and grasping hold of the frame.

"I'm gonna go back to my fucking tent and do some serious drinking now. Don't call if you need me," she said.

"Jane, he's better!" Trixie said. "Fever finally broke, and he's sleeping peacefully. We're all just enjoying the moment."

"Come see for yourself," Sol said.

Jane walked over to the boy's cot and was looking down at him when his eyelids fluttered. "Miss Jane?" he said.

"Well, look at you. Those damn lesions have finally started to ripen and will soon dry up and go away. You're gonna be okay, sweetie," she said, wiping a tear from her eye.

"I told you the Lord would not let us down, Jane. He's always there when we need him most."

Jane put her hand on the boy's head. His hair was damp, but his head no longer felt hot. "Well, I guess he did not reckon it was your time to go," she said. She did not say what she thought about this supposed divine entity allowing a child to go through such horror in the first place.

And then there was the business of Bill's death, which she intended to take up with this god, assuming she ever got a chance to talk to him. Which, she thought, will be never because he doesn't fucking exist.

"Miss Jane, I'm a bit hungry. Do you think I could have something to eat?" Gary asked.

Jane laughed. "You can have anything your dear heart desires, little one," she said.

"A biscuit would make me very happy," Gary told her.

"Then a biscuit it is!" Jane said.

"I'm going to leave to get some supplies, Jane," said Seth. "We do have a few biscuits left, but I thought those who are recovering and ready for some food might benefit from some sausage and gravy to pour over them."

"Yes, please!" Gary said. It seemed with every passing minute he was heading farther away from death's door, where he'd been just hours ago.

"That's mighty kind of you, Mr. Bullock," Jane said. She was wondering how many of the town's residents Doc had been able to inoculate, but did not have to wonder for long.

Doc walked in the door, looking as tired as he had when he left. He told them that they had run out of the first of the vaccine that had been brought back yesterday noon, but that two other riders had returned with more later in the day.

"I was starting to get low about nine last night, with a long line still left to inoculate, when the final two men arrived with another supply. I vaccinated the rest of the town, and finished the last man standing in line shortly before dawn this morning. And we have some left. I do believe we have stopped this disease from felling any more men, women, or children in this camp."

"Wahoo!" Jane cheered. She looked around the room and said, "Now all we have to do is get the rest of our little family here well."

After assuring Doc, Trixie, Seth, and Sol that she could handle caring for the four who were still bedridden, Jane was left alone to nurse the remaining patients. Seth went to fetch supplies, Sol to tend their store, Trixie to get back to her job at The Gem, and Doc to get some rest.

Jane made her rounds, emptying bedpans, filling water glasses, putting fresh wraps on one of the men's hands to keep him from clawing at his sores, and offering words of comfort where needed.

"Jane," Marcus Smith said, grabbing her by the hand, "I don't think I am going to make it. I can tell. But before I go, I want to thank you for the care you've given me."

"It has been my pleasure to serve as your nurse in this trying time. And, as such, I do not fucking intend to let you leave this world after all the hard work several of us have put into getting you better. So just stop with the *I can tells* because what I can tell, Mister, is that you are turning a corner and soon will be out swinging that pick and striking it rich," she said.

"You're an angel, Jane. You swear a bit much, but I don't care because you're an angel. A living, breathing angel," he said.

Marcus drifted off to sleep and Jane walked over to the cot where Russell Hines lay moaning. The poor man had the misfortune of getting sores under both of his eyelids. The lesions created corneal ulcerations and caused permanent blindness.

"It's dark! I'm scared!" Hines shouted repeatedly during almost every waking moment.

"I know it's dark, Russell, but your mind can still see all of the sights it has stored for you in your memory," Jane told him. "You can still picture that new buggy you admired a week ago. You can still see your wife's sweet face. And you know that baby the two of you have on the way? You now have a special sense of touch that will allow you to see your newborn through your fingers. I read up on this when I learned my sweet Bill was going blind. We had plans for finding a way to deal with that, and you can make some of your own, too. I'd be mighty happy to help you with that, if you'd like, as soon as you're well."

Russell had quieted down while she was speaking, and seemed to be taking to the idea of finding a way to live with this new affliction.

"Yes, Jane. I'd be most honored and indebted to you for helping me learn how to find a different way to see," he said.

"Good!" she said. "Let's start now. Relax and think about all the things you have already seen in your lifetime and let yourself picture a

147

few of them in your mind, as you drift off to sleep. You have turned a corner in this battle against smallpox, and rest is going to take you all of the way toward healing," she said.

Jane patted the man's hand, then got up to check on the boy. He was sound asleep, so she decided to step outside to take in some fresh air. She was just about halfway out the door when she fainted.

Chapter 27

Doc was just returning to the cabin as Jane was passing out of it. Literally. He saw her fall and ran to help. He pulled some smelling salts from his bag and roused the stricken woman within seconds.

"What the hell?" Jane asked, as Doc helped her sit up.

"I think you might be suffering from some serious exhaustion, Jane. And it's no wonder. You've been taking care of everyone but yourself," he said.

"I know I'm immune to smallpox," she said, "but could it be possible my immunity has run out? I've been vomiting a lot lately, too. And no, it is not from fucking drinking which, I'll thank you to know, I've had little time to do lately what with people dying, screaming, going blind, and puking all around me."

"I don't think immunities have a limit," Doc said.

"Well, then, I guess I'm just tired and grieving. That can make a person sick, right?"

"Yes, it most definitely can. But just to be sure it is not something more serious, as soon as Trixie comes back to relieve us, I'd like you to accompany me to my office where I can give you a thorough examination," Doc said.

"And just what kind of thorough examination do you conduct on a person who's grieving, tired of living, and tired of being tired?" Jane asked.

I just want to check your vital signs. Pulse. Temperature. Listen to your heart. That sort of thing," he said.

"Why can't you do all that here?" she asked.

"Truthfully, I can. But I thought getting you away from this environment for a bit might do you some good," he said, then added, "You stay seated a bit. I'm going to go check on our patients, make sure no one is in urgent need, and then come back out with some coffee and a biscuit for us to share. I need to take my own advice and get some nourishment myself," Doc said.

Doc returned a short time later with two cups of coffee and two biscuits. He handed one of each to Jane and then sat on the ground next to her.

Jane took a sip of the coffee and said, "You know, Doc, I had a strange dream about Bill last night. Don't know what it might have meant."

"My belief, Jane, is that dreams mean nothing more than the fact that we have something weighing heavy on our mind," he said.

"Yeah, that's what I have always thought, too. But my mind never, not in its most intoxicated state, considered the idea that Bill might be trapped in a beautiful waterfall, ringed with fire," she said.

Doc looked at her, and the only thing he could think to say was: "Eat some of that biscuit, Jane."

They were enjoying a quiet moment when Marcus Smith cried out from inside the cabin. Both Jane and Doc got to their feet and raced inside. The man was clutching his chest with both hands. When he saw Doc and Jane, he lifted his head slightly off the bed, said the word "angel," then fell back. It took only a few seconds for Doc to confirm that he was dead.

"No!" Jane cried. "I told him he wasn't going to die, Doc! I've lied about some things in my lifetime, but I would never have lied about that! I was sure he was going to make it."

"It's beyond our control, Jane," Doc said. "We can only do so much. But we have managed to nurse twelve people back to health in the last few weeks. Twelve people, including that boy over there, who would not be alive now were it not for your efforts and that of others. Focus on that, not on those we couldn't save."

Jane sat down in one of the chairs at the table she had shared with Bill. She suddenly felt she lacked the energy to ever stand up again.

"Just how many did we lose, Doc? I didn't count," she said.

"We buried as many as we've helped walk out of here. But with the vaccine administered, and more of it in storage for newcomers, I am certain the worst is behind us," Doc said.

"You know what, Doc? I've never felt so goddamn tired in my entire life. Too much sadness in too short a time for a soul to bear. Wears you out and makes you puke and have to pee too much," she said.

Doc put his hand over his mouth and looked at Jane.

"Please tell me you're not about to be sick now, too, Doc," Jane said.

He ignored her question. "Jane, do you keep track of your female cycles?"

"What the hell kind of a question is that for you to ask me? I don't embarrass easy, but that just about makes me want to blush."

"I'm going to ask you again, Jane. It's important. I want you to think back and tell me when your last menstrual period took place," he said.

"Jesus, Doc. If you must know, I haven't bled since shortly after I joined Charlie Utter's wagon train. Why the fuck do you care?"

"I care, Jane, because I have a suspicion about exactly what it is that may be ailing you," he said.

"Well, spit it out," she said.

"Jane, has it occurred to you that you may be with child?" he asked.

Jane was not able to answer that question. For the second time that day, she fainted dead away.

Chapter 28

Jane spent several days cleaning and disinfecting the cabin after the last of its patients had gone. Star and Bullock provided her with a few containers of ammonia and laundry soap that she added to water from the creek that she heated on the wood stove.

Almost everything inside the cabin that had been used to care for the smallpox victims had been burned or buried. All that was left was the table and two chairs, the wood stove, and a few personal possessions that Jane had moved outside when she set up her tent.

She scrubbed with all her might, insistent that the place had to be unsoiled during her pregnancy and the birth of Bill's child.

After Trixie had returned to the cabin on the day Doc told Jane she might be with child, Jane and Doc made a hasty retreat to his office. Once there, Doc explained the method he used to determine if a woman was expecting a child.

"Jane, most doctors don't use this sort of examination, because the issue of privacy," he said. "I use it when a woman allows, because it's been proven reliable. So, I need to ask: would you allow me to examine your vaginal area to see if you might be with child?"

"Are you telling me that you can look down there and see a baby, if it's there?" she asked. "Isn't it too little to see yet?"

Doc scratched his head. "No, Jane. What I can tell is if there is increased blood flow in the area, which would indicate pregnancy," he said.

"Seeing as how you have never looked at my area, how would you know if the blood flow there is increased, decreased, or same as always?" Jane asked.

"Jane, it's called Chadwick's sign. About six to eight weeks into a woman's pregnancy, certain parts of the female reproductive area—"

"Exactly what parts are we talking about, Doc?" Jane interrupted.

"To be specific, Jane, the cervix, labia, and vagina are the parts I need to examine. They take on a dark bluish or purple-red hue about

152

six weeks or so after a woman is impregnated, which tells me there is increased blood flow. I'd rather stop talking about it and just get this done, if you don't mind. If you do mind, we can just wait and see if your belly begins to swell."

"How long will that take if I choose to wait as opposed to finding out this Chadwick way you mention?" Jane asked.

"It's different for everyone, but if this is your first pregnancy—"

"Yes, damn it! This would be my first fucking pregnancy, if it is a pregnancy," Jane interrupted.

"So being your first fucking pregnancy, it could be a few more months, based on what I assume was the beginning of your sexual activity with Bill occurring about six to eight weeks ago," Doc said with an edge in his voice.

"Well let's get it done, then, because I sure as hell am not going another few months without knowing, now that you have got me thinking about it," she said.

After Doc examined Jane, he told her he was certain she was expecting a baby. She showed little emotion when he gave her the news and said only, "You and I both know I'm not fit to raise a child, Doc."

"I know nothing of the sort," Doc said. "You certainly were fit to take care of some very ill people the last few weeks. I have no doubt you could do the same good work with a child."

"I couldn't have done that for as many years as it takes to see a child through from a baby to an adult. I'm a drunk, Doc. There are times when I don't know where I'm at, or how I got to be there. I function pretty well about half the time, but that's about it for me," she said.

"You could stop being a drunk, Jane," Doc said.

"Really? Can you stop walking around with a johnson dangling between those legs?" Jane yelled.

"So how do you expect to get through carrying this child, if you are not able to keep from getting shit-faced drunk during the next seven months you have left to go?" he asked.

"Well, I figure if I am carrying the baby in my belly, no matter where I wander off to, the baby will have to ride along with me," she said.

"Well, that may mean this child ending up in the bottom of that creek that runs out back of your house, were you to stumble and pass out into it, too drunk to know that was happening. There's also the danger of the effects of the alcohol in your system causing harm to this child," Doc said.

"And just how the fuck can alcohol cause harm to a child who is not drinking it?" Jane said.

"This baby will feed off you, Jane. Whatever you put in your body can and will affect it."

"So, this baby, Bill's baby, could be born a drunk like me?"

"That has the potential of happening. Also, if you drink to excess, the child could be born mentally or physically damaged. I've only seen it happen once or twice, but since most of the pregnant women I treat don't drink at all, it is rare," he said.

"You treat plenty of prostitutes and dance hall girls, and drinking is part of their lives," Jane argued.

"Jane, I rarely have a prostitute or dance hall girl come to me requiring care during a pregnancy because they end their pregnancies as soon as they learn of them."

"Oh," she said. "I don't think Bill would want me to do that. Even though he agreed not to have babies, this is different."

"How so?" Doc asked.

"It's the only part of Bill that is left here on earth," she said.

Both were quiet for a few minutes, and then Jane said, "Well, if what you say is true, I guess I have no choice but to stay sober for a few months, assuming I can even do that. However, as soon as it's born, I will thank you to have a nice, well-situated couple lined up who can raise a child better than I ever will and happy to do so. I want Bill's young 'un to have the best life possible."

Doc nodded his agreement. Secretly he wondered if Jane might change her mind when the baby was placed in her arms.

Now, four weeks later, Jane had stayed true to her promise not to get drunk. She did take small sips a few times a day, whenever she started to shake and sweat, but that seemed to be happening less and less as her body adjusted to functioning without booze.

Right now, her hands were trembling and she needed a break from cleaning. Her back ached something fierce, and she was always tired. *Thank the fucking universe the puking part of this has become less frequent,* she thought.

Jane pulled a bottle down off a shelf, poured a shot, and slammed it down her throat. She set the glass down and took a seat at the table.

She looked around the newly cleaned room and thought about what it had looked and smelled like a month ago. Her little cabin had seen so much pain. Beginning with her tears over losing Bill to the suffering of a couple dozen critically ill camp residents. Many of them had walked out of the cabin, but just as many were carried out. From the time smallpox came to visit until it was gone, a dozen new graves had been added to the Deadwood cemetery.

Scant months ago, she was a government scout, never in a million years expecting to again see the only man she had ever loved. Then he appeared out of nowhere, or so it seemed.

After he had told her he was married and there was no hope for them to rekindle a relationship, that very thing had happened, and quickly at that. Then came their time together, perfect in every way this time, and him telling her he was going to ask his wife for a divorce, so he could marry her.

Then he died. Just like that. In the blink of an eye, all her dreams were shattered to hell. And now this. She wouldn't have asked for this. She had not wanted a child—not even Bill's. She was fond of little ones, but not as a steady diet. She'd spent her whole life trying to take

155

care of herself and, although she did well during temporary situations of caring for the ill or downtrodden, she couldn't maintain that level of being a responsible human being on a permanent basis.

Jane leaned back in the chair and closed her eyes. She placed her hands on her belly and said, "My love for you will be proven in my willingness to hand you over to someone who can take good care of you, little one. You will not have to live through the horrors of having a poverty-stricken, alcoholic, useless parent."

Jane opened her eyes and looked around the room. Then she said, "I reckon this cabin is clean enough for us to move back into it. I'm gonna take down the tent, bring my things back inside, and then lie down and take a nap."

A half hour later she was sound asleep on the fur coat that she and Bill had once shared.

Chapter 29

Jane was waking up earlier than usual these days. She thought it was probably because she wasn't drinking and thus not hung over. She had reduced her alcohol consumption to a fraction of what she was accustomed to drinking.

At first, this deprivation caused her all sorts of misery. Being nine-tenths sober meant she was fully aware, always, except when sleeping, that her life was now miserable and lonely. And the exception, the part about sleeping and getting some relief from her pain—well, that was not as easy to come by nowadays as it was when she could down a bottle and pass out, oblivious to the world and all its problems circling around her, like buzzards waiting to feast on soon-to-be carrion.

The night Doc told her she was pregnant, she hadn't gotten a wink of sleep. She had gone home and paced back and forth between her tent and the cabin, checking on the sick and fretting about the state of her own body. Several times she had picked up the bottle and then set it down again.

How much drink would be too much for this baby to be born healthy? How little could she get by with drinking to prevent sweating and shaking uncontrollably? She had sworn, paced, sworn some more, and finally lain down, covered up, and rode it out. She so wanted sleep to come and give her a respite from both her physical and emotional pain. That didn't happen. Just before sunrise she got up, blanket still wrapped around her, and got the bottle out of a bag she kept in the tent. Three gulps later she felt some relief and a whole lot of remorse.

This scene was repeated several times over the next several months. Go without, suffer the consequences. Give in, feel the guilt. She hated this unsolicited responsibility she now carried. First it made her puke from morning till night. Now it was forcing her to stay as sober as possible. And sometime down the road, god help her, it was going to squeeze itself out of an area that Doc told her might need to be cut open and stitched together afterward. Still, she tried as hard as she could to do what was needed to allow this child to come into the world with a fighting chance at a decent life.

Her days and nights were filled with torment, and it wouldn't be long before her belly began to stretch as the baby within grew a little each day. Jane wondered how it was possible for a woman to endure this kind of torture repeatedly. And how was it that something like skin, that fit so tight over the body, could expand as greatly as she had seen in other pregnant women who were close to giving birth. Why didn't it rip and tear open, spewing the child and the contents of its mother's abdomen all over the ground? Jane wondered if this ever happened and made a mental note to ask Doc about that the next time she saw him.

Also, she knew, because Doc had told her, that if all went well, the part of her that the baby would roll out of, the birth canal it was called, expanded like a piece of elastic to get the baby through, thus usually eliminating the need to cut and stitch.

"And then what?" she had asked Doc. "Does it just snap back the way it was, like a rubber band when you stretch it between two fingers and then take one finger away?"

"Not quite the same as before, but enough to allow a woman to function down there the way she did before giving birth," he had told her.

She would never tell Doc this, but she had taken both hands and tried to stretch herself the way the baby would when it came out. Didn't happen, hurt like hell, and she could not fathom how this was even possible.

Was he lying to her to ease her fear? She'd never tended to a woman birthing a baby before, nor had she been present when one was born. She wished she had more firsthand knowledge of this process.

She wasn't taking to the notion that all females, human or animal, delivered their babies in the same manner.

"Jane, have you never witnessed the birth of a calf?" Doc had asked.

"Yes, but I ain't no fucking cow!" Jane responded.

"No, you're not, but the process is the same," Doc said.

"That's just gross," Jane told him.

Doc had just sighed and given up for the moment. He knew Jane had been on her own, working, drinking, shooting, and riding wild since she was a child. Yet, in some ways she was so naïve.

Chapter 30

Jane had expected that awaiting the birth of her child would be as boring as watching snails walk across a blanket. And for her, it was exactly that. She couldn't drink, much. Certainly, she couldn't get drunk. Doc told her that hard activity would not be good for the baby, either. So, she had to be content with riding Buddy at a slow pace twice a day. Charlie took the horse on a good run every couple of days. For that she was grateful, albeit jealous.

It was out of curiosity and a desire to do something besides sit in her cabin and stare at its four walls for days on end that she accepted an invitation to join a quilting group. It turned out to be a less than desirable experience for all who attended that day. When speaking of it years later, Jane would have this to say:

"This activity, if that's what you could call it, amounted to sitting around a table, cutting a piece of fabric into squares, sewing them back together, and talking about such fucking scintillating topics as how to get gravy stains out of a tablecloth. Or how to get a two-year-old child to go to sleep at night. Oh, and this one's hysterical: The best way to keep a house made of sod from getting dirty. That one made my head want to whirl like a spinning top. But the most riveting topic of all was: How to teach your newborn baby to latch onto your nipples for breastfeeding. The quilting busybodies, like everyone else in Deadwood, knew I was with child, so were trying to steer some of their conversation toward me. It was an act of kindness that I, being me, saw as more of an annoyance. Still do."

Jane had caused a bit of a stir when she argued that there was nothing to teach. That feeding a baby anything was a natural occurrence and just happened as nature intended.

"I would think, ladies, that if a human baby is hungry enough, there would be no more need to teach the little pooper how to latch onto a breast than there is to teach a newborn calf to grab its mother's udder. Or any species, for that matter," she said.

160

And that simple comment started the women in on a litany of stories about how one or the other of them had a dreadful time getting her baby to wrap its little mouth around their mammary glands.

Jane's loud, sudden, and profane reaction to pricking her finger with the needle she was using to sew a red plaid flannel quilt square to a solid color green square cut the discussion short. The woman had a high threshold of pain when it came to being shot with arrows or taking a rock to the head, but not so much so when the pain came from a needle stab.

"Holy fucking mother of god!" Jane yelled, causing a few of the women to nearly fall off their chairs.

"What happened?" asked Margaret Gray, whose story had been silenced by Jane's profanity.

"The goddamn needle nearly severed my fucking finger, that's what happened!" Jane cried.

Margaret got up and walked over to Jane. "Let me see," she said. "Um, it is just a pin prick. No real blood beyond the tiniest of drops, or two," she said.

"Well it sure as hell *felt* like a knife wound," Jane said, a bit embarrassed for having caused such a scene.

"Would you like me to wrap it, Jane?" Margaret asked.

"Oh please, Margaret!" broke in Grace Davis. "And maybe we should apply a tourniquet to keep the poor woman from bleeding to death," the woman added, causing a ripple of snickers to roll around the quilting circle.

That comment and the group's subsequent laughter at her expense infuriated Jane, who was already fuming. Margaret glared at Grace for having made such a remark, but before she could defuse the volatile situation, Jane picked up one of the delicate teacups off the table and hurled it at the nearest wall.

"In retrospect," Jane would later say, "that was a rather rude thing to do. But then I asked the delicate flowers assembled around that table just how many of them had ever ridden into war, with no fucking

161

regard for the safety of their own person, and ridden out again carrying a high-ranking officer all the while enduring the pain of several arrows affixed to their very own bodies—including having one graze their much-revered mammary glands.

"Margaret Gray stared at me as if I was some sort of creature. She said, 'I'll have you know that the cup you just destroyed in your disgusting profanity-laced demonstration of a childish temper tantrum belonged to my great-grandmother, Maud Smith, and was to have been passed down to my daughter, should I ever be lucky enough to have another someday.' "

It was common knowledge that Margaret had given birth, so far, to three children—two boys and a girl. The little girl arrived too early and her lungs were not able to function outside the womb. She died an hour after she was born.

"'I'm mighty damn sorry about that,' I told her. 'Sometimes my temper just gets the best of me.'"

At this point Jane would pause in her retelling of the story, shake her head, and claim, "Well, Margaret just sighed and said one of the fucking dumbest things I had ever heard. She said: 'Jane, your behavior is off because you are, after all, pregnant. We've all experienced this.'"

Jane recounted that an unenthusiastic murmur of agreement had flowed throughout the room.

"I told them thanks, and once again, that I was so sorry about my bad performance. I said, 'I will find the finest teacup cup around and replace it, I promise.'

"Margaret told me that it was okay and not to bother because the cup could never be replaced, but that she forgave me anyway. Yeah, well, that made me feel a whole fucking hell of a lot better. But I didn't say that out loud.

"Then Grace stood up and began clearing her work area and pretended her back had started bothering her. She suggested we call it a day for that reason. Like anyone was buying the pile of malarkey she was selling.

"But everyone agreed and, after helping put things away, I said my good-byes and with a great sense of relief with every step that took me farther away from that gathering of blanket makers, I headed back to my peaceful little cabin."

This is where Jane would insert another pause in her story to add her assessment of the ancient fine art of quilting:

"Quilting. Making a covering to keep one warm piece by fucking little piece. Hell! Why go to all that trouble when all you need to do is sew two large pieces of cotton three-quarters of the way round, fill it with goose feathers, and then sew it shut. Simple. Effective. Devoid of any of the boredom that comes with cutting a large piece of material into dozens of little squares and then sewing them back together. Does it fucking even occur to the idiots who waste their time making these piecemeal blankets that there is a much simpler way of achieving their goal of producing a cover to keep the body warm?"

Jane would conclude this story of her most boring time ever by adding that she never went back to spend time with that group or any that engaged in such nonsense. As for the group of ladies she had spent time with that day, this arrangement suited them just fine.

Chapter 31

Hey, Jane. Are you home?" Trixie called one Saturday morning about a week after the disastrous quilting party. "Behind the cabin by the water, Trixie," Jane yelled back.

Trixie was the closest thing to a female friend Jane had ever known. The woman could be a pain in the ass, what with the straight way she shot the words out of her mouth sometimes. *Kinda like I do,* Jane thought. But Trixie also was kind, caring, and fun to have around.

"Hey there," Trixie called as she approached her pregnant friend.

Jane's belly was starting to expand, and Trixie was fascinated by being so close to what she hoped to experience herself someday.

"Hi yourself," Jane said. "What brings you out here, away from the hustle and bustle of your two very different places of employment?" Jane asked. She was sitting on the edge of the creek bank, dangling her feet in the water, watching it flow by her.

Trixie smiled and sat down beside her friend. "Well, if you must know, the one employer gave me the day off and, as of last night, I ceased being employed by the other."

Jane frowned. "Please tell me *the other* is the slimy one."

"That would be the one," Trixie laughed. She was downright giddy.

"Well, praise whatever mysterious forces rule this fucking universe!" Jane said. "Did the cocksucker fire you, or did you remove yourself from that deplorable situation of your own choosing?"

Trixie laughed. "Well, though you may be the self-proclaimed queen of storytelling, I have a script to rival any of yours."

"Does it involve getting shot at?" Jane asked.

"Nope."

"How about saving lives?"

"Maybe. At least mine."

"Hmmm. Okay go ahead and tell away. I don't mind if you want to try and top my tales of derring-do, but keep in mind that you will

164

never have a story the likes of any told by this one, *Calamity Jane*. I fear boredom coming on, but that's okay when I'm expecting it, and I've nothing else to do now except sit and watch my belly grow," Jane said.

"You're so funny, Jane," Trixie laughed.

"So I've been told," Jane agreed. "Well, go on, now. Commence to tell your story."

"Okay. Well, last night Sol and I went for a walk while I was on break from my duties at The Gem."

Jane yawned long and loud. "That's about as interesting as watching flies graze on horseshit."

"C'mon, Jane. Give me a chance. It gets better. I just have to set the scene," Trixie pleaded.

"Okay, but speed it up a bit. This baby is gonna want to come out in a few months and, when it does, I doubt any of us will be listening to anything but the sound of me screaming, from what I've been told of this barbaric process that god, there he is again, decided to visit strictly upon females," she said.

"We openly held hands, Jane, because it just seemed like the natural thing to do," Trixie began.

Jane smiled. She liked seeing her friend so happy.

"We walked along in silence, just enjoying the feeling of holding hands, right out in public, you know?"

Jane nodded.

"I knew I was being gone from my duties longer than I should have, but the moment was so perfect, and I wanted it to last as long as I could make it do that. Have you ever felt that way?"

Jane nodded, and Trixie regretted asking the question she should already have known the answer to.

"I'm sorry, Jane. Of course, you've felt that way," Trixie said, reaching out to put her hand on Jane's.

"Always treasure those moments because they don't last forever," Jane said. "Nothing does."

The two were quiet for a few seconds. Then Jane said, "Well, is there more to this so-far not-so-exciting narrative?"

"Trixie laughed. "Oh Jane, so much more," she said. "I finally told Sol we should start back. I knew Al was going to be furious with how long I was gone and didn't want to push him over the edge. That is when Sol said, 'Why even go back to The Gem? Why not stay with me, Trixie?' "

"I knew it!" Jane squealed.

"Well, I have to admit *I* didn't see it coming. Damn, Jane, I've known for a while now that he was attracted to me as something more than just a convenient lay, but I didn't entertain any thoughts of being something he would want to live with, as man and wife," Trixie said.

Jane corrected her. "Someone, not something. And any man would be a fool not to want the likes of you there beside him for all of his days and nights."

"I told him, 'I would stay with you forever, Sol, in a heartbeat, but you live at a place of business you own together with a partner—'"

"That would be 'My lips only turn one way and that's toward my boots' Seth Bullock," Jane said, impersonating Bullock's dry tone of voice, wrinkled forehead, and frown.

Trixie laughed. "Seth would have a conniption if Sol moved me into the store."

"Well, Mr. Cranky Pants will just have to adjust his thinking, is what I would say," Jane said. "It is as much half of Sol's place as it is half of Bullock's, after all."

"Turns out it doesn't matter. Sol told me he has purchased a house and asked me to marry him and live in it with him—as his wife!" Trixie squealed.

Jane reached out and grabbed her friend, giving her a hug that nearly crushed her ribs.

"Easy there," Trixie said. "I know Sol's getting a soiled dove, but at least I'm not a broken one."

Jane took Trixie by the shoulders and, using the stern tone of a mother chastising her child, said, "Don't you ever call yourself a soiled dove around me or anyone else. You are a kind, beautiful, intelligent woman who deserves to be loved and revered by the finest man alive."

Trixie blushed. "Well, you've got some of that right. Sol is one of the finest men I've ever known. I feel honored he wants to make me his wife. And, one other very important detail is, I'm in love with him."

Jane smiled. "He is a good man at that. And a wise one for choosing you. Now, if I remember our conversation the day we met, you have achieved two of the three goals you stated that day we sat by the creek and talked. One, you have a profession involving numbers; two, you have found a good man you also happen to love and who loves you back. Have you changed your mind about the number of poopers you want to raise?"

Trixie grinned. "Children, Jane. And we'll be happy with whatever we're given. But yeah, the more the merrier," she said.

"Oh, Trixie. It warms my heart to see you so happy," Jane said.

"I have one more thing to tell you," Trixie said.

"And what would that be?"

"If you're not too busy, you know—sitting around and waiting for your belly to grow and all—Sol and I would love for you to attend and bear witness to our nuptials."

"A wedding! Of course, I'll be there. When is the big day?"

Trixie blushed. "Wednesday."

"As in the one coming up?"

"Yes. We don't want to waste a second, now that we know we are going to be man and wife. And Sol told me about this little verse that says Wednesday is the best day to get married, so that is what we chose."

"I never knew there was one day better than any other to tie the knot," Jane said.

"Neither did I, but listen to this:

Marry on Monday for health,
Tuesday for wealth,
Wednesday the best day of all,
Thursday for crosses,
Friday for losses,
Saturday for no luck at all."

"So how come Sunday isn't in there somewhere?" Jane asked.

"I asked that, too. Sol said he doesn't know why, but it probably is prohibited because Christians see it as a day of rest. And I guess getting married isn't very restful."

"Some superstitious crap, if you ask me. But if I was to believe it, I'd steer clear of Thursday, Friday, and Saturday for sure," Jane said, then thought: *There might be some truth to this, considering Bill and I got unofficially hitched on a Saturday.* Out loud she said, "Well, I did have some plans to stare at my four walls this coming Wednesday, but for you I'll be happy to change them. My plans, that is, not my walls."

Trixie laughed. "Oh, Jane, you should be in the entertainment business."

"That was part of the plan Bill and I laid out for ourselves. But I don't want to dwell on that. What I really am interested in hearing is how the slimy limey reacted when you gave him the news you were quitting," Jane said.

Trixie laughed. "I don't know which of us will enjoy this story more: me telling it or you hearing it. Either way, I guarantee you're gonna love it. And before you ask, there are no guns or rocks involved, although there is a bit of violence I think you'll enjoy."

"Just a bit?" Jane asked.

"Yeah, but it got the job done!"

Chapter 32
The Night Before

I'm going in with you," Sol told Trixie as they neared The Gem. Sol had just asked Trixie to be his wife and she had accepted, which meant she was no longer in the business of being a whore. Which meant Al Swearengen was about to find out that his favorite prostitute was quitting the business to get married and become a respectable woman. Which meant a substantial loss of revenue for him, among other things.

"You're a sweetheart, but I'd rather do this by myself in my own way," Trixie said, squeezing his hand and smiling up at him.

You are so gorgeous, Sol thought, looking down at his soon-to-be wife.

"I'm afraid he's going to hurt you," Sol argued. He knew how ruthless Al Swearengen could be when things didn't go his way. Trixie had told him about some of the past beatings she had taken at the tyrant's hands for even the smallest of infractions.

What would he do to her when he learned he was losing the woman who managed his prostitutes and brought in a fair amount of money for her own sexual favors? She meant dollar signs to Swearengen, and he did not like anything or anyone interfering with his ability to make as much money as possible.

"Well, I will approach him in the open, and if you want to wait out-side and come to my rescue should the need arise, I would be most beholden to you." Trixie's smile was so sweet and so convincing that Sol didn't feel he had much choice but to do as she asked.

In truth, Swearengen scared the bejeezus out of her at times. He could be an almost kind man, when the mood struck him, but when he was riled it didn't matter who or what you were. He would make you pay, one way or the other. There was more than one occasion Trixie could recall when someone went into Al's office to confront him or be

169

confronted about something, and had to be carried out and prepared for burial.

Then there was the added complication of Al seeing Trixie as his personal wench, whom he called to his own bed often, at least before Seth came into her life. She had once seen this as an honor, and lorded it over the other working girls at The Gem. Now she saw nothing but shame in it.

Sol and Trixie stopped shortly before reaching the door of the saloon. She stood on her tiptoes and gave him a kiss.

"I will go to my room and get my belongings before asking to talk to Al," she said. Trixie had not come to Deadwood with much personal property, but she did have a few mementos from childhood that she treasured and would not want to lose.

"Then I'll ask Dan to go call Al down, assuming he is in his office, and wait at the bar. You can keep an eye on me the whole time if you stand in this doorway just so," she said. She took Sol by the arms and positioned him at a vantage point where he could see the area she intended to confine herself to.

That seemed to satisfy Sol. Trixie gave his hand one more squeeze, took a deep breath, and walked into the saloon. But Al was not in his office. He was standing at the bar and as soon as he saw her, he began a tirade.

"Well, lookee here, if it isn't the prodigal prostitute coming back home after taking twice the time allowed to go on break," Al shouted.

Trixie froze. She would have to change her plan.

"Accompany me to my office, and tell me all about why it took you a fucking hour longer than allowed to do whatever the hell it is you were doing in your generously allotted to yourself free time?" he said, roughly taking hold of her upper arm and pulling her toward the stairs leading to his office.

Sol heard every word Al said and was ready to barge in the door when Trixie said, "Al, I have some good news, but I have to go back and use the chamber pot. Wait for me here, please? You're going to love this!" She pulled out of his grasp and whisked by him before he had time to react. Trixie went into the back room she shared with five other women and quickly gathered her things. She put everything she owned into a small bag, putting her finger to her lips to caution the girls present not to ask.

"I'll explain tomorrow," she whispered.

Meanwhile, Al told Dan to pour him a shot while he waited to hear Trixie's news.

By the time Trixie came back into the bar area, Sol had walked in and ordered two shots—one for him and one for her.

"Join me, Trixie?" he asked when she reached the bar.

Al growled. "No, Jew boy, she is not going to join *you*. She is going upstairs with me and tell me why the hell she was late."

Before Sol could respond, Swearengen noticed the satchel Trixie was carrying.

"Going somewhere, are we?" he asked. His voice was loaded with menace as he reached out to yank the bag from her hand.

Trixie didn't miss a beat. She tossed the bag to Sol, who caught it and held tight.

"No, Al, *we* are not going anywhere. But me? I'm leaving this hell hole tonight, and I don't intend to ever come back," she said.

Al sneered. "Well, well, well. Looks like the Jew boy wants this whore for his very own self. The problem is, she's not for sale."

"No, I'm not," Trixie said. "I'm not your property, Al. I accepted your offer for employment and I am now quitting that employment. You are going to be minus one of your resident cocksuckers tonight, Al. Maybe you will need to fill in until you find another, seeing as how you are one."

Al looked stunned, then began to laugh and clap.

"So, let me get this straight. You are going to be given room and board in that hardware store across the way in exchange for working this Jew boy's dick as well as his books. Do I have that right?"

Sol took a step forward. The man was known for being a pacifist, but listening to Al insult his woman drew some latent rage to the surface.

"I have never punched a man in the mouth before, but if it is true what they say about there having to be a first time for everything, I reckon this is dangerously close to that time," he said. "For your information, I have asked Trixie to marry me. I have purchased a home in which we will live, so you don't have to concern yourself with her and she will no longer do your bidding. She will be a great asset to me in the business due to her talent in accounting matters, as well as a loving wife and, God willing, someday, the mother of my children. That's all you need to know."

"Well," Al said. "I guess congratulations are in order, then. Hell, Trixie, I wish you only the best. In fact, Dan, drinks on the house for all who have witnessed this declaration of love. It's not often, hell! Practically fucking never will one see a Jew boy walk into a saloon and ask a pimp for a dirty whore's hand—"

Whatever else Al might have intended to add to that speech was stopped short when Sol's fist connected with the saloon owner's mouth. Al recoiled and covered his bleeding lip with the back of his hand.

"The next time you speak of the woman I love, I will thank you to do so with the respect and dignity she deserves," Sol said.

"Get out of my saloon and take the woman with you. Neither one of you are welcome here again," Al growled.

"I will be only too fucking happy to eternally recuse myself from this hell hole," Trixie told him. She turned, picked up the two glasses of whiskey Sol had purchased for them, handed one to her future husband and raised the other. "To freedom," she said.

Sol and Trixie drank, set their glasses back down on the bar, and walked arm-in-arm out of The Gem. Neither one of them ever went back.

Chapter 33

Jane nearly fell over laughing when Trixie finished telling her about Sol's fist bloodying Al's mouth. "So, I take it you need a place to stay until your wedding day?" Jane asked. She would welcome having Trixie's company for a few days.

"Actually, Sol said I should stay at our new home and put some of my own decorative touches on it and he will sleep at the hardware store, as usual," Trixie said.

Jane tried not to let her disappointment show. "Well, that seems like a good plan," she said.

"Although why we can't just move in there together tonight makes no sense to me whatsoever. It's not like we haven't fucked dozens of times already," Trixie said.

"See, this is why I love you, Trixie. You are a woman who thinks a lot like me!" Jane said.

Trixie laughed. "Yeah, I guess we both are cursed with seeing things in a straightforward sort of way. Don't know why people have to take something so simple and make it all complicated," she said. "But there is a silver lining to this prim and proper adjustment. Jane, I would like you to come stay with me in my new home for the next three days, and maybe help me prepare for my wedding and set up housekeeping," she said.

"Trixie, I would love to keep you company, but if you think I know how to do either of those things you need help with, you don't know me as well as I thought you did," Jane said.

Jane had never expected her own wedding, when she and Bill made it legal, to be any different than the first one, except for the preacher who would say some words and sign a piece of paper. She treasured their nuptials spoken out in the open, the wedding dinner of chicken, making love on a blanket under the open sky. She wouldn't have changed a thing.

"Well, I do know you are the best friend I've ever had, and if there is any woman I want by my side to help me muddle through these challenges, that woman would be you, Jane," Trixie said.

"Oh, Trixie. Don't you know that you hadn't oughta give a pregnant woman reason to get all emotional?" Jane said, a few tears running down her cheeks.

"No, Jane, I don't know anything about a lady's emotions when she's pregnant, but I can't wait to find out," Trixie said, putting her arm around Jane's shoulders and holding her close.

Chapter 34

Jane and Trixie spent the next few days choosing the bride's wedding ensemble and planning for the reception. Jane was going to wear one of her two "perfectly acceptable" dresses and Trixie was fine with that.

"You're the one people are going to be looking at, anyway," Jane told her.

The two women paid a visit to Martha's Dress Shoppe, the shop where Jane had bought the yellow dress that was now packed away, still covered in Bill's blood. Jane didn't have the heart to wash it or throw it out.

"Good morning, Jane, Trixie," Martha greeted them when they walked into her store. "Have you come to look at some of our new arrivals?"

"Trixie here was hoping you might have a wedding dress or two on hand," Jane said.

"Oh!" Martha's shock was easy to see. She had been clothing Trixie for the last month, and the dresses Trixie chose had made her occupation obvious.

"Sol Star has asked for my hand in marriage, and I have accepted his proposal. So, I will need a proper dress befitting a proper betrothed lady," Trixie explained, mindful of what must have been going through the storekeeper's mind.

Martha recovered in an instant. "How wonderful, Trixie. He is known to be a very good man. You are quite the lucky little lady," she said.

"Not to mention that Sol is beyond fucking fortunate himself, to get this beautiful, kind, loving, intelligent woman," Jane said. Her tone made it clear that Trixie deserved a good man, and no one had better suggest otherwise, at least not in Jane's presence.

"He most certainly is," Martha said, smiling. "Now, I have four dresses in stock suitable for a proper lady such as yourself, Trixie. I

175

will bring them out and, if none of them strikes your fancy, I have a catalog you can order from. We can have any dress in stock here within the next month."

"Better bring out what you have," Jane said. "The wedding's in two days."

"Oh!" Martha's mouth dropped open before she could get a grip on it.

"No, Martha," said Jane gruffly. "Trixie is not with child. They just love each other and don't want to wait. I'm the only one in this room with a biscuit baking on the oven." It was clear from Jane's tone, if not her words, that she was annoyed at Martha's reaction.

"Jane!" Trixie interrupted, glaring at her friend. "I'm sure Martha registered surprise because most brides, I'd guess, don't wait until two days before their wedding to purchase their dress. Right, Martha?"

"That is certainly what I was thinking." Martha said. "It is very unusual to wait this long. What if we don't have what you want? There is no time for mail order."

"It's okay. I'm pretty easy to please, and the important thing is that I'm marrying the man of my dreams," Trixie said.

"Yeah," offered Jane, "sorry I got a little heated under the bustle. My emotions are pregnant. Anyway, Trixie here would look gorgeous wearing a potato sack. I'm sure one of your fine dresses will fill the bill."

An hour later the two women left the dress shop arm in arm. Trixie had chosen a sky blue taffeta and embroidered dress with a light blue silk sash, long train, low square neckline, low waist, and tight bodice. Martha told her the dress made her look like a bride straight out of eastern high society. Jane was amazed how closely the color of the dress matched the blue in Trixie's eyes. Very few alterations were needed, and Martha promised to begin working on them immediately. The dress would be ready for Trixie to pick up at noon the following day.

"You've got to stop being so protective of me," Trixie said. "From the look on poor Martha's face, you scared the living daylights out of her."

"I just didn't like what I thought she may be implying," Jane said.

"Then again, Jane, she may not have been implying anything other than what she explained. Besides, I am already expecting there will be some who have a difficult time forgetting what it is I used to do. I've just told myself I must be patient. You can take the cock out of a whore's mouth, but it takes a while to wash away all the traces of it being there in the first place."

Jane laughed. "Yeah, well, it will go a lot faster with me around to remind people of who and what you have become. It's not just the getting hitched to a real gentleman part that matters to me, Trixie. It's the fact that you set out to make something of yourself career-wise, stayed the course, and now realize your dreams. I'm so proud of you, my little friend," Jane said with a sniffle. "Damn those fucking pregnant emotions!"

Trixie laughed and hugged her friend. "Come on. I'm hungry. I'll buy you lunch at the hotel, and then we can talk to management about what we want to serve wedding guests following the ceremony."

Sol and Trixie decided to have a brief, mid-morning nuptial in the hotel lobby, followed by a celebratory lunchtime meal. The lobby would be closed to the public for the affair. The tables were to be topped with crisp white linens and the hotel's best china. The three-tiered wedding cake was to rest on a table set in the center of the room. After everyone had viewed the cake, the staff would cut it up and set pieces inside individual boxes to be handed to guests as they left. Food would include bacon, gravy served over sausage and biscuits, an assortment of cheeses, some pork pies, mushrooms, and fruit salad.

Jane and Trixie chatted and giggled like a couple of schoolgirls while they enjoyed their meal of steak, potatoes, and bread.

"I swear I'm eating for ten, not two," Jane exclaimed as she downed the last bit of food on her plate.

"I *know* I am, and I'm not even with child!" Trixie laughed.

After they finished eating, Jane and Trixie approved the menu and the other plans for Sol and Trixie's big day and then left the hotel. They headed to the hardware store, where Sol was working on inventory and Seth was placing orders for items that needed to be restocked as Sol called them out.

Sol looked up when Jane and Trixie walked in the door. His face lit up like a sky full of twinkling stars on a cloudless night. "Well, this is a nice surprise," Sol said. "I thought the two of you would still be shopping and planning."

"No, we got those boring parts over with and now we're just walking," Jane said.

Both Sol and Seth grinned. Jane ignored their reaction.

"Say, Seth," Jane said. "Might you mind keeping watch on the store while Sol, Trixie, and I take some air? I have something I want to talk to them about."

"Not at all, as long as it's not too long. We have to finish this order by the time the mail goes out this afternoon," he said.

"Thanks, Seth. I'll be back soon," Sol said.

Jane directed the two lovers to a bench outside the couple's new home. The house was two doors down from the hardware store, so it was the closest place to sit and talk in private. Now, Jane felt very much like sitting. The baby was getting heavy to carry, and right now it was adding to her discomfort by kicking both feet against the walls of her abdomen, as though it was trying to break free.

"Whoa, there. You're not going to get out that way, no matter how hard you try," Jane said. She put her hand on her belly and rubbed softly. Sol and Trixie exchanged glances and smiles.

"I can't wait for your blessed day," Trixie said.

"I sure can," Jane retorted. "I'm not at all looking forward to the process involved in getting this little one from where it's at to the outside world."

"It will be fine, Jane." Sol tried to reassure the anxious mother-to-be. "Women do this all the time, and most have no problem whatsoever."

"Yeah, well, as my dear Bill pointed out many times, much to my delight at those times, I'm not like most women."

Sol and Trixie remained silent out of respect for Jane's grief, while Jane stared away for a few minutes, blinking her eyes a few times to keep the tears from falling.

"Damned emotions!" Jane said. Then she cleared her throat and looked at Sol and Trixie. "You know, I didn't ask you to walk with me to talk about my fears of childbirth. I have something much more important to address with the two of you, and I would much appreciate you hearing me out."

"Of course," Sol said. "Go ahead."

Jane took a deep breath and said, "Okay. As I have told Trixie and she no doubt has conveyed to you, being her lover, confidant, and soon-to-be husband, I plan to give this baby up for adoption as soon as it shows itself outside the womb."

Sol and Trixie both gave her a solemn nod.

Jane continued. "I know this is not what you or Doc or Charlie want me to do, but it is what is best for this child. I asked Doc, some time ago, to search for a family who would love, take proper care of, and educate this baby. I also asked him not to tell me who it was and not to give them any information about me." Jane stopped, took another deep breath, and then continued.

"Lately, I've been thinking there may be another, better way that will benefit not only this child, but also others."

"Are you changing your mind about keeping this baby?" Trixie asked.

"No, but I would like to see this child grow up with a loving couple in the best situation for him or her possible. I would like to watch from afar and interact as a friend of the family's. But to do that,

I would need two loving, caring, decent people who have the means to feed, clothe, and educate a child.

"Sol, Trixie, I may not have the means to buy you a wedding present to put on that gift table come Wednesday morning, but if you can wait a few months, Bill and I would like to place our baby in your loving arms for you to adopt and raise as your own." Jane sighed. That was harder to say than she had imagined it would be. "Take your time and think ..."

"Yes!" Sol and Trixie answered in unison after exchanging a quick glance and broad smiles.

"Yes?" Jane asked.

"Yes, yes, yes!" Trixie said, jumping to her feet and grabbing both of Jane's hands in hers.

"We'd be honored. And very happy, Jane," Sol told her.

"I promise on the grave of my child's dead father, I will not interfere," Jane cried. The relief washed over her like a warm, rainbow-colored waterfall. She remembered her dream about Bill and smiled. "I know he will be pleased about this."

Two days later Sol and Trixie were married and moved into their home together. They planned to take five days for a honeymoon, most of that to be spent decorating a nursery and buying baby equipment.

Jane went back to her cabin, at peace with her decision. At peace with her life. At peace with herself and the entire universe.

Chapter 35

Sol and Trixie's wedding dawned bright and promising. Trixie looked ethereal in her gown, and Sol's eyes lit up when he first saw her in it. Sol wore a semi-fitted brown thigh-length coat. His white shirt featured a stiff collar with the tips turned down into wings. The two made a stunning couple.

Sol had requested that Jewish vows be exchanged, but told Trixie she was not expected to adopt his religion. Sol planned to give her the ring that had once belonged to his mother. When Sol repeated the words, "With this ring you are made holy to me, for I love you as my soul. You are now my wife," he slipped it on her finger. The ring featured cut diamonds, a sapphire, and two ruby accents, all arranged in a cluster in a multi-band gold setting.

Trixie placed a plain gold band on Sol's finger and repeated the words, "With this ring, you are made holy to me, for I love you as my soul. You are now my husband."

After the brief ceremony, the couple shared a feast with their guests and then retreated to their new home. As she was leaving, Trixie gave Jane a long hug and whispered in her ear, "This former soiled dove just turned into a beautiful swan."

One morning, a few months after Sol and Trixie's wedding, Jane decided to pay Charlie Utter a visit at his store. It was February and chilly, but the bright sun this day made for an enjoyable walk. Jane could no longer fit into the buckskin britches she loved wearing, but two women in Deadwood had loaned her their maternity dresses and Jane was happy to have the warm and comfortable attire.

On this day Jane was wearing Bill's long buckskin coat over an olive-green, wool lined dress and jacket. The dress had a high neck, puffed sleeves, and a lined bodice that had a long, hidden front-lacing tie to enlarge the center front from beneath the bust down to the hem. Double metal hooks kept the lacing secure. The bustle skirt had a front-pleated expansion panel with many ties to adjust the waist as it increased in size. Jane wore long wool stockings under the dress, covered by her well-worn pair of boots.

After her work with the camp's smallpox patients, several residents had come forward and bestowed Jane with gifts, most of which consisted of food and some monetary support. They knew that when Bill had died she was all but penniless. A short time later, word spread quickly around Deadwood that the woman who called herself Calamity Jane was expecting Wild Bill Hickok's baby. It was a common belief that this woman who stepped forward in her hour of grief to care for so many, deserved all they could do to help her out in her time of need.

The sun had raised yesterday's very icy ten degrees Fahrenheit to a tolerable thirty-five degrees by noon. Snow covered most of the ground, but another five degrees would take care of that in no time at all.

Jane had an idea she wanted to run by Charlie, something she had been mulling over for the last two months. She would be willing to carry her idea through all by herself, if she were able. But to pull it off, she would need Charlie's help.

It seemed Charlie was always willing to come to Jane's aid. Whether it was to bring her food or to make sure Buddy was getting the exercise he needed, Charlie made sure it was done. Charlie watched over her like a mother hawk, and Jane found it ironic that this man she so despised when they first met had grown to be one of her closest friends. In fact, Charlie Utter had turned out to be one of the finest people Jane had ever known.

Jane was nearing The Gem where, as was often the case, Al was standing on the deck outside his second-floor office. Sometimes he had a coffee cup in hand, other times a bottle. Today it was a bottle.

"Good afternoon, Jane," Al called. "Fine sunny day to be taking a walk."

"Hello, Slimy," Jane called back, without looking up.

182

"Would you care to come inside and have a drink on the house?" he asked.

"I would not care to come inside and have a drink or anything else you have to offer, free or otherwise," she said.

Jane kept walking but could hear Al laughing as she put The Gem behind her.

"Always a pleasure, Lady Jane," he called out. Why Swearengen thought her insults were a pleasure was a mystery to Jane.

"Jane!" Charlie said when she walked in the door. "Good to see you taking some air on this gorgeous day!" he said.

"It's good to be out," Jane said. "My purpose of doing so was to both visit with you and talk to you about something I could use your help with," she said.

"You know if I can do it, I will, Jane," he said. When his friend Bill died, Charlie had made a promise to both himself and his dead friend to help Jane with whatever she needed. He was there for her both because he had grown to love the woman as a friend, and as a tribute to Bill. How he missed Bill Hickok!

"Well, Charlie, I've been thinking. You know I intend to give this baby to Sol and Trixie to raise, right?"

"Sadly. I heard that," he said.

"It's not sad for the little one, Charlie. You know I'm not the mothering type. I don't have the means. I don't have the desire. And most of all I'm a lifelong imbiber who still drinks three shots a day, even if it might cause me to unwittingly bring harm to my child. I just can't go without. Hell, I don't even want to try. I have not been falling-down drunk once since Doc warned me what might happen to this baby if I blacked out. It's one thing for me never to wake up again after drinking myself into a stupor, but the baby would die right along with me. So at least, I have managed to do that much. Not what most would consider a paragon of parenting," she said.

Charlie was silent.

183

"So, what do I do when the kid leaves my belly and is at an age when he or she might wander off and be harmed? What if I have just three shots and forget to watch or feed it? What then?"

Charlie still did not respond, so Jane continued her rant.

"Doc thinks I'll change my mind once the baby is born. And Sol and Trixie say they will understand if I do. But I can tell they are over the moon about becoming parents right away. And I know they will not only love, but also feed, clothe, and educate this child, who deserves no less. Hell! No child deserves less," she sighed, and then she asked in an abrupt change of subject: "Why are you so damned quiet?"

Charlie sighed. "What you say makes sense, Jane, but it still troubles me."

"Well, look at it this way, Charlie. You will get to watch Bill's kid grow up, assuming Sol and Trixie stay in Deadwood. And I will get to see the child whenever I want. Trixie told me so," Jane said.

"Do you intend to tell the child you are the birth mother?" Charlie asked.

"Still trying to figure that one out. I mean, I would not be so inclined, but I think it should be left up to Sol and Trixie to decide that. Everyone in Deadwood knows whose baby this really is, and there are always some who will talk. It might just be inevitable," she said.

"Well, I can tell you one thing for sure. Whatever yours and Bill's child needs from me will be freely given with great pleasure," he said.

"Thanks, Charlie," Jane said. She knew she could always count on him.

"Hey! Where are my manners? You walked all the way here in the cold, and I have not so much as offered you a hot cup of coffee," he said.

"I was just about to ask," Jane said.

While Charlie saw to making the coffee, he and Jane talked about a variety of subjects. Charlie told Jane business was going well and asked if she would consider a job as a mail carrier.

"You would be carrying mail between here and Cheyenne, over some pretty rough trails," he said.

"Oh, Charlie! I would love that," Jane said. "I've done this job before in other towns with similar rough terrain. I could do this with two hands tied behind my back and my eyes closed!" she said.

Charlie laughed. "Well, I'd rather your hands and eyes were fully functional because the important thing is to get the mail delivered promptly and intact."

"Yeah, well, just trying to make a fucking point," she said.

Charlie handed Jane her coffee and sat down beside her. "If you've done this before, you know there are robbers often waiting along these routes, who want nothing more than to steal packages and any money you may be carrying from one point to another," he said.

"Yeah, and there ain't one I ever encountered who did not leave my company dead or severely damaged," Jane said.

"You know what, Jane? That's something I truly believe, even if it did come out of your mouth." Charlie was on to Jane's way of hoisting a tale up over its original fencepost.

"Shut up and drink your coffee, Charlie Utter," she said.

"Okay, I'll shut up. But please, tell me what it is you need me to help you with."

Jane took another sip of coffee, set the cup down on his desk, and said, "I need you to help me write my story."

"Your *story*?" he asked.

"Yeah, my fucking life story. In a book. To be published for everyone to read so they can learn about all my adventures," she said.

"You know, Jane, that would be an amazing story, but you have to be able to prove what you say is true, and how're you going to do that?" he asked.

"Well, Charlie, seeing as how it is my fucking life story and I fucking lived it, I would think that would be proof itself." Jane glared at him, then continued. "I will call it: Life and Adventures of Calamity Jane, by Herself."

"Um, *herself*? Why not by Martha Jane Canary? Or by Calamity Jane?" Charlie asked.

"Charlie, everyone who writes a book about themselves says 'by' and then their name. As is my custom, I want to do something a bit outside the norm and just say: *Herself*. Is that okay with you? Seeing as how it is *my* book, not *yours*?"

Charlie wanted to say that it would not be *anyone's* book if he did not agree to pen it for her. But he didn't.

"Whatever you want, Jane. I will write down what you say, but I do not want to be associated with your accounting of events, some of which I fear will not be entirely true," he said.

"Okay, then. When can we start?" Jane asked, ignoring his comment about truth.

"How about tomorrow? You will have to come here, since I have work to do. And we will have to work around my customers. Except on Sundays, when I can come to your place," he said.

"Mighty beholden to you, Charlie. What time would you like me here?" Jane asked.

"Well, later in the day is best for me, so how about coming around three? We'll work until I close at six, and then we can head over to the hotel and get some dinner, and I will walk you home," he said.

"Dinner would be great, but I can get myself home," Jane said.

"I'd just feel better knowing you and that little one are safe. The streets of Deadwood after dark can be a dangerous place for a woman," he said.

"Okay, Charlie. I'm getting too fat, too slow, and too tired to argue," she said.

Jane left Charlie Utter's store and headed back to her cabin. The weather had turned a bit colder, so she was happy to get home, light a fire, and eat some beans. The sky was just beginning to darken when Jane lay down and fell right to sleep.

Chapter 36

Over the next two weeks Jane and Charlie met almost every day, and he wrote down what she told him. The book began: "My maiden name was Martha Canary, was born in Princeton, Missouri, May 1, 1852."

"Let me see," Jane demanded when Charlie was barely done inking the date at the end of the first sentence. "You spelled my surname wrong," she said.

"How do you spell it?" Charlie asked.

Jane knew the spelling was right, but wanted to show that she had full control over the book's contents. "It's spelled C-a-n-n-a-r-y," she said.

"Jane, whenever I've seen your name in print, it is spelled with one n, not two," Charlie argued.

"Well, then, it was spelled wrong," Jane spewed. "I should fucking know how to spell my own name, shouldn't I?"

"You should, but you don't," Charlie muttered.

"I heard what you mumbled, and I choose to fucking ignore," Jane said.

"Okay, so you want to just put down statistics, instead of writing in full sentences?" Charlie asked.

"What I gave you was a full sentence," Jane said.

"No, what you gave me was a statement followed by a *was*." Charlie argued.

"Huh?" Jane asked.

Charlie sighed. "Well, for instance, instead of just saying: 'My maiden name was Martha Canary, was born in Princeton, Missouri, May 1, 1852,' how about something that reads more like this: 'I was born in Princeton, Missouri, on May I, 1852. My parents named me Martha Jane Canary'?"

"That's exactly what I said," Jane spewed.

"No, it's close, but far from exactly," Charlie argued.

Jane stood up and started yelling. "Charlie Utter! I am not feeling all too well today! This baby kicked my insides out all night long and I'm feeling a lot of pressure where it is not pleasant to be pressed. I have to pee two hundred times a day, and I am not in the mood for you today!"

"Sorry," Charlie said.

Jane walked to the door, opened it, and yelled, "I'll see you tomorrow and I hope you will have adjusted your fucking annoying attitude to the point where I can stand being around you."

It's safe to say their first day of collaborating on Jane's life story did not go as well as either would have hoped.

Day number two had Charlie wondering if Jane would show up. She had left pretty riled up, and he felt kind of bad about that. He made a promise to himself that he would remember to take Jane's physical state into account if she returned to work on her book.

Jane walked in the door of Charlie's store a little before three, wearing a smile and another one of the maternity dresses she had been loaned.

"Sorry if I'm a little early, Charlie," she said sweetly.

"It's okay, Jane. I just finished packaging the last of the boxes that go out today. Now I'm just waiting for my rider," he said. "I fixed us some fresh coffee, and purchased a couple of rolls from the bakery, if you would like to join me," he said.

"Thanks, Charlie! I'd love to," she said. While Charlie poured the coffee, and put the rolls on plates, Jane sat quietly. After he handed Jane's to her, she said, "I want to apologize for my outburst yesterday."

"Let's not worry about it, Jane. I shouldn't question your telling of your own story. From now on, I am simply to serve as a conduit for getting your story told however you want that to be, and however you want the words spelled," he said.

188

"Thank you, Charlie. As a matter of fact, I need to tell you something you might not like and, if after I tell you, you decide not to continue with this project, I will understand," she said.

"Okay. What is it?" Charlie asked.

"As you know, I have led a very interesting and action-packed life. But nothing in my twenty-six years has been any more exciting or important to me than Bill is—was. I want to share our love story with the whole world, but to do that I will have to break another woman's heart."

"Agnes," Charlie said.

"Agnes," Jane confirmed. "See, I considered it a final act of love for Bill to show compassion to his legal widow, to protect her from learning the truth, and to make it possible for her memory of him to remain as untainted as possible. If I wrote about Bill being anything but my friend, and she were to read it or hear about it..."

"That's a good point," Charlie agreed. His respect for Jane grew even greater at that moment.

"So, I'm going to exaggerate my relationship with Bill, only I'm going to exaggerate it backwards," Jane said.

Charlie laughed. He knew what she meant, but had never heard it put that way before.

"What's so funny?" Jane asked.

"You are, Jane. You are one of the funniest and most wonderful women I have ever known," Charlie said.

"Well, you certainly didn't think I was either of those things when I first made your acquaintance," she said.

"Well, I didn't know you then, now did I?" Charlie said. "It's safe to say that you have grown on me."

"Why, Charlie Utter, if I didn't know you better, I'd think you were flirting with me," Jane said.

That day and the days that followed were a pleasant experience for both the one telling her life story and the one writing it down. Jane showed up at Charlie Utter's office at three o'clock every day but

189

Sunday. They worked until dinner time or until one of them was too tired and wanted to quit for the day. On Sundays he would take meat, cheese, potatoes, and vegetables to her cabin and he would write while she cooked them dinner and dictated her story.

They covered a lot of ground in a short time, and Charlie learned more about her than even Bill probably knew.

"As a child," Jane related to Charlie, "I always had a fondness for horses, which I started riding at an early age, and continued to do so until I became an expert rider. I could ride the wildest horses even as a young child.

"In 1865 we left our home in Missouri and traveled by land to Virginia City, Montana. It took us five months to make this journey. I spent most of my time during that trip hunting alongside the men. By the time we reached Virginia City I was hailed as a remarkable shooter and fearless rider, especially for someone my age." Charlie wrote down what she spoke and enjoyed the story she was telling.

Jane recounted that her mother died in 1866 and her father a year later. She was left to care for her siblings. She left out the part about working as a whore to provide for them, as well as the part about meeting Bill in Cheyenne.

"So, up until this time I had mostly worn the costume of a woman, but when I joined Custer ..."

"Custer?" You fought alongside Custer?"

"Just write what I say, Charlie. Questions make me lose my place," Jane said.

"Your place?" Charlie asked.

"There you go again. Another fucking question!" Jane yelled, getting up off her chair and starting to pace. "Yes, my place, as in the place I am at in the story I am trying damn hard to tell without wanting to kill you!"

"Sorry," Charlie mumbled. "Carry on."

"As I was saying, up until that time, I wore the uniform of a soldier. It was a bit awkward at first, but it didn't take me long to feel right at home in men's clothes."

And so it went, day in and day out, as the unlikely couple worked to make a permanent record of Jane's life story. One Wednesday afternoon, shortly after Jane arrived at Charlie's, she recounted the story about how she got the name Calamity.

"It was in Arizona in the winter of 1871 when I had a great number of dangerous missions. But whenever I was in a tight spot, I always succeeded in getting away safely, and for this reason I was considered the most reckless and daring rider and one of the best shots in the west."

"The entire west?" Charlie asked.

"Yep," Jane said, her voice filled with pride.

"Well, after that I went several places and performed all sorts of brave acts. But it was at Goose Creek, Wyoming, that I acquired the name Calamity. Captain Egan was in command."

"Yeah, I think I heard this story sitting around a campfire one night," Charlie said.

"Well, then, smarty-pants, you should be able to write it yourself," Jane said.

"Don't mind if I do," Charlie said, and then continued Jane's narrative: "Well, despite having twenty-five arrows, two bullet holes, five knives, and a hatchet stuck in various parts of my body, as soon as I saw Captain Egan get shot I galloped toward him, lifted him to my horse in front of me, and succeeded in getting him safely back to the fort."

Jane didn't want to, but she burst out laughing when she heard Charlie's exaggerated account of the wounds she sustained at Goose Creek.

Charlie was pleased he could make her laugh.

"Okay, Charlie. If you're done mocking my bravery, I'll be happy to continue."

"Yeah, I think my point was made," Charlie said, grinning.

Jane ignored him and picked up where she had left off. "When he was able to talk again, Captain Egan told me: 'I name you Calamity Jane, heroine of the plains.' "

"I don't remember you saying he added the word heroine," Charlie told her.

"And I don't remember saying that I was fucking carrying in my body twenty-five arrows, two bullets, and five knife wounds," Jane told him.

"It was something like that," Charlie said.

"You know what, Charlie, I think we're done here for the day. The pressure in my body has gotten worse, probably because of your incessant arguing, and I believe I will now allow you to buy me dinner and walk me home. Can you do that much without giving me any more reason to want to put my fist in your mouth? And don't underestimate my ability to throw a knockout punch just because I'm pregnant," she said.

Charlie laughed. "Aw, I was just teasing you, Jane. I'm sorry you're feeling so poorly. Never having been with child myself, I can only imagine how uncomfortable that must be."

"Yeah, well fucking *imagine* this: Imagine how I feel having a boulder the size of a large jackrabbit pushing against the inside of my female privates. And every day it seems to push just a little bit harder until I would not be at all surprised if one of these days it just decides to yell, 'Coming on through.' *Imagine!*"

"I am capable of imagining that would be a bit uncomfortable," Charlie said.

"A *bit*? A bit, Charlie Utter? *Uncomfortable*? You fucking moron! Try imagining that it hurts like a motherfucker, because it does! Quite a bit more than a *bit*," Jane yelled.

"Okay, Jane. Why don't we mosey on out of here and get you and your little one some nourishment?" Charlie tried to change the subject.

192

"For all the room the supposed *little* one is taking up in my tummy, about all the food I can manage these days is a spoonful of whatever is on my plate," Jane said.

Charlie wondered if Jane could get any crankier, but didn't have to wait long to find out. As they were sitting down to eat, Jane turned her attention on two men sitting nearby.

"What are you cocksuckers looking at? Never seen a pregnant lady before?" she spewed.

One of the men took offense. "I wasn't looking at you, and ladies don't use words like cocksucker," he said.

"Jane, let it go," Charlie said. "They weren't even looking at you. Let's just eat and get you home to rest. I've heard the last few weeks of a pregnancy can be difficult to endure. You just need to rest."

"Sorry, Charlie. I just truly am miserable. And, not having experienced this supposed joy of being with child before, I don't know whether some of the things I'm feeling are normal, or if something is wrong."

"Maybe you should have Doc look at you," Charlie said.

"Yeah, it couldn't hurt. What am I saying? Anytime that man examines me it does hurt!"

Charlie laughed. "Yeah, Doc's kind of known for making it worse to make it better."

"Oh, I could tell you some things, but I won't since we're eating," Jane said. "I think instead, what I would like to do when we're done here is go home and get some sleep and then pay him a visit before I come to your store to work on the book tomorrow," Jane said.

"That sounds like a good idea," Charlie agreed. "I'll stop by when I get up tomorrow morning and let him know to expect you."

Their walk to the cabin took longer than usual this evening because just about every step seemed to be painful for Jane. When they got there, Charlie helped Jane lie down on her fur bed and told her he would see to the fire.

Jane was too tired and too sore to argue.

Once the fire was going, Charlie asked Jane if there was anything else he could do.

"Yeah, Charlie. Would you please stay with me tonight? I'm feeling really scared and I'm not exactly sure why."

"Of course, I will, Jane," Charlie said.

Jane told him to grab one of the extra blankets and Bill's pillow out of a chest in the corner.

"You can share this part of the fur bed my huge body is not taking up, if you'd like. I'm sorry, but that's all I have to offer," Jane said.

"It's a very kind and considerate offer, Jane," Charlie said. "But I don't want to take a chance of bumping into you and maybe hurting you. I will be fine rolled up in this blanket with Bill's pillow beneath my head," he said.

But Jane didn't hear. She was already fast asleep.

Charlie sat and watched her sleep a while before settling in himself. He felt sad about all that Jane had gone through and was sorry she was feeling so poorly. Maybe once the baby was born and she was feeling better, he would risk telling her about an idea he'd been having of late. An idea that could make both of their lives much happier and, if not that, at least a lot less lonely.

Chapter 37

Jane was perched at the top of a steep cliff, rocks everywhere as far down as her eyes could see. There was barely room for both of her feet to stand on the flat surface that made up the peak of the mountain. She had no idea how she had gotten there, or how she was going to get down.

In addition to the precarious position she found herself in, her stomach was on fire and she felt like vomiting.

Afraid to move for fear of falling, Jane called out for help. She could hear Charlie's voice in the distance, telling her he was going to get help.

"Charlie," she yelled. "Don't leave me alone like this!"

"I have to, Jane. I'll be back as soon as I can," he said.

A few seconds later, darkness fell over the entire area, the only points of light seemingly coming from a fire suspended in the air in front of her and a kerosene lamp hanging off to the side. She reached out for the lamp and lost her balance.

"Nooooo," Jane cried quietly as she fell off the top of the cliff. Her body tumbled head over foot for what seemed like an eternity. She hit rock after jagged rock on her way down into a deep, dark pit. Finally, she reached bottom, and found herself lying in a shallow pool of water. Warm water that seemed to be gushing from her body. That's when she started to scream.

Charlie awoke to the sound of Jane's screams in the pitch-dark cabin. "Jane! What's wrong?" he asked, rushing to where she was lying.

Something's wrong. Or maybe the baby is coming. Oh my god! The pain!" Jane answered.

Charlie immediately lit the kerosene lamp. The fire had gone out, so he put more wood in the stove and started that, too. All the while Jane kept screaming and pleading for him to make it stop.

195

"I hurt so motherfuckin' bad and I'm peeing all over the place," Jane screamed.

"Jane, I have to go get the doc. I think you're ready and I don't know the first thing about delivering a baby," Charlie told her.

"Oh, sweet Jesus! Don't leave me here alone, Charlie. I think I'm dying."

Charlie was torn. He didn't want to leave her, but he couldn't help her, either. He had to make a split-second decision.

"I'll be back as soon as I can," he said, and took off running out the door.

Jane felt like her insides were being twisted, squeezed, and pulled every which way. The searing pain in her lower back felt like she was being stabbed—repeatedly. Knife shoved in. Knife pulled out and then shoved back in again.

Waves of nausea rocked her body. It took everything she had to try to ride it out. She wished she had thought to keep a bottle of whiskey close by, so she could grab it and drink away the pain.

A half-hour later, after what seemed like days to Jane, the cabin door flew open and Doc Cochran rushed in.

"Oh, thank god you're here, Doc. Hurry! Get this motherfucking baby out of me! I think it's trying to kill me," she screamed.

Jane, you have to calm down, so we can work together to make this happen," Doc told her. "I'm going to give you some laudanum to ease the pain a bit. Then I will need to examine you."

Doc poured a little water into one of Jane's shot glasses and then added a few drops of the opium-based drug. He put one hand under Jane's head to raise it just enough so she could drink, and used his other hand to raise the glass to her mouth and tip it. He prepared a second dose and administered that as well.

"You should start feeling some relief soon," Doc said.

While he was waiting for the drug to take effect, Doc set a pot of water to boil on the stove. Then he took a knife and cut away the skirt of the dress Jane was wearing.

"Jane, do you have a freshly cleaned sheet or piece of cloth?" Doc asked.

Jane pointed a finger at the same chest where Charlie had found the pillow and blanket. Doc retrieved a clean sheet and covered Jane with it.

"Okay, Jane, I need you to spread your legs and pull your feet back toward your body, so your legs can tent this sheet," he said.

The laudanum seemed to have taken effect because Jane's constant screaming had changed into frequent yelps and moans. Doc helped her position her legs and then checked to see if she was dilated.

"Where's Charlie?" Jane asked.

"I came on ahead while he stopped to wake up Sol and Trixie. I thought you would want Trixie here," Doc said.

"I do, thank you!" Jane said. "And please, keep the laudanum coming. I can still feel these damned rolling pains, but it's a lot better than feeling them without the help of your reddish-brown miracle liquid."

"I'll do what I can, but I can't give you too much, Jane. I need you conscious to push this baby out."

"Mother of all fuckers!" Jane screamed. "That one was bad! Doc, I feel like the baby is tearing me apart down there!"

"Jane, your cervix is ninety percent effaced and four to five centimeters dilated. The cervix must be one hundred percent effaced and ten centimeters dilated before a vaginal delivery. But your baby is turned, and the head is not where it should be," Doc said.

"Can you get it to where it should be?" Jane asked.

A knock on the door came before Doc could answer. Doc opened the door, saw Charlie, Sol, and Trixie outside, and told Jane he would be right back. Doc shut the door behind him and told the group, "We have a problem. The baby is not situated where it belongs. It's in a breech position," he said.

"What does that mean?" Trixie asked.

"It means I either need to turn the baby so its head, not its feet, is positioned to come out first, or perform a type of surgery called a Caesarean section. Bringing the child out feet first will quite probably pull the child apart, causing its death and possibly the death of its mother."

Trixie gasped. "What can we do?" she asked.

"You can come inside and help me try to turn this child, which will cause Jane no small amount of pain, and Sol and Charlie, you can go back to my office and bring me back a box labeled surgical tools," Doc said.

Sol and Charlie set out to retrieve Doc's tools and Doc and Trixie went back inside the cabin, where Jane was beginning to panic.

"What the hell were you telling Trixie outside so as not to allow me to hear?" Jane asked.

Trixie took Jane's hand and said, "It isn't a secret, Jane. Doc was just asking for our help," she said.

"Our?" Jane asked.

"Yes, Jane. Sol, Trixie, and Charlie are all here for you. I did not figure you would want your privacy invaded by Sol and Charlie, so I sent them on an errand for some surgical tools I may need to assist you in bringing your child into this world," he said.

"Surgical tools? Surgery? What? Oh, holy hell! Here comes another one and it's huge," she screamed as another, much stronger contraction hit.

Doc administered another two doses of laudanum to calm her down.

"Listen to me, Jane. Your baby is trying to come out feet first, and that is not good. Trixie and I are going to try to turn the child, and it's going to hurt. If that fails, I will have to cut around your belly in the shape of a 'C', pull the baby out, and then stitch you back up. The only other option would be to attempt to pull the child out by its legs, and that almost always results in death," Doc said.

"Holy mother of god, Bill! What have you done to me?" Jane cried. Then she screamed at Doc and Trixie, "What the fuck are you waiting for? Turn this baby. I will not have you pull Bill's child apart to get it out of me!"

"Okay, Jane. I'm going to give you a little more pain medicine and we will begin," Doc said.

After a few minutes, when Jane seemed to be sedated enough for them to proceed, Doc instructed Trixie to do exactly as he said.

"Jane, Trixie and I are going to try to perform an external cephalic maneuver, which means we will attempt to reposition this child by pushing on your abdomen and the baby's head. It's like a deep abdominal massage and it will be painful," he said.

"Do it," Jane said. The extra medication was helping, but she had no idea how much this procedure was going to hurt, even with the help of the pain drug.

"Trixie, the head is here. I want you to place both of your hands right here, and gently but steadily push when I tell you to," Doc said. "Do not stop, no matter how tired you may get."

"Gotcha, Doc," Trixie said. "It's going to be okay, Jane."

Trixie placed her hands where Doc had instructed. Doc put one hand on Jane's cervix to try to push the feet back and one hand on her abdomen against the baby's rear end.

"Okay, Trixie, slow and steady," Doc said. "I know it's hard, Jane, but the more you relax your body, the better this will work."

Jane nodded. The pain was on the rise again and it was not easy to do as he asked.

Ten minutes later, Doc, Trixie, and Jane all felt the baby do a kind of somersault. Doc and Trixie yelled with joy. Jane managed a smile before passing out.

Chapter 38

Sol and Charlie returned with the tools Doc requested in the event he needed to perform surgery to save Jane and her baby, They were delighted to learn the tools would not be needed after all.

The three men waited outside the cabin while Trixie tended to Jane. Doc examined Jane every thirty minutes or so and made sure Trixie knew to call him inside if labor started speeding up.

For her part, Jane had learned to ride out the pains, but still longed for the baby to be out of her body, although she wondered if it would ever be out of her system.

"Trixie, I think I need to poop," Jane said suddenly, prompting Trixie to yell for Doc to get inside.

"Okay, Jane. I think it is time to deliver this baby," Doc said after checking her out. "What you are feeling is the need to push, and you are feeling this way because your baby is ready to come out and see the world."

Jane and Trixie looked at each other and smiled. "Well, Trixie, are you ready to become a mama?" Jane asked.

"I am so ready, Jane!" Trixie said.

Her answer was cut off by Jane's scream. "I can't take much more of this!" she howled.

"You won't have to if you do as I say," Doc told her. "When I say push, bear down like you are having a bowel movement and hold it until I say stop. Understand?"

Jane nodded.

"Okay, Jane, it's time. Push!" Doc ordered.

Jane clenched her teeth, raised her head off the pillow, squeezed Trixie's hand so hard she nearly broke it, and pushed with all her might.

"Stop!" Doc said.

Jane let her head fall back down on the pillow and panted. "Oh, I feel like I'm on fire down there," Jane said. "Is everything okay, Doc?"

"That feeling is normal, Jane. The baby is crowning after one push, so it is not going to take much more for it to tumble into my hands," Doc said.

"Don't let it fall on the ground, you hear me, Doc?"

Trixie and Doc looked at each other and grinned. "Never happened to me before. I am not going to start my habit of dropping newborn babies with this one. I promise, Jane," Doc said. "Okay. This is it, Jane. One more strong push."

Jane raised her head back up off the pillow, clenched her teeth, screamed, and pushed with all her might. The next sound she heard were the cries of her baby girl.

"Oh, Jane," Trixie said. "Look what you've done. Calamity certainly does not describe your newest act of courage!"

Doc cleaned the baby off and wrapped her in a blanket. "Jane, you should be the first to hold her," Doc said.

Jane shook her head. "I do want to hold her, but her mama should be first. Please hand the baby to Trixie."

There were tears in Trixie's eyes as she looked down at her daughter. "Oh, Jane, she is so beautiful," Trixie said.

"Well, of course she is. Look who made her," Jane laughed.

While the two women continued to admire the child, Doc delivered the placenta and began to clean up. He started to clean Jane, although she was embarrassed and said she could do that herself.

"I don't want you on your feet any more than necessary for the next few days," Doc said. "This was a rough delivery and you need to rest. However, there is something I can't do for you, and that is breast-feed. Have you given any thought to how this child is to be fed, Jane? Trixie?"

Jane and Trixie looked at each other and smiled.

201

"As a matter of fact, Doc," Trixie said, "Jane has agreed to be the baby's wet nurse for the first few months of her life. Jane will stay with Sol and myself in our home during that time. Now if you don't mind, would it be okay for my husband to come in and see his new baby girl?" Trixie asked.

Doc had finished ministering to Jane and had put a blanket over her naked extremities. He looked to Jane for approval and she smiled and nodded her head.

Trixie and Sol shared some sweet moments introducing themselves to their new daughter while Charlie, Doc, and Jane chatted.

"Sorry I had to leave you to get the doc," Charlie told Jane.

Good thing you did, Charlie, or that baby may not be here right now," Jane said. Then she reached out, took his hand, and added, "I'm eternally grateful, dear friend."

Charlie blushed and grinned.

"Jane, I think it's wonderful that you are going to breastfeed this baby," Doc said. "But you do know that you absolutely cannot ..."

"Get drunk. Yes, I already know that. But do not expect me to one hundred percent abstain. I plan to time my still-limited amount of drinking after nursing to give the alcohol time to be out of my system," Jane said.

"Damn it, Jane, or you could just give up the booze for three months!" Doc exploded. He was tired of this woman thinking she couldn't live without her whiskey.

Sol and Trixie broke the tension by joining the three and asking Jane if she had a name in mind.

"Well, if it was a boy, I was going to ask you to please name him Bill. But I don't really think that would work for a girl. So, I guess not," she said.

"Well, Jane, Trixie and I have an idea for a name, but we want to make sure it's okay with you," Sol said.

"Whatever the two of you decide is fine with me," Jane said. She was feeling a little hurt over Doc's outburst, and tired from having worked so hard to give birth.

"Jane, we have chosen the female version of Bill, Billie, for our daughter's first name," Trixie said.

"Oh! I never thought of that!" Jane said. "I love it."

"And her middle name will be Jane. Billie Jane Star," Sol said.

"That's a beautiful name," Charlie said.

Doc agreed, and Jane was too choked up to say anything.

"Would it be okay for me to hold Billie Jane Star for a bit now? And if you all don't mind, I would like to be alone with her," Jane said.

"Of course," Trixie said, putting the baby in her birth mother's arms.

"I need to get back to my office," said Doc. "I left a note on the door, in case anyone needed me, and since there have been no apparent emergencies, I think I just might take a bit of a rest before there are."

"Yeah, I must get back to work, too," Charlie said.

"Doc, I'll walk back to your office with you. I need to borrow your medical sled so Trixie and I can take Jane to her new temporary home a little later," Sol said.

"I would like to go purchase some new bedclothes for you to wear. Will you be okay here by yourself for the next hour or so, Jane?" Trixie asked.

"I will be okay, Trixie, and I'm not alone. I am holding a part of my beloved Bill in my arms. How could I not be okay?" Jane said, looking down at the best thing that had happened because of her love affair with Bill Hickok.

Chapter 39

When everyone had left the cabin, Jane opened the top of her dress and helped Billie Jane form a seal with her mouth around Jane's nipple. There was no milk yet, but Jane had heard that the sooner a baby begins to suckle, the sooner a mother's milk will begin to flow.

She had also heard that some women had a difficult time with this. She had to laugh when she thought about the quilting ladies' dire warnings about how difficult a task it could be to learn to feed your baby. Billie was already getting the hang of it. Her little lips were pulling on Jane's nipple something fierce.

Jane gently rubbed the top of the child's head and then leaned down and kissed her. The baby had quite a bit of yellow—almost white—fuzz on her head. Her eyelashes were long and darker than the hair on her head. She had blue eyes, but Jane knew that all babies' eyes were blue at birth and then gradually changed into their permanent color. She hoped that Billie's permanent eye color would be blue, like Bill's.

The baby's skin was softer than anything Jane's fingers had ever touched. It was hard for her to believe that this perfect little human had once been inside her belly.

"Sorry I complained about you so much, little one, but in all fairness, you do have a ferocious kick, kind of like your—kind of like me," she said, interrupting herself. She knew she would have to stop thinking of herself as this child's mother.

Jane felt a basket full of emotions. There was a strange kind of peace and happiness. There was pride intermingled with humility. Accomplishment. Exhaustion. Relief. All these feelings hovered around her, like hummingbirds poised above a cup of syrup.

She moved the baby to her other breast and held her close. She didn't know who their daughter looked like. A little bit Bill, maybe? A little bit Jane? It would be nice if she bore some resemblance to both of her birth parents. Then again, whether she looked like them or not, it was a certainty that this child had the blood of two extraordinary human beings running through her veins.

Jane reveled in the warmth radiating off Billie. She could feel Bill's energy in this tiny body. It was so strong and more than a bit unnerving. Did he know? she wondered. Could he see her?

"Oh, Bill! Look what we did! When you died I felt so sad that we would never be able to carve out a life together, but I didn't know then that we already had done that. We created a life that is now living and breathing because of us. We will live on together in the body and soul of this beautiful little girl. We did good, sweetheart."

Jane closed her eyes and allowed herself some time to enjoy holding this bundle in her arms.

I have to remember this moment. These few seconds when she is all mine, Jane thought.

Then she addressed the child. "Hey, little one. You are going to have the life your mama only dreamed of having. You will live in a nice home and never wonder where your next meal is coming from. You'll get to go to school and play with your brothers and sisters and wear pretty dresses—or britches, if that's what you want." Jane made a mental note to talk to Sol and Trixie about that.

"You will be loved and kissed and held. Your mother and daddy will walk with you, each holding one of your hands. They will tell you every day how much they love you. And when you grow up, you will find someone to love as much as I love your daddy. My gift to you, my beautiful daughter, is that I am providing you with the best life by the only means I have at my disposal.

"That grumpy old Doc has no idea that I would give up my drinking in a heartbeat for you, if I had the rest of the mother package to go with it. But facts are facts. I have no money. I'm not well educated. To make the money I would need to feed and clothe you, I would have to do the only things I know how to do, dragging you along with me, which is no life for a child.

"So, my gift to you is to let you go to people who will take much better care of you. I just want you to know, and I place this notion in your mind and heart today where I order it to stay for as long as you live: No one will ever love you more than the woman who gave you life. No one."

Chapter 40

Jane settled into her role as Billie's wet nurse as though this was something she had done all her life. She loved her private time with Billie, and felt good about the fact that she was providing nourishment for the child.

It also was gratifying to watch Trixie and Sol settle into their new roles as parents with the same sort of ease, comfort, and pleasure. Jane loved the way the two of them talked to Billie, as if the infant really understood what they were saying, and maybe she did. After all, this baby was destined to be brilliant, considering her heritage.

Every morning Trixie would lift the baby up out of the cradle Sol had made for her, change her soiled diapers, then bring her to Jane's bed for her morning meal. What a joy it was for Jane to wake up in the morning to the sight, sound, and smell of this heavenly package. Every day there was something new to marvel over.

Billie's eyes were open wide and alert three days after she was born. Her hand and arm movements, though jerky, gained coordination as each day passed. Four weeks after she left the womb, Billie surprised Jane with a tentative smile that, within days, grew to a full turning upward of the lips. Once she mastered the art of wearing that happy face, the little girl made frequent use of it.

Sol and Trixie held and touched the child during most of her waking hours, which thrilled Jane. Billie was stimulated, rocked, and talked to in the most tender tones by her parents, and the child's every need was met as soon as it arose.

Since the hardware store was so close to the couple's home, Sol stopped by to see Trixie and Billie every chance he got. Even Uncle Seth dropped in every few days, and the usually somber man's eyes lit up whenever he saw the baby. His smile was wider than Jane could remember it being before.

Charlie visited every day, at first. He and Jane continued to work a bit on her life story, but she seemed to have lost interest, at least for the time being—and he wasn't going to push the issue.

The plan that Sol, Trixie, Charlie, and Jane had agreed upon was for Jane to remain at the couple's home for the first three or four months of Billie's life. She fed the child every three hours for the first several weeks, and Billie put on the appropriate amount of weight as Jane's reward for her efforts.

Once Billie got to a point where Jane would need to feed her only a few times a day, Jane planned to move back to the cabin and work at Charlie's store, sorting mail, packaging goods, and running errands, for which he would pay her enough to live on. At six months, Billie Jane would be weaned off Jane's milk and Trixie would take over all the feeding, freeing Jane to work as Charlie's assistant.

While Jane was eager to get back to a more adventurous daily routine, she was not sure how she felt about the idea of not waking up with Billie every morning. She knew that was going to take some getting used to. But her decision had been made before Billie was born, and she felt happy that she got to see Sol and Trixie in action before weaning herself from a daily life with her and Bill's child.

One evening, when Billie was about two months old, Jane and Trixie were sitting in Trixie's parlor after the baby was asleep for the night. As was customary since Jane had moved in, she and Trixie were spending some time together while Trixie waited for Sol to close the hardware store and come home. Doc had said a glass of whiskey before bed, once the baby had begun sleeping through the night, would be safe for Jane to drink. So, she and Trixie each imbibed and chatted. These were times Jane would cherish for the rest of her life.

Most nights, the topic of conversation between the two women was the baby they both loved.

"I think she knows me by name, now," Trixie said. "Last night when we were holding her in bed, Sol said. 'Where's your mama?' and she turned her head and looked right at me."

"She is a smart little bugger," Jane agreed.

"That reminds me, Jane. I have never heard you call her a stinky pooper," Trixie said.

"Yeah, ever since I had her, I have looked back with regret upon having referred to babies as... that. Although, you know, she certainly is one!"

Trixie laughed. "Oh, yeah! A few days ago, Sol insisted on changing her diaper and I saw him gagging something fierce. I had to come to his rescue before he vomited all over the poor child. That's the last time he ever offered."

"You know, I've smelled some disgusting things in my lifetime, but that girl's dirty diapers are by far the worst," Jane said.

"Her smile, though. Isn't that just the best thing you ever laid eyes on?" Trixie asked.

Jane nodded and raised her glass to Trixie. "Amen to that, girl!"

Jane and Trixie sat in silence for a bit, enjoying their separate thoughts. Jane was the next to speak.

"Trixie, I've been meaning to ask you something about Billie's upbringing. I'm just wondering whether you and Sol will object if somewhere down the line she decides she would rather wear britches, instead of dresses—like I did. I mean, maybe it's in her blood, you know?"

"I've never thought about that, Jane. But I can tell you something Sol and I have agreed on and that is if Billie does no harm to innocent people, we will support whatever she wants to be and whatever path she wants to follow. How she needs or wants to dress to be able to do that is not something I can imagine troubling us," Trixie said.

Jane smiled. "I'm so happy to hear that."

When Sol came home a short time later, Jane told the couple she was going to take the air for a while. "I'll come in quietly, so I don't wake any of you," she promised.

It was a brisk May evening, and Jane was happy she had grabbed a shawl to put over her dress. Sol and Trixie had surprised Jane with a new wardrobe shortly after she moved in with them. Jane had said that during the time she nursed Billie, she planned to dress as a woman. She didn't tell them it was because she wanted to feel like a mother during this time in her life. As soon as she took the job at Charlie's, she would go back to wearing britches.

Jane decided to walk out to the edge of town to her cabin. She wanted to sit by the creek and talk to Bill for a bit. She'd stopped worrying about whether he could hear her. She figured probably not. But it comforted her some to talk to him anyway.

She felt a sudden chill as she approached the cabin. It was almost as if someone had opened the door to a gust of cold wind and then closed it again. She stopped for a minute to get her bearings, and the night air returned to the temperature it was before.

Jane walked around the cabin to her favorite spot by the creek. Tonight, she did not feel like sticking her feet in the water, so she didn't remove her shoes. Instead she sat cross-legged and closed her eyes. Then she spoke quietly.

"Good evening, sweet Bill. Sometimes when I close my eyes like this and imagine hard enough, I can almost smell you, and feel your hand holding mine. Of course, I would prefer you were here doing that in person, but this is all I've got to work with.

"Do you remember me telling you I did not want to have children? If you still have such a thing as a memory, you probably do. Well, I regret that now that I have given birth to our sweet Billie Jane. I didn't know 'til then what a wonderful feeling it is to hold your own baby in your arms.

"Oh, Bill, she is the definition of perfection! A handful, at times, but she no doubt comes by that naturally."

Jane laughed. *Of course she does*, she thought.

"If you are still able to see and hear things happening in this world, then you know that I have given our daughter to Trixie and Sol Star to raise as their own child. It was a decision based on wanting her to have a good life, which I alone can't give her. Hell, I doubt the two of us together could have provided for her the way she deserves.

"Anyway, as you may or may not know, I have been staying with Sol and Trixie and breastfeeding our daughter. Who knew my breasts were intended for more than you, wrapping your hands around them or stroking them gently?"

Jane shuddered, remembering how Bill's touch had made her feel.

Jane's body reacted to the mere thought of their passionate love-making. Nothing had ever made her feel so good. Nothing ever would again.

"Damn you for dying!" she cried. Jane was quiet for a spell. Her eyes were leaking the way they did when she longed for him to hold her. She sniffled and closed her eyes again. It lasted only a second or two, but again she felt a sudden blast of icy air. Her eyes flew open.

"Was that you, Bill? Do it again now if it was. Do it right now!" she demanded and once more closed her eyes.

Minutes passed, and nothing happened.

"I didn't think it was you. Just a coincidence. Damn!" she said.

After a few more quiet moments Jane again addressed the love of her life.

"You know, Bill, I once told you I would never love anyone as much as I loved you. Never. But I lied. The truth is, I am in love again. Her name is Billie Jane and it is possible I may love her even more than I loved you. I just can't help myself. And I'm pretty sure if you were here, you would love her just as much."

Thinking about Billie had made Jane's breasts harden and trickle a bit of milk. Jane laughed and said, "You'd be proud of me, Bill. I think I could probably feed a dozen hungry babies a day. Guess I finally found something womanly I'm good at."

Jane stood up and brushed off her clothes. It was a clear night, and she looked up at the sky to take in a million little twinkling lights. She chose to believe that her Bill was one of those stars.

211

Jane turned and began her walk back to Sol and Trixie's. She was feeling tired, suddenly, and the expulsion of her milk made her want to feed Billie. She decided she would wake the baby when she got back, change her diaper, and give her a little midnight snack before rocking her back to sleep. Now *that* was something to look forward to.

Chapter 41

Jane's days with Billie flew by, and before long it was time to say good-bye and go back to her own cabin. Sol and Trixie told Jane she could stay with them as long as she wanted. But Jane thought it would be best to move aside and give the couple a chance to enjoy their baby all by themselves.

Four months after Billie Jane Star's birth, Jane packed her belongings—of which she had many now, courtesy of Sol and Trixie's generous nature. In addition to a feminine wardrobe Trixie had chosen for Jane, Sol also made sure she had several pairs of britches, shirts, vests, and jackets.

Sol and Seth had made improvements to her cabin, including a comfortable bed and a down-filled mattress and comforter. They bought her some kitchen utensils and dishes, installed a new wood stove, and built a cupboard. A few days before Jane's planned departure, Sol and Trixie asked her to tend the baby and slipped away to hang curtains that Trixie had purchased by mail order.

On the day she left, Sol and Seth intended to take Jane home in a horse-drawn wagon, telling her it would be easier to transport her new wardrobe and other things she had acquired. When Jane balked at the idea that she needed to be driven home, Trixie said she and Sol also wanted to take Billie to visit her place of birth.

"Are you saying you think she will have a clue where she's at and what you are talking about?" Jane asked.

"No, but I'll know that we visited what is now to me this sacred place where she took her first breath," Trixie argued.

Jane gave in, and the four of them set out for the drive across town. When they arrived, another wagon was parked in front of the cabin and Charlie Utter was sitting up on the clapboard, holding the horses' reins. The wagon was full, and it was covered with a tarpaulin.

"Charlie, what are you doing here?" Jane asked.

Charlie hopped to the ground and secured the reins. "Well, Jane, I just wanted to welcome you home and..."—he pulled the tarp back and finished—"deliver a few food supplies to get you started. I know you don't have any money yet and it will be a week before your first pay from me. I just wanted to help."

"Oh, Charlie! You are too fucking much!" Jane squealed and threw her arms around Charlie's neck, making him blush.

"Jane, Trixie, and Billie—you can go on inside while Charlie and I bring in these supplies." Sol said.

"I certainly can help," Jane said.

"No, Jane. I want you to be with me when I tell Billie that this is where she was born," Trixie said.

Sol walked over to the door, opened it, and said, "After you, ladies."

Trixie walked in first, followed by Jane. Sol and Charlie followed behind. The look on Jane's face was something none of them would ever forget, and the fact that she was speechless for a full minute said it all.

Jane walked around the room, touching each new piece of furniture. Running her hand along the top of the new stove. Picking up pans and dishes and turning them over and over in her hands. She had never seen such beautiful things.

Finally, Jane spoke, blinking back the tears in her eyes. "This is exactly how I pictured the inside of the cabin all decorated and furnished," she said. "Look at this gorgeous bed, the curtains, the cupboard. So nice. So comfortable. This is what I imagined Bill and I would do to this place when we had some extra money someday—which I did not expect to happen—the extra money part, that is."

"Seth contributed to everything in here. He is mighty grateful to you for making him an honorary uncle," Sol said.

"I don't know how to begin saying a proper thank you for all of this," Jane said.

"How about just assuring us that you will invite us for dinner occasionally?" Trixie said.

"I can verify that this woman can cook," Charlie said. "Sol, let's get the supplies brought in, and then we should clear out and let Jane enjoy her peace and privacy. She starts work at my store tomorrow and I think a good night's rest will be helpful."

When that was accomplished, Trixie asked Sol and Charlie to give Jane their goodbyes and then wait outside for her and the baby.

Jane was exhausted for all sorts of reasons. Her body was still healing. Her emotions were conflicted over leaving Billie, and the prospect of spending her first night without the child in the next room was almost terrifying.

"I am so grateful to all of you for everything you have done for me. You are the best friends I have had in my entire life. I don't know how I can ever repay you for all of this"—she swept her hand around the room— "but mostly for agreeing to give this beautiful child a wonderful life. Words just don't..." Jane stopped and burst out in tears.

"Get some rest, Jane," Charlie said. "I'll see you at the store tomorrow after you stop at Trixie's to feed Billie." He gave her shoulder a squeeze and then went outside, got on his wagon, and left.

"Jane, you have given Trixie and me a greater gift than you will probably ever imagine," Sol said. He gave her a hug and went outside to wait for Trixie.

"I agree with Sol," Trixie said to Jane. "You're more than a best friend to me. You're the sister I never had." She handed Billie to Jane. "I think this little one could use another feeding before we take her home, if you don't mind."

"Mind? It will be my pleasure," Jane said, holding the baby to her chest.

"I'll wait outside. Take all of the time both of you need and bring her out when you're both ready," Trixie said.

Jane spent the next twenty minutes sitting on her new bed and feeding Billie, gently rubbing the top of the baby's head. When Billie had her fill, and drifted off, Jane took another few minutes to watch her sleep, memorizing the tender moment. Then she got up, went to the door, opened it, walked outside, and placed the baby in her mother's arms.

Chapter 42

For the next few weeks Jane worked for Charlie and nursed the baby three times a day. The first night she had spent away from Billie was not as gruesome as she had thought it would be. That was probably because she was drained and fell asleep shortly after her friends had left the cabin.

Waking up to rock-hard breasts overflowing with milk was not pleasant, but she quickly rushed off to Sol and Trixie's, took care of that problem, and then went to Charlie's to begin her first day of work.

"Hey'a, boss!" Jane called as she walked in the door of Charlie Utter's delivery service. Charlie looked up from a table where he was preparing some packages for their journey to Custer—a fifty-mile ride over one of the roughest trails in the Black Hills country.

"Good morning, Jane. The name's Charlie, not boss. And I'm happy to have you here. I'm a little behind in sorting and packaging for this afternoon's run."

"Just tell me what to do," Jane said, eager to begin working.

During the next thirty minutes or so Charlie showed Jane where to find all she needed to box items and affix labels. She was quick to learn, although no one would describe this task as a difficult or complicated process.

Soon the two of them were hard at work making sure every package intended to leave Deadwood that day was ready to go when the rider returned.

They finished the last of the packages with a half hour to spare.

"How about some coffee?" Charlie asked Jane as she sat down to rest.

"Don't mind if I do, Charlie."

"How was your first night in your new, improved home?" Charlie asked as he handed her a full cup.

"Slept like a baby," Jane said. She took a sip and sighed in appreciation. "You sure make some mighty fine coffee, Charlie."

"So I've been told. Bill especially used to like the way I made his coffee," Charlie said, then added, "I still miss him every day."

Jane just nodded. She understood that feeling.

"There's really nothing more to do here today, Jane," Charlie added. "If you want to head home, or to Trixie's to feed the little one, if it's time, feel free to do that when you finish your coffee."

"Don't mind if I do, Charlie. I will go feed Billie, then go home and cook a fine dinner with the vittles you provided."

"I'm happy to have done that," he said.

"I'm thinking something, Charlie."

"What's that, Jane?"

"I'm thinking with all of that fine food and the beautiful dishes to put it on that it would be real nice if you would agree to join me for dinner tonight."

"I'd be delighted," Charlie said. The words didn't come close to describing how happy her invitation made him feel.

Chapter 43

Dinner was a good time for both Jane and Charlie. Jane made a beef stew using the meat, potatoes, carrots, leeks, and onions Charlie had provided the day before. She also made biscuits to dip in the stew. Charlie brought a bottle of whiskey, and the two spent three hours laughing and reminiscing about how and why they met.

The two felt comfortable with each other. Charlie's reserved, gentle manner made it easy for Jane to be around him. For his part, Charlie had gotten used to Jane's occasional outbursts. It could even be said that he enjoyed the woman's feisty temperament.

For the next two months Jane and Charlie worked side by side and enjoyed many dinners at Jane's house. Sometimes, when the Deadwood Hotel was serving something special, Charlie would invite Jane to join him in a meal there.

They went riding together, although Charlie was no competition for Jane when it came to speed and showmanship. But that didn't matter to him. And if she cared about it, she didn't let it show.

All the while she was working and enjoying Charlie's companionship, Jane was also fitting Billie into her days every way she could. The child was growing so fast, and Jane couldn't get enough of her.

Trixie had mentioned on a few occasions lately that she thought Jane should start thinking about ending her wet nurse duties. But whenever Trixie brought it up, Jane changed the subject and refused to address it.

Then the day came when Jane showed up at Trixie's to feed Billie, and Trixie gently but firmly let her know that the time had come for Billie to be weaned off Jane's milk.

"You've been eager to start your delivery job and get on the road again," Trixie reminded her. "And Billie has thrived on what you have done to nourish her. We're grateful, Jane. But the time has come for me to take over and you to have the freedom to live your life the way you want."

"Please, Trixie, give me one more week of feeding her," Jane pleaded. "Doc says I will need to wrap my chest tight to stop the milk, and I can do that gradually over the next seven days." But her request had nothing to do with milk flow. She just wasn't ready to stop doing the single most fulfilling thing she had done in her life—aside from giving birth.

"Well, if that is better for you, Jane, I can't see how one more week will make much difference to us. I just worry a bit that she has gotten attached to you to the point of missing you when you're not around."

"Why do you think that?" Jane asked. She was thrilled to hear it, but didn't let Trixie know.

"The last couple of weeks when you have handed her to me, after you were done feeding her and then left, she has cried, and I haven't been able to quiet her. I'm sure she is crying for you," Trixie said.

Jane had noticed that the child whimpered a bit when she handed her over to Trixie, and had wondered about that.

"I just thought that, maybe, she had not gotten enough milk," Jane said.

"Whatever the reason, I think the sooner she is weaned, the better for her emotionally," Trixie said.

"I see your point," Jane said. "I will start wrapping my chest to-night and within a week, according to what Doc said, my milk supply should be dwindled to little or nothing. Then I will just stop by once a day to see her, if that is okay with you."

"Actually Jane, I think once a week would be better, so she can establish who her mother is going to be," Trixie said. "I'm not trying to be selfish with her. I just need to find my own footing as Billie's mother."

220

"I understand," Jane said. "I'm going to be riding back and forth from here to Custer delivering the mail, so I wouldn't be able to stop by much more than that, anyway."

For the first time since declaring themselves friends, Jane and Trixie experienced an awkward silence. Jane broke that silence when she said, "So, I should feed her now, so I can get home and cook dinner before Charlie arrives in his usual famished state of being."

Jane laughed and handed Billie to her.

"So how is that going?" she asked as Jane walked over to sit on the sofa.

"How's what going?" she asked.

"Your relationship with Charlie?" Trixie said. She hadn't talked to Jane about it before now, but the two spent a lot of time together these days and many around town assumed that theirs was a budding romance.

"My *relationship* with Charlie is the same as it has always been," Jane said, her tone a bit terse at what she imagined Trixie to mean.

"Oh. I heard you were spending a lot of time together and I guess I just thought..."

"Thought what?" Jane asked, although she knew.

"Um, I thought the two of you might be getting close—as a couple —romantically. But you're not?"

"No, Trixie, we're not. We're just two people who miss their best friend who is now dead in the ground and who sometimes enjoy not having to eat or ride alone. Or talk to ourselves," she said.

"I think you might be missing something here, Jane. I've seen the look in Charlie's eyes these days. There's a lot of light and happiness that wasn't there before."

Jane took Billie off her left breast, raised her up to burp her, and then said, "Trixie, while I'm holding this sweet baby in my arms, I'll need to ask you to stop your speculating about what may or may not be going on with Charlie Utter's eyes.

"I, for one, don't care to know if there is anything there concerning any feelings he may or may not have for me because I will tell you now that I do not harbor any such feelings for him and if you keep yapping about it I am liable to get fucking angry and a person shouldn't hold an innocent child when they're angry." And with that said, Jane placed Billie on her right breast and glared in Trixie's direction.

"Okay, Jane. I'm sorry. I didn't mean to upset you. I just want you to be happy."

"Happiness and me parted ways when Bill died. The only other person I have come close to loving as much, if not more, is this little girl."

Billie Jane had finished her meal and was asleep in Jane's arms. Jane handed her over to Trixie, adjusted her dress, and stood up to leave.

"Do you have to go?" Trixie asked.

Jane looked at Trixie for a few seconds and then answered that question. "Yes, Trixie. I must go. I think it's time."

While Trixie thought Jane's departure was a little abrupt, she never dreamed that would be the last time the two would ever see each other.

Chapter 44

When Jane got to Charlie's store, he was locking the door. "Jane!" I was just on my way to your place for dinner," Charlie said. He was surprised to see her back there.

"Charlie, I haven't been home yet, and I have nothing prepared for our dinner tonight."

"That's okay, Jane. Why don't we just eat at the hotel tonight?" he said.

"That would be good, Charlie. Thank you."

Jane began walking toward the hotel. Charlie turned and followed.

"You're walking kind of fast, Jane. You must be really hungry," Charlie observed.

Jane stopped and pivoted to face him. "Charlie, I need to talk to you about something," she said.

"Okay. How about we do that over dinner? I could eat an entire buffalo. That's how hungry *I* am," he said.

Jane laughed at that. "Yeah, okay. Let's get some food."

The two sat at their usual table and, for the first time since she and Charlie started making dinner together an almost nightly thing, Jane noticed people smiling at them.

Charlie seemed to be used to it, nodding at several tables of diners who were looking at them.

"Am I the only one who didn't know what people were thinking of our friendship, Charlie?" Jane asked.

"You just might be, Jane," Charlie said. He smiled warmly at her and then added, "You say you have something to talk to me about. I have something to talk to you about, too."

Jane sighed. Then she said, "Charlie, I appreciate everything you've done for me. You are one of the dearest friends I have ever known. I enjoy spending time with you, laughing, riding, talking. But if you have any illusions of us becoming more than good friends, I need to tell you now—"

Charlie didn't want to hear the rest. "Jane, if you're talking about us becoming lovers in the biblical sense of that word, I have no such aspirations," he said, keeping his true thoughts to himself.

"I'm relieved to hear that," she said.

"I do enjoy your company and would like as much of that as possible," he said.

"Is that what you wanted to talk to me about?" she asked.

It wasn't, but Charlie no longer held out hope that she would react favorably to the proposal he'd had in mind. So, he lied again. "Yes, Jane. That's what I wanted to talk to you about."

Jane signed and set her fork down on her plate. "Charlie, I've decided to leave Deadwood."

"Why?" was all Charlie could manage.

"I think it's best for everyone. Billie needs to grow up unencumbered by the presence of a person she may or may not be getting too close to. Sol and Trixie need to be able to raise her without any interference from me. Sometimes I think my hanging around makes Trixie nervous, like she's afraid I will want to take Billie away from her. And you..." Jane reached across the table and took Charlie's hand in hers. "You should not have to live with false hopes."

"Jane, I would be satisfied for things to remain as they've been these last few months, with no expectations beyond that," he said. His eyes were pleading with her to stay, even if the words were not issuing from his mouth. "And what about the delivery job I promised? I thought you were looking forward to that."

"I was, or so I thought. But looking back, I realize that's a hard and dangerous life that I've already lived once. I don't think I want to do it again," she said.

"What do you want to do, then?" Charlie asked her.

"I think I'd like to roam a bit and then maybe get into the entertain-ment business. Maybe find a performin' job at some saloon or theater," she said.

"Jane, is there any way I can talk you out of leaving?" This time Charlie's voice did the pleading for him.

"I'm sorry, Charlie. I will genuinely miss your company, but my mind is made up. This is what I need to do," she said.

Jane got up from the table and asked, "Walk me home one last time, Charlie Utter?"

Charlie stood and said, "It would be my pleasure."

The two walked in silence, each with their own thoughts and fears. Charlie wondered how he was going to function without Jane, now that he was so accustomed to having her around. Jane wondered where she would go, what she would do, and how she would continue to live without seeing her baby.

When they reached the cabin, Charlie gave Jane a big hug. "Take care of yourself," he said.

Jane hugged him back. "I love you, Charlie Utter."

"I love you, too, Martha Canary." He had intended to tell her that tonight, just not in the process of saying good-bye.

"Do me a favor, please, Charlie? Would you take over this cabin as your residence? As you well know, it is set up quite comfortably and beats sleeping at your store."

"I would be happy to stay here," Charlie told her, although he wondered how he would do it with so much of her memory lingering here.

"And look after the little one, please? I know she'll be fine with Sol and Trixie, but a girl can't have too many fine upstanding men in her life."

Charlie nodded. "Will I ever see you again?" he asked.

"Well, I guess we will have to leave that up to the almighty universe that decides these things for us, Charlie." And with that, Jane turned and walked into her home.

Charlie wiped a tear from his eye as he walked away. Once he got back to the store, he tried to sleep, but tossed and turned all night. Finally, as dawn was breaking, he couldn't take it anymore. He got up and rushed to the little cabin to beg her to stay. But Jane had already put miles of distance between her and Deadwood.

Chapter 45

October 9, 1895
Deadwood, South Dakota

Seventeen years later, Jane rode back into Deadwood. She was forty-three years old and had spent much of her time away in and out of relationships, in and out of various types of employment, and more in than out of saloons.

Jane rode into town on Buddy, who was twenty-eight years old now and a shadow of the magnificent steed he had once been. Her reason for coming back to Deadwood was twofold: she wanted to visit Bill Hickok's grave, and she hoped to lay eyes on the girl. Only one of those things happened.

She soon learned that Sol and Trixie had moved out of the area several years earlier. In addition to Billie, Trixie had four babies of her own while they were in Deadwood. One of their five children, a girl, had died from the flu. No one could tell Jane what that child's name was, but folks said Trixie had taken her daughter's death hard, and was never quite the same afterward. Sol decided they should move, hoping that getting away from the memories that surrounded them in Deadwood might help Trixie get some of her old spark back. No one had heard from them since.

Although Jane asked everyone she talked to, not one person could tell her how many of the Star's children were boys and how many were girls. Nor could they tell Jane the age of the child who died or when the death had occurred. She would never know whether the child who died was her own daughter.

Charlie Utter, also, had moved on at some point since Jane left. No one could tell her anything about him or his whereabouts. They did know that he was in Deadwood in 1879, when he oversaw the relocation of Bill Hickok's body to the Mount Moriah Cemetery. Jane went there to visit the grave upon her return to Deadwood, and several times thereafter.

Three years before she died, a professional photographer took a photo of Jane standing in the weeds in front of Bill's gravestone. She was holding a daisy in her left hand, and her hat on her head with her right, as though fearful that a gust of wind would come along.

Jane wore a drab ruffled dress with a large white collar. Long gone were her days of wearing britches.

Her hair was stringy, and her face had the texture of the leather she was once fond of wearing on her body. Her nose appeared to have taken a good amount of punishment, either from intoxication or punches.

"Can you please take the fucking photo and leave so I can have some private time here with Bill?" she snapped at the photographer.

After he left, Jane pulled a flask from a large pocket in the dress and took a swig before addressing her dead lover.

"Don't have much to say, Bill. I haven't led a very productive life, as you may well know. But I did have me some fine adventures, you being the finest of them all. I have to go now, and I will not come back to this spot until they bring me here in a box to rest beside you for all eternity. I'm figuring it's not too many years off. Until then, my love..."

Two years later, after spending a day sitting with Buddy in one of their favorite spots—*sun shining through the branches of the pines painting the ground with shadowy fans of all shapes and sizes, birds chirping almost loud enough to raise the dead, just enough wind to lift the edges of your hair*—Jane got up intending to ride Buddy back to the stable for the night. Then she had a sudden change of mind and took her pistol out of its holster, instead.

Jane walked over to the old horse and put her arms around his neck. This animal was the last friend she had left in this world, and she wanted to do right by it.

"I love you, dear friend," she said. Then she let go, stepped back, raised the pistol and shot the horse in the side of the head. He died instantly, most likely never knowing what hit him.

Jane dropped the gun, fell to the ground, and sobbed. "Have a good rest, my Buddy! You deserve it more than most of the people I have ever known."

A year later, in a hotel in a small town a few miles from Deadwood, Martha Jane Canary died of acute alcoholism. She was alone and broke. Her wish to be buried beside Wild Bill Hickok was honored. Her funeral was one of the most widely attended Deadwood had ever seen.

A man in his early thirties remained behind after almost all the attendees had gone. He stood looking down at Jane's grave, hat held to his chest, tears streaming down his face.

A man standing nearby asked, "You related to her, or something?"

Gary just shook his head.

"Why're you crying, then? She was just an old drunk who never amounted to anything," he said.

Gary looked at the man and asked, "Why did you come to her funeral?"

"I don't know. Curiosity, maybe," he said.

Gary looked back at Jane's grave and said, "This woman you say never amounted to anything sat by my bed round the clock and cared for me when I was a child dying of smallpox. I'm here today because of her, and I'm only one of many she helped in various ways throughout her lifetime."

Gary put his hat on his head and said, "She amounted to something, all right." Then he turned and walked away.

ACKNOWLEDGEMENTS

I want to begin by thanking my mother, **Pauline Davis Adams**, who encouraged me to write from an early age. She had the talent and desire to be a writer, but not the time. Not with birthing and raising seven children while helping to manage my father's dry-cleaning plant. It was the 1950s and, unlike Calamity Jane, my mother married a man whose gender bias was written in stone. Shortly before she died, she told me she couldn't remember what it was I did for a living. I mentioned a bunch of things, but she just shook her head and repeated "No, not that." Years later, I realized what she was asking. "I write, Mom. That's what I do!" I don't think it's too late to tell her that.

To **Michael Neff**, the man who encouraged me to write this book at a writer's retreat three years ago on Whidbey Island and who continued to meet and mentor me for a year or so after. I am mighty grateful for all your help, Michael. Oh, and I'll never forget the day an irate woman approached our table and accused you of being a bully for talking to me in your best Gollum voice. I did ask you to stop, as the angry woman pointed out, but it was only because I was laughing so hard I was afraid I was going to pee my pants. We both know you're not a bully.

To **Gerrit Hansen**, my friend and fellow writer who also attended the same retreat as well as those mentoring lunches. You are the best and most patient writing partner ever. And such a peacemaker when Michael and I disagreed. I appreciate you, as I'm sure does Michael.

To three voracious readers and amazing people in my life, who donated their time to read and comment on the original manuscript.

Stephen Radney-MacFarland, Ryan O'Neill, and **Sue Weinlein—** your comments were helpful, and I am deeply grateful.

To **DARLENE** an artist, writer, and dear friend of forty-two years, who talked me into self-publishing this book. Who did the work to get these pages into publishable form, whose amazing artwork appears on the cover, and whose illustrations decorate the story. Thank you, dear friend.

To my husband, **Kim Mohan,** whose red pen has perfect aim, who forty-three years ago was my editor at the Beloit Daily News in Wisconsin, and who served as my editor on this project—not just because he came free of charge, but because I have reason to believe he's the best, and I'm not alone in that. I love you so much, sweetheart!

Finally, I want to thank **Martha Jane Canary**, "Calamity Jane." A real woman with real challenges who had the courage to stand up to her male counterparts and insist on being treated as their equal. I wish I had met you then.

231

ABOUT THE AUTHOR

Pamela Mohan spent years in court as the felony crime reporter for the *Janesville Gazette,* a daily newspaper in southeastern Wisconsin. To this day, it is her favorite writing gig. Ever!

She gave it up to move to Seattle, Washington when her husband, Kim Mohan, was offered a job at Wizards of the Coast, a game company located in Renton, Washington. Pamela joined the staff at Wizards as the Associate Editor of *Amazing Stories* Magazine—at the time, a 70-year-old science fiction magazine— and then as the managing editor of the company's game convention publications.

She co-wrote a young adult science fiction trilogy based on Gary Gygax's *"Cyborg Commando"* roleplaying game with her husband and, together with Kathleen O'Neill, wrote a nonfiction book called *"A Man Worth Knowing,"* based on the life of Dr. Herbert Ross Reaver.

She lives in Seattle with her husband and their dog, a Chiweenie named Charmander who, despite having been named after a Pokémon card, has never played the game.